THE PROMISED HAND

THE PROMISED HAND

VEVISHAAL

JHAVERCHAND MEGHANI

Translated from Gujarati by
ASHOK MEGHANI

SAHITYA AKADEMI

The Promised Hand : English translation by Ashok Meghani of *Vevishaal*, a novel in Gujarati by Jhaverchand Meghani. Sahitya Akademi, New Delhi, 2002.

Sahitya Akademi

Rabindra Bhavan, 35 Ferozeshah Road, New Delhi-110 001
Sales : 'Swati', Mandir Marg, New Delhi-110 001

Regional Offices

Jeevan Tara Building, 4th Floor,
   23A/44x, Diamond Harbour Road, Kolkata-700 053

Central College Campus, University Library Building,
   Dr. B. R. Ambedkar Veedhi, Bangalore-560 001

172, Mumbai Marathi Grantha Sangrahalaya Marg,
   Dadar, Mumbai-400 014

Chennai Office

C.I.T. Campus, T.T.T.I. Post, Tharamani, Chennai-600 113

First published, 2002

RUPEES ONE HUNDRED THIRTY

ISBN : 81-260-1174-2

Typeset & printed at Sita Composers Pvt. Ltd., New Delhi.

Author's Note

One Tuesday ten months ago, I started writing this story to serialize it in the weekly issues of *Phoolchhaab*. I did not have the entire story sketched out, not even in a skeletal form. The process of a story's creation works in two ways : some authors develop the skeleton of a whole story and then proceed to add the flesh and blood to give it the final form; and then there are many others like me who start out writing with nothing more than a powerful idea in their head—the characters and the plot taking shape as if on their own. When you think about it, this latter seemingly blind process of story-writing is not something that happens quite by chance as it may appear. Invariably, it is the experiences and thinking of a lifetime that help provide the form and the substance of a story; the raw but refined cotton is all there, ready to be spun out.

On the other hand, it will be wrong for me to say that I had struck out and trekked through this story totally blind. The readership of *Phoolchhaab* took an active part in its development. The letters started arriving soon after the first installment appeared and continued to come as the story progressed. From near and far, from villages and cities, the college-educated and commoners, man and women alike, wrote to me and suggested the direction the story should follow. Publication of those letters here could shed new light on the art of creative story writing. It is regrettable that the predetermined price of *Vevishaal* can not bear the cost of those additional pages. All I will say is, lucky is the writer who receives such affectionate support for his creation from so many.

Did I succeed in telling everything I wanted to tell in *Vevishaal* ? I don't know. What I do know is my firm belief that the author should include what he wants to in his story; he has no right to use the preface to try and make up for his failure to do a complete job of his story. His first—and the last—duty is to tell the story, a good story and only the story. If I make a claim about *Vevishaal*, it is to have told a story and only the story.

One admission I must make: I have not been happy with the remake of Vijaychandra's character in the later chapters. My attempts to undo the damage have been totally unsuccessful; I have failed to erase what was written.

... I gratefully acknowledge all the people that have taken such interest in the writing of this story. The thought that I may have been unable to do justice to their imaginative ideas makes me shudder. Among them there are many that consider this story to be incomplete without the climax of a wedding. I want to tell them that to include the elements of a wedding and its aftermath — a happily married life complete with children — is forbidden by the rules of the creative world. The story about a *Vevishaal* (betrothal) must stay within the bounds implied in that title.

January 14, 1938   JHAVERCHAND MEGHANI

Translator's Note

It was in 1937 that the thirty-seven chapters of *Vevishaal* first appeared as installments in the Gujarati weekly *Phoolchhaab*. They came out in the book form in 1938. Hugely popular, the book has since seen two more editions and ten reprints, the last of them in 1996, forty-nine years after the author's death and in his birth centenary year.

Since reading it in my early teens, I revisited Vevishaal in the Fall of 1996 after a gap of almost four decades. I had just finished translating into English a couple of my father's short stories. Being in that frame of mind, my first impulse after reading *Vevishaal* was to sit down and work on translating my favourite episode from the novel, the dying moments portrayed in the twenty-fifth chapter. I lived that chapter for the following two days. The resulting translation seemed good enough to me to be read to my two brothers whose intimate understanding of my father's works and honest appraisal I could count on. Their enthusiastic reaction was beyond anything I had expected. I was virtually ordered to drop everything else and to concentrate all my energy on the rest of the book. Nobody has ever accused me of following good advice and it took me over two years to finish the task. But, better late than never, and here it is!

A couple of points are worth mentioning here. While working on the translation, the audience that I had constantly in mind was the young readers, Indian or otherwise, that cannot read Gujarati. My own two children are the prime examples of that intended audience. Bela and Sagar both grew up in the United States and, although they speak and understand it, do not read Gujarati. I believe that their generation, Indians and foreigners alike, is quite comfortable with the

contemporary American English and that is what I have
tried to use in my translation. I have also tried to provide
footnotes to help cross the generation, geographical and
culture gaps the readers might face in reading this
translation. Sagar and Bela's help in checking my work
out from both of those angles has been invaluable.

I would never have started with this work without the
encouragement I received from my brothers
Mahendrabhai, Jayantbhai and Vinodbhai. My wife Asha
supported me in the two long years without showing her
frustration about my various moods that kept me from
working consistently. But for her well-deserved prodding,
I would not be writing this note today. Dr. Sitanshu
Yashashchandra, who I can scarcely believe I have known
only a few months, has provided not only encouragement
but active help in the publishing of this book. I owe
them all my deep gratitude.

November 20, 1998   ASHOK MEGHANI

1

IT was approaching midnight on that Saturday. A full inventory of the firm's merchandise was being prepared. *Mota Sheth* was seething with concealed rage.

He had learnt upon his return from a trip to their village that, in his absence, *Nana Sheth* had instituted a weekly Sunday holiday for all employees. In private, Mota Sheth had thoroughly chewed his younger brother out, but the two brothers valued the firm's prestige too much to air their differences publicly. The biggest tragedy of the situation was not only that the Sunday holiday grant had been made in writing, but that Nana Sheth had also given his blessings for the creation of an employees' Social Club. Mota Sheth knew better than to abruptly rescind those concessions. He was waiting for an opportune moment when the employees themselves would volunteer to give up the Sundays and ask to return to the one-day-a-month New Moon holiday. Mota Sheth genuinely believed that the free time on Sundays didn't do anything good for the employees, but actually caused harm. They tended to go out with their families and waste good money that they should be saving. He also knew from his own experience that it was difficult to concentrate at work on Mondays after being idle for a whole day. But the staff had to come to this realisation themselves. The prolonged Saturday night assignments were aimed at securing this result.

On one such late Saturday evening, a call from the office informed Mota Sheth that Sukhlal had a severe nosebleed and that he was almost unconscious.

"What a wimp! Good for absolutely nothing. Thinks I owe him because he is my future son-in-law; wouldn't strain that delicate body of his one bit. I am sending the car, get him to the hospital." Mota Sheth barked into the phone. Sukhlal was taken to a hospital and admitted. His stay there would not be short.

The young Sukhlal was actually Nana Sheth's son-in-law-to-be. His engagement to Nana Sheth's daughter dated back to the times when the two families belonged to the same social stratum in the small village of Thorewaad. The two brothers and Sukhlal's father had struggled to make a living on groceries they sold from their little shops. While Sukhlal's father was forced to stay in the village to care for his ever-ailing wife, the two brothers, with the blessings of a Jain priest, had moved to Mumbai and made a fortune selling imported textiles. Much had changed since then. Sukhlal's betrothed's old-fashioned name Santok had changed to Sushila. The Sheth brothers' wives had shed their traditional village attire and donned the more fashionable five-yard sari and blouse. The younger brother's wife had learned to mispronounce the 's' sounds as 'ch's as befitted the *nouveau riche* of Mumbai. Santok-turned-Sushila had three tutors teaching her music, Sanskrit and English at home. From a young age, Sushila had started wearing full length sari unlike the girls of her age in her old village.

The only disturbing thought that remained : did it make any sense to honour the stupid old arrangement that tied the beautiful and cultured Sushila with that country-boy Sukhlal?

Many attempts were made to convince Sukhlal's father to send Sukhlal to Mumbai where he could be educated and trained for an appropriate vocation. His father had advised Sukhlal : "You should go if this means a better future for you." But Sukhlal had been reluctant. His father needed help in providing constant care for his mother who was seriously ill. Who would cook for the younger siblings if he left? Who would keep the barely surviving shop going?

When Sukhlal had refused to listen to his father, his mother called him to her bedside one day and said : "Who knows, my son, but it is possible ... these rich people ... if they lose interest ... they may call off your engagement. If that happens, our lives will not be worth living."

This had come as a complete revelation to Sukhlal. He had not realised that the previous five years had created credible reasons for nullifying his engagement. His mother had further clarified :

"Their new affluence is only one factor. The other is, hey are spending a fortune on educating the girl, bless her soul! Everyone comes back from the city with the news that she has blossomed into a smart and beautiful young lady. We have to think about all that, son. I don't want anything to get in the way of your getting settled with her; I don't need anyone to look after me. I want you to stop worrying about me; go and let your father-in-law help you train to be a good match for the girl."

"Ba," Sukhlal's mouth had gone dry, "I will not like it there."

"And why not?" his ailing mother's face beamed with a big smile, "She will be there with you!"

"That's exactly why, Ba!" Sukhlal's handsome face was not smiling; his eyes had turned moist.

He was unable to explain his feelings. Had he had sufficient vocabulary, he would have used words like 'That Santok-turned-Sushila will keep taking my measure all the time; I'll be doing nothing but striving to be worthy of her and I'll be very uncomfortable.'

"Whatever you may be considering, son," it had taken all her energy to speak, "if the unthinkable happens, it will not only turn our lives to dirt, we'll be so disgraced that nobody will even look at your brother and sisters for marriage. And if that angel of a girl goes somewhere else after fifteen years of attachment here, your father and I will not be able to survive that shock at our age. Now that you understand how I feel, my son, I beg you to go there."

And the final straw had been the hard-hitting letter from the older in-law :

'If you insist on keeping Sukhlal confined there, take this as our final warning. Our daughter was not sold to you and we do not intend to deliberately consign her to a wretched life. If Sukhlal wants to marry her, he will have to prove himself deserving of her. After coming here, if he wants to further his education, we will be happy to help him; if he wants to get into business, there are plenty of opportunities here.

On the other hand, if you take Sushila for granted, we want you to think again! You should understand that we did not raise and educate our only daughter to send her to your dusty Thorewaad shack to breathe the smoke from the cow-dung cakes burning in your kitchen. We would like your decision so that we can announce it to our community.'

The threat was unambiguous and unmistakable. Sukhlal's father could not eat that day. Seeing her father and older brother so depressed, the young Sooraj—forced into cooking duties because of her mother's illness and barely able to hold *rotla* in her small hands—did not eat either. Sukhlal's younger brother went off to school on a half-empty stomach.

Four days later Sukhlal left for Mumbai. He had got collared shirts and long jackets tailored in haste from a nearby township. He wore new shoes with his new clothes. When Sooraj put the *chaandalo* that ran down his forehead, she had not liked his new attire. His mother had struggled to sit up with her husband's help; she had touched Sukhlal's bowed head and managed to whisper her blessings for a long life.

2

"YOU don't plan to bring him here, do you? Let's not frighten poor Sushila unnecessarily." Sushila's mother had advised Nana Sheth, her husband, the night before Sukhlal's arrival.

"If that's what you want, we'll put him up at the office." Nana Sheth had acquiesced rather quickly.

In the morning, Nana Sheth ordered the car out to meet Sukhlal at the railway station. Mota Sheth immediately jumped on him : "Why do you want to pamper him like that? Ask one of the men to hire a horse-cart and go get him."

"I thought ... er... I will ride out to the station and get him to the office." Nana Sheth's discomfort was evident.

"You will not go; and you will not start spoiling him! And, who knows what the future holds! We are not going to jump blindly into anything but consider what is good for Sushila. No harm is done, yet. We have to look for a way out of this mess. Fortunately, time is on our side."

While this was going on, Sushila entered with their tooth-brushing equipment. The customary smile was missing from her face. She placed the containers of water, fresh *daatuns* and some table salt in front of each of them and left without a word.

"Did you see how pale she has turned already?" Mota Sheth observed as he chewed on his *daatun*. The younger brother said nothing as he worked on his own *daatun*.

"Praaniya!" Mota Sheth instructed the office employee who had just returned from the market with fresh vegetables, "Sukhlal is arriving from Thorewaad. Go to the railway station and bring him to the office. He is going to live and work with you people there."

"I really should meet Sukhlal!" The trembling Nana Sheth expressed his desire one more time.

"Didn't I say there was no need to?" The elder brother's facial expression matched the hardness of his voice, "Why don't you just do what I say? Do you think this is a joke?"

Nana Sheth remained quiet for the rest of his *daatun* ritual. They left for the office after a quick breakfast. Sukhlal had arrived and was waiting for them. His greeting to the two elders was respectful but quiet. Mota Sheth responded with nothing more than a terse nod.

The empty cup and saucer next to Sukhlal appeared to be from a restaurant. He apparently had been treated to a breakfast of tea.

"Where is that dumb ...?" Mota Sheth took his anger out on the office servant. "What are you waiting for? Get this dirty cup out of here."

Even the inexperienced Sukhlal could tell that he, not the servant, was the real target of that rebuke. He picked up the offending items and handed them to the servant.

"Get a wet mop and clean up over there." Mota Sheth's instructions continued. The non-stop orders he issued to everyone around him were the signs of his newly acquired affluence and stood out like new unwashed clothing that did not quite fit. What irked him most was Sukhlal's occupation of one small corner of his spacious *gaadi*.

Sukhlal had no particular desire to sit there; the employee who brought him to the office had pointed to Mota Sheth's *gaadi* to him upon arrival. Sukhlal himself, whether in deference or out of fear, had tried to minimise this transgression; but Mota Sheth's disapproving glance repeatedly went to his left where Sukhlal sat. Finally, that visual shoving had made Sukhlal slide down from the *gaadi* on to the bare floor.

"How is your mother's health?" Mota Sheth asked after a long and deliberate pause. His tone implied resentment of Sukhlal's mother's sickness—as if she had committed a crime or, worse still, the whole thing was a scam.

"She is OK." Sukhlal decided it would be considered uncivilised to dwell on—even mention—his mother's sickness by the rules of Mumbai society. He added while he had the opportunity, "My father and mother have sent their regards to everybody."

Mota Sheth did not think it worthy of a response and got busy with the mail which had arrived just then.

Nana Sheth had retreated to his own smaller office in the back. Having finished with the mail, Mota Sheth entered that office. As he sat down, he asked his younger brother :

"Well, did you get a good look at him?"

"He seems to have lost weight. Five years ago, he looked ..."

"Who cares about five years ago? Let's worry about now. Do you see anything good in him? One good thing?"

"Give him time and he will be alright."

"Are you out of your mind? There's nothing to wait for. I won't play games with my only daughter's future."

Sushila was the only child between the two brothers. Mota Sheth and his wife were childless. Sushila was the centre of their universe. Well-wishers had advised a second marriage to Mota Sheth but he had refused to follow that path to producing an heir. Every person's life has brighter and shadowy sides; Mota Sheth's inner light had manifested itself in his strict belief in monogamy. He had considered Sushila to be his sole heir.

"I don't see what we can do." Nana Sheth sounded reluctant.

"We must do something! But for now, let's put him to work. I think it's as hopeless as trying to squeeze oil out of sand, but let's put him through the mill anyway." And Mota Sheth's words had almost become reality. Sukhlal was pushed into heavy work like any other low ranking employee. Sukhlal, for his part, was determined to prove his worthiness to be a son-in-law and had jumped in with both feet. He pushed any thoughts of self-respect to the background. Every night at bed-time, his mother's voice kept echoing in his mind ...

"If they break this engagement, it might as well be a dose of poison for us."

3

SUKHLAL was in Mumbai almost three months before he got his first glimpse of Sushila.

In those months, he had been invited to his in-laws' place for dinner a couple of times. But every time, he was driven back to the office—his place to live—as soon as the dinner was over. Once he heard a voice in the other room instructing the chauffeur to come back immediately after dropping Sushila off. He had wondered where the girl was going. To study? For embroidery or music lessons perhaps? Shopping for new saris and brooches? For the rest of the dinner, his imagination had taken him roaming all over Mumbai.

Sitting in the front seat next to the chauffeur on his return trip to the office, Sukhlal had pictured a stylish Sushila in the back seat. His olfactory sense worked overtime to conjure up the intoxicating scent of perfume left behind by a previous occupant of the car. Sukhlal, the simpleton, would never be able to verbalise his feelings from that experience; and no self-respecting poet would ever have the time to describe this villager's mental suffering.

Sukhlal was jealous of the chauffeur who he thought must know every minute detail of Sushila's life. He obviously saw enough of Sushila every day in the rearview mirror. He must be the only one to feast on the fragrance of perfumes and flowers worn by Sushila!

In the following days, with great difficulty, Sukhlal suppressed the naïve urge to talk to the chauffeur about such things and immersed himself in his work.

Three months went by and it was the prime mango season in Mumbai. The monthly 'New Moon' holiday was approaching. The painful abscess that Mota Sheth had long suffered from had finally receded and, in celebration, he had ordered a staff picnic. A mountainside bungalow in a remote western suburb of Mumbai was borrowed for a day from some friends. The young staff members spent the prior evening and most of the night transporting all the provisions including baskets filled with mangoes.

Sukhlal was one of the participants in that backbreaking ordeal. His time in Mumbai had not been kind to his health. His constant brooding about his family back in Thorewaad on one hand and about Sushila on the other had not helped either. That night he had worked extra hard in anticipation of seeing Sushila at least briefly during the all-day picnic. Spurred on by that burst of artificial energy, Sukhlal had lugged the heavy loads back and forth all night. That night he had felt the first snap in his chest.

That pain was the messenger bearing the reward for the inhuman drudgery at the office. It was also the result of the skill with which the other employees pushed their work off on him.

"Has anyone seen Sukhlal Sheth?", "Is Sukhlal Sheth available to help?", "This job is right up his alley," and other similar phrases were used by the other employees if they ever found Sukhlal catching his breath between assigned tasks. These utterances, always loud enough to be heard by Mota Sheth, caused Sukhlal to immediately jump to the task at hand. His fellow workers employed this trick regularly, making Sukhlal the implement of their enjoyment and relief from their own workload. Sukhlal had feared about this happening at the picnic, too. To fend that off, he had approached the resident jester Pranjeevan, a.k.a. "Praniya" and begged to be assigned the relatively light task of extracting mango juice.

"Give me a break, Sukhlal Sheth!" Praniya had teased him, "All this is going to be yours one day! You are just trying to make us look bad."

Sukhlal knew that these people meant just the opposite of what they said. But he had considered any discussion of that totally futile and just repeated his request with "Please! Please!"

"Then, listen." The staff jester—and the 'boss' of the pack—had pulled him aside and whispered, "I know that you are up to no good today."

"What do you mean?"

"You think I don't know?"

"'What are you talking about?"

"You... are... planning ... to... meet... Sushilaben... here... today." Praniya emphasised every word.

The second spasm shook Sukhlal but he continued to laugh. He just said : "Please let me sit and work; and please, for God's sake, leave me alone."

"Then give me your word."

"What?"

"That you will not see her."

"I am dying here and all you want to do is joke about it?"

"No deal then. Promise that you will not speak to her even if she approaches you!"

"Pranjeevanbhai, please leave me alone."

Encouraged by Sukhlal's pitiful tone, Praniya raised his voice, "And you will not exchange handkerchiefs or rings."

"Please..."

"And will not pass love letters!" In a loud voice that was deliberately unintelligible to others, Praniya continued. "Agreed?"

"Whatever you say. Who is going to give anything to anyone anyway? Just let me be, please, Pranjeevanbhai." Sukhlal doubled up in pain as another spasm hit him.

Pranjeevan had mercifully relented. Sukhlal sat down with the mango group of fellow workers and Pranjeevan issued strict instructions : "Don't anybody ask Sukhlal Sheth to do anything else. He is not well and will stay right here."

What Sukhlal really needed was to lie down and rest. His chest pain worsened as he sat up and worked on the mangoes. Afraid of the bully Pranjeevan, the others didn't dare bother him directly but found one excuse or another to keep Sushila as the central topic of conversation.

"I tell you, the best mangoes are the ones that Sushilaben picked out."

"I don't see how she does it. Sushilaben must have a sixth sense about mangoes."

"Certainly not something you can learn!"

"If Sushilaben had not been with me yesterday, I would be a dead man by now! She stopped me from buying the 200-pound lot that I had selected; 'Dayal, deep down, I can smell the tartness in these', she said. We bought only ten pounds from that lot and, would you believe it, every single mango turned out to be sour!"

"Her mother's family owns a whole mango grove; could be the time she spent there."

"Oh really! Our Otamchand's in-laws have a grove too. Why can't his wife pick'em?"

"This Dayal can't stop talking about Sushilaben."

"That's because she is smart. Knows what she's talking about. Nobody can fool her!"

Sushilaben's name had become the sustenance everyone needed to continue working as also the chief source of entertainment. They kept their eyes on one another as they talked. All except Sukhlal, who was in intense pain. Unable to bear it any longer, he finally asked , "Would you guys mind if I laid down for a while? My chest hurts."

"But of course, Sukhlal Sheth! You are, after all, the son-in-law. Want me to make your bed? On second thoughts, why don't you just move into that bedroom over there?"

The sarcasm was totally lost on Sukhlal. He stretched out on the bare floor right where he was, lying on one side, his hand clutching to his chest.

A messenger came and called out, "Come on you guys, Mota Sheth wants everyone out there to swim in the lake as soon as you are done with the mangoes."

"Let's go, this is going to be fun!" The rest of the juicing was completed in a hurry and everyone left for the lake, leaving Sukhlal sleeping. Someone showed some pity for him, "Let the poor man rest!"

Noticing that Sukhlal had dozed off, another was more candid : "What an idiot! He still has illusions of marrying that girl. He doesn't know Mota Sheth! He will eventually be tossed out like a dog."

"Then what are they holding him here for?"

"To get his release papers."

"What release papers?"

"A signed statement admitting to his impotence ... and, get this, willingly asking for an annulment from his betrothal with Sushilaben."

"That will be the end of him! Who is going to marry him after that?"

"Are you kidding? If Lady Luck smiles on him and if he goes home with some serious dough, eligible girls' fathers will be lining up outside his door. It is the money, not manhood, that gets the girl!"

This conversation continued out the door and all the way to the lake. All the men got into the spirit of the picnic and jumped into the lake. It was as if they had traveled back in time to their childhoods in the various

Saurashtra villages; they repeatedly jumped off the trees, some splashing water all around, others diving deep into the water. The noise was deafening. The two cooks also joined them after completing their cooking chores.

Half an hour after everyone had left the building for the lake, Sukhlal was startled out of his nap by the sound of someone asking "Where is the cook?" from the next room. He opened his eyes to find a young woman before him. "Do you know where he went?" she asked. Embarrassed at being caught napping, Sukhlal sat up and immediately reached for the one or two mangoes still left there.

The young woman was, of course, Sushila. She saw Sukhlal, at first sleeping and later distressed at being seen sleeping. She was about to leave but stopped and asked : "Isn't the cook here?"

"I don't know."

Sushila went out of the kitchen where Sukhlal was and stopped in the adjoining room. She had recognised Sukhlal—her betrothed. This was the first time she had met him alone. Previously, in her quick glances at him from a distance, he had seemed gaunt and nothing much to look at. But, today she had seen him from close and his sleeping face had seemed guileless and wholesome; she had heard his voice after he woke up. The incessant talk at home had painted Sukhlal as a village idiot incapable of even putting a sentence together. It was hard to believe that those things had been said about this person!

"I am sorry I disturbed you. I didn't really need anything." She said, making no attempt to leave.

Wanting her to stay, Sukhlal said : "I had some chest pain and had just stretched out for a while. I was done with my assigned work anyway."

His obvious awareness of the need to prove his worthiness, even at the cost of his health, was the reason behind that remark.

"You have lost weight!" Sushila continued nervously from the next room.

Sukhlal had guessed that the girl was Sushila. Now convinced by that remark that it was her, he responded quickly : "Oh no, I haven't ... By the way, my mother sent you lots of love."

"How is Ba?" Sushila asked after a perceptible pause and Sukhlal's heart resumed its beating again. Even a moment's silence from Sushila, in response to the words from his mother, had naturally seemed like the lull before an eruption to Sukhlal. Now it was Sukhlal's turn to pause and think. His *my* mother had evoked a "How is Ba?" response from Sushila. The difference between the two expressions was unexplainable but quite clear. Sushila's respectful mention of 'Ba' could not have been faked and had to have come from her heart.

"She couldn't even get up when I left three months ago. She had blessed me from her bed. I haven't heard from them since then."

Sushila felt like she had stepped into a strange new world. How could these musical utterances be coming from a man who had been described to her as nothing more than a wretched stray animal? The future mother-in-law's long illness had been the subject of constant cursing and calling of names in Sushila's house. Her family had helped create such a frightful image of the mother-in-law's disease in Sushila's mind that she could almost smell the stench emanating from the sickbed. But the news brought by this young man created in her a feeling of compassion for the sick mother-in-law. The person that tried to rise from her bed to say goodbye to her son ... that had to settle for blessing him without standing up ... that sent me her love ... how could she be a monster?

"Don't you write to them?" she asked, standing beyond the door, her eyes on the floor and thinking about these things. Her eyes darted to the doors on both sides, wondering if anyone had seen her.

"Now I will."

"Why now?"

"To send them the news of your well-being ... and to tell Ba that you asked about her." Sukhlal looked at the room where Sushila was as he washed his mango-stained hands. He had to make sure that she was well before he could send such news home!

She looked very well indeed. Her complexion was slightly on the darker side but had a healthy glow to it. Her eyes were unusually clear. He hardly had time for a detailed look though. He knew the perils of staring at any young girl. In this case, the stakes were even higher.

But Sushila didn't move from her spot. Sukhlal began to be concerned about his predicament. Every young man has this natural fear that, if and when caught, the girl will invariably lay the blame on the boy to save herself; she will lose no time in telling lies and shedding false tears. Sukhlal didn't know this girl well and was worried. Could she be setting him up for something? The sooner she left, the better, he thought.

But Sushila's feet seemed to be glued to the floor. Meanwhile, the lake echoed with the sounds of bodies splashing in water, fountains erupting as people jumped off the tree branch. The bathers frolicked; people who wanted to get out were being dragged back into the lake. Mota Sheth and Nana Sheth were both at the lake and could be heard all the way inside the bungalow. Mota Sheth's voice cracked in the fashionable way as was required of the neo-affluent.

The roar of a car's engine cut through all that noise. Several voices joined in the chorus of welcome : "Hurry up and change, Vijaychandrabhai! We've been waiting for you."

Mota Sheth personally went to receive the newly-arrived, cultured-looking young man. The conversation between the two went like "What made you late?" "I had an appointment with the Hon. Setalwad. Sir P. had strongly recommended that I see ..." as they made their way to the bungalow and went up the steps.

Mota Sheth called out : "Where are Sushila's mother and *Bhabhu*?* Vijaychandra has arrived. Ask the cook to get ready to serve lunch. Where is he?" On his way to the kitchen, he entered the room where Sushila was before she could leave. Her eyes and face looked troubled as she walked out. Mota Sheth instructed her as well : "Sushila, my dear, can you arrange to have lunch served immediately? Vijaychandra is already here."

Sushila left without answering and entered the room on the other side of the bungalow where the other women were. When Mota Sheth looked towards the kitchen and looked for the cook, it was Sukhlal who answered : "I'll go get the cook right away."

Seeing his worst fears realised and extremely worried now, Sukhlal ran towards the lake. Mota Sheth's face turned red seeing him coming out of the kitchen. Is that why the lowly stooge had stayed behind—to see Sushila? Did he intimidate Sushila into coming here? Why did she look so disturbed? ... Enraged by such thoughts, he lost his self-control. He was going to get some answers even if that killed the entire picnic. Ignoring Sukhlal, he charged into the room full of ladies and started his 'inquisition'.

"Why was Sushila in the kitchen? Who called her there? Who made her cry? Who is threatening her? I will flay the son-of-a-bitch alive! Who does he think he is? What right does he have to call her there? He does

---

*   A man couldn't address his wife or a younger brother's wife by name.

not even have the right to step inside my house and he
.. he dares to order my daughter around? That ... that
scumball ... bully ... hoodlum!"

"Calm down, please," his wife admonished him in a
low voice. "We don't even know what has happened."

"What is there to know?" Sushila's mother spoke out
for her brother-in-law from behind the veil formed by
the end of her sari.* "The girl is sobbing her heart out,
Bhabhiji! We must find out who did this to her."

"Mother ... please, mother ...you don't even know ..."
was all that could be heard between Sushila's sobs. She
couldn't even form a sentence. Her mother's
interpretation of her broken words was just the opposite
of what Sushila had intended.

"Bhabhu ... please ... call ... Bhabhu ... here." The
exasperated Sushila looked for her one confidante.

She loved and trusted Bhabhu. The childless wife of
Mota Sheth was a grand woman with much culture and
had been the real influence in Sushila's balanced
upbringing.

"Bhabhu is the one that made you into the simpleton
you are." Her mother called for her sister-in-law :
"Bhabhiji, your precious Sushila wants *you*."

"What's the matter, honey?" Bhabhu was calm as could
be.

"Please tell Mota Bapuji not to scold anyone."

"Not scold anyone? You want him to put up with this?
Wasn't he ashamed to call a girl of her age here, all
alone? Is anyone going to look at the root of this
problem?" Sushila's mother was not going to let that
pass.

And her words were not lost on Mota Sheth who stood
outside. "You just wait and see. Your brother-in-law has

---

* Women of the time would not show their faces nor would speak
  directly to elder men in their husbands' families.

learnt a thing or two in his years in Mumbai. He knows how to unlock all doors. Just sit back and watch the show now. Do you think I like this any better than you do? But I have had to swallow my pride and wait. If my own wife hadn't held me back, do you think I would have let it go this far?"

"Now, now, slow down. Let's not be hasty." His wife repeated her earlier plea for patience.

Mota Sheth's angry words had been heard very clearly at the lakeside and all the frolicking had stopped. Nobody knew what had transpired. Sukhlal was the only one who knew and was scared out of his wits. The only question in his mind was : what role had Sushila played in this whole episode? Each answer provided by his overworked imagination seemed as dreadful as the other. Sushila's last words to him in the kitchen had been :

"Why is everyone trying to get the annulment? When did I ever ask for it? Nobody has even bothered to ask me what *I* want. It has hurt me to know how they have treated you and worked you like a slave. For God's sake ... why don't you look after your health?"

Mota Sheth had entered the room just as she had finished saying those words and started crying. What reason did she give them for crying?

Could he trust this girl?

4

A S the big feast was being laid out, Mota Sheth called Pranajivan aside and whispered to him : "Praniya, don't let that Romeo sit anywhere near me!"

"No problem, I will take care of it."

As Mota Sheth watched Pranajivan shuffle Sukhlal around to the remotest corner of the assembly, the authority with which Praniyo did the job left no doubt in Mota Sheth's mind that it was a matter of time before the rascal became a partner in his business! Meanwhile, Pranajivan seated himself next to Sukhlal and started elbowing him; elbowed him and whispered : "Looks like you have been a naughty boy! Broke your promise, didn't you? Start packing your bags, Casanova, and so long!"

Closer to Mota Sheth, the young VIP Vijaychandra had become the centre of attention. People watched as he very carefully removed his jacket and his silk hat and hung them on a hook conveniently close to his seat. Everyone else had left their coats and hats in the outer room. He had set himself apart from the crowd even with a little matter like that. His bare head was the epitome of neatness with every single hair in its assigned place with military precision. Having locks of hair flowing over his forehead was not Vijaychandra's style. His shirt got the loving care worthy of a living companion and hugged his body with perfection in return. In fact, every stitch of clothing on his body was a testimony to the meticulousness of its owner with no trace of a 'nobody is going to notice' attitude.

Mota Sheth made sure that Vijaychandra sat right next to him and got to know quite a few details of his life. Lost both parents in early childhood; brought up by his sister and brother-in-law; tutored other students to pay for his own education. "Had to quit studies twice to work full time or I would have graduated from college at 20. Sheth M.B. is sending me to England for further studies. They plan to have me help develop one of their new businesses."

"How long will you be in England?"

"A couple of years."

"Not planning to settle abroad, are you?"

"Absolutely not, sir."

Vijaychandra turned out to be a native of Saurashtra as well. The talk revealed a lot of close links between their two families. And, although Mota Sheth thought Vijaychandra's family did not measure up to his own family's stature, the young man's own abilities and prospects impressed him a great deal.

"Come, let me show you around." After lunch, Mota Sheth invited Vijaychandra for a walk around the estate. Vijaychandra donned his jacket and cap with the same care that he had exercised in removing them. Each of his immaculate coat-sleeves seemed to cry out even to those not watching : 'Come on, I dare you to find one wrinkle in me!" The amazing thing was that all this neatness gave no appearance of any overt showiness or affectation. What can one not do by trying? This may seem to be a contradiction, but is it not true that looking natural is but the result of working at it? It was the result of hard work in Vijaychandra's case for sure, because how else would he not look showy with the scented silk handkerchief peeking out of his jacket pocket? Not only did it look tasteful, one actually felt that his handkerchief should show and show only that much. And it had to be scented; if not, Vijaychandra's personality would seem, well, incomplete.

As they strolled, Mota Sheth made more small talk and asked, "Does this look like a good bungalow to buy?" and navigated him towards the room where the women sat. He introduced Vijaychandra to his wife : "You know this young man's family well. Isn't it a small world? He is being sent to England by Mansukhlal Balabhai's firm..."

His wife, known to the staff as Mota Shethani, looked up and sized Vijaychandra up in that one look. After that, her steady eyes did not move from her husband's face. Childless at forty, she looked no older than thirty. The impression she made on everyone she met was that of a person who could serve as the living ideal of grand womanhood and, if preserved, as the ideal for a millennium.

"Where is Sushila?" Mota Sheth tried to sound casual but everyone, including Vijaychandra, knew his real intent behind the question and in bringing this guest all the way to the women's room.

"I'm here." Sushila didn't move from where she stood.

"Why, Sushila, what are you doing up there? Come here, my girl! Did you eat yet? Did you try the mango juice? Our Sushila is a poor eater in general, and even worse with mangoes."

Sushila was totally nonchalant as she stepped into the room. Mota Sheth was chagrined to notice that Sushila had not washed her tear-streaked face from half hour ago. Vijaychandra, on the other hand, found her unwashed face a lot more appealing. Even in his young age, he had concluded that nature had provided women with bottomless reservoirs of tears behind their eyes only to help them refresh their feminine appeal at will.

The picnic broke up late in the evening. Vijaychandra was invited to drive back with Mota Sheth and his family in their car. He sat next to the chauffeur and sensed rather than saw that Sushila sat between Mota Sheth and his wife in the back. Mota Sheth helped out by talking to him all the way back, forcing him to turn and look back. While talking to Mota Sheth, his eyes didn't have to move much to look at Sushila; to his credit, the wise young man looked straight at Mota Sheth without letting his gaze move even a millimetre. Some people have the natural gift for a steady stare.

He had asked to be dropped off at Sir P.'s residence and Mota Sheth had the chauffeur make a detour around Malabar Hill to comply with that request. There they parted with Mota Sheth inviting him to visit his home some evening to talk about business.

On their way home, Mota Sheth told his wife : "Had it not been for this young man's presence, today's picnic would have been a total disaster. The son-of-a-bitch showed his true colours today!"

Sushila looked away and Bhabhu chose not to reply, hoping for a quiet ride home. The fuming husband's frustration remained unvented, the lack of a response killing his desire to talk.

As Sushila reached home and while Vijaychandra's shirt collar swayed in the cool Malabar Hill breeze, Sukhlal was toiling away at the picnic bungalow. He ran around taking an inventory of the pots and pans, re-packing the leftover condiments and gathering up the cutlery while the office-colleagues directed their ridicule at him. The cooks claimed they had earned their right to rest and to chew their tobacco; Pranajivan believed his duties now consisted of firing instructions while he stretched out; most of the others declared that "After all, this stuff belongs to Sukhlal Me'ta, not to us. If one little cup is missing and if the Nana Shethani gets mad,

Sukhlal Me'ta, we'll tell her that you, her son-in-law, were the one in charge of it all."

When it was all loaded into a truck, the whole staff returned to the Mumbai office. The third day after that was a Saturday. That Saturday night, Sukhlal's head finally exploded into a nosebleed that would not stop.

And he landed in the Harkishandas Hospital.

5

LYING in a charity-ward bed in the basement of the hospital, Sukhlal thanked his lucky stars for his illness. He had assumed that the around-the-clock care that he received from the hospital staff was the result of his influential father-in-law's instructions. His constant thought was of how quickly his mother would get well, if she were to be treated at such a great hospital, where he couldn't even turn over in bed without a white-clad nurse rushing over to help! He had not been touched by that many women in his entire life.

The nurses that sponged his body with hot water and then soothed it with fragrant talcum powder seemed to him like angels sent from heaven. He prayed for a prolonged stay in the hospital.

All the neighbouring patients had someone or other to keep them company and visitors who came daily by the dozens. Sukhlal attracted attention by the total lack of visitors. Women—young girls and older women alike—noticed the forever lonely young man and asked each other in whispers : why haven't we seen a mother or a sister visiting? Isn't he married? Did he not have friends or anyone to see him at all?

The patient in the bed immediately next to Sukhlal was a man in his fifties. It was difficult to say what his ailment was. He called out "Nurse! Nurse!" even to turn on his side. After a nurse helped him sit up, he constantly barraged her with questions in his broken English : "Are you married yet? Are you going to work like this all your life? Why don't you get married? ... Will you help me sit outside? ..."

Sukhlal had noticed that the man needed no help to sit up. When his wife visited him in the afternoons, he never asked for any help.

Even the nurse would occasionally lose her cool and tell him : "Grandpa, I don't see why you keep coming back to the hospital. There is nothing wrong with you!"

"Why do you call me grandpa?"

"Why? Because you are old enough to be one."

Sukhlal did not understand why it bothered this man to acknowledge his age. Could it be that he was too humble to accept the deferential treatment reserved for the elderly?

The nurse's name was Leena. It never failed to amaze Sukhlal that a name could sound so musical every time the other nurses called out for her with the elongated "Lee...naa...".

The old man in the next bed resented the special attention that Leena gave to Sukhlal. He cautioned Sukhlal more than once about getting too close to these nurses : "They wouldn't think of blackmailing you for all you're worth."

Not knowing how much of that advice to believe, Sukhlal would try to keep his distance which caused Leena to pay even more attention to him. She would appear from nowhere at breakfast time and threatened and cajoled him into drinking a whole glass of milk. She would caress him and say :

"Smarty, my dear! Why don't you let me make an egg for you every day? You are weak and the egg will be very good for you. Come on, Smarty, we need to get some flesh on those bones!"

At the mention of eggs, Sukhlal would just lay there and smile his patient smile. That smile looked so sweet on his thin, pale face that Leena would repeatedly bring the topic up just to see that smile.

"Why do you call me 'Smarty'?" he asked once.

"All my patients who keep smiling even when in pain I call 'Smarty'. It's English for both neat and intelligent. But if it bothers you, I won't call you that."

Sukhlal wouldn't respond to the implied query. He wondered if the man that everyone at the office thought of as 'sickly' and 'lazy' was the same man this woman was calling smart!

But, as soon as Leena's back was turned, his self-appointed guardian angel from the next bed would whisper : "When she has you eating eggs, don't tell me I didn't warn you!"

Leena appeared to be thirty-ish. A bundle of joy, she seemed to laugh more than she talked. Sukhlal constantly compared her face with Sushila's. He had seen Sushila only once and didn't remember her face very clearly, but he tried to complete the missing details in that mental canvas with broad strokes borrowed from Leena's facial features. His clumsy attempts at this creation resulted in blurring of both pictures in his mind; so much so, that even when Leena's face was in front of his eyes, what his confused mind visualised was an absurd caricature.

The hospital rules permitted only the closest family members and no general visitors with the patients in the afternoon. One afternoon, the new wife of the neighbouring 'Grandpa', half his age, peeled an orange for him and offered a plateful to Sukhlal as well. For someone who asked for a nurse's assistance for the slightest movement, 'Grandpa' turned quickly in his bed to observe the exchange between his 'Navi' (new wife) and Sukhlal. As Sukhlal declined the offered fruit with a smile, the 'Navi' asked him : "Don't you have any family here?"

"You! get back here, you low-li ..." but the 'Navi' was back before "Grandpa" could complete his contemptuous phrase. All Sukhlal could do was to watch his neighbour

heap abuse at his young wife. Although he couldn't
understand everything 'Grandpa' said in his Kutchhi
dialect, Sukhlal caught some words meaning 'You are
going to pay for this when I am home, you ...'

Sukhlal was no more the naïve person that had come
out of his village. Accustomed to blaming himself for
everything, he was itching to jump in with an explanation
but kept quiet for fear of making the sensitive situation
even worse than it was. At that moment, Leena arrived
to see his unhappy expression.

"Temperature!" She stuck a thermometer in his mouth
and in one quick motion lifted his arm to take his pulse
and her own to look at her wristwatch. Her impassive
face did not reflect the hundreds of things her mind was
racing to sort out.

Her readings done, she pulled the thermometer out
and asked him gently in English : "Why aren't you
smiling, Smarty?"

Then she realised that Sukhlal, with his inadequate
English education, had not understood her question and
asked him in Hindi.

"That's what I like to see. Stay that way." Seeing the
characteristic Sukhlal smile, she turned around and saw
an unlikely sight ... a visitor by Sukhlal's bed! A young
woman stood there and nervously looked all around.

"Who are you looking for?" Leena asked, first in English
and then in Hindi. She couldn't believe that a beautiful
girl like that would wait all these days to see Sukhlal;
she had to be here to see someone else.

"Him." was all that the visitor said. Sukhlal's face
was turned the other way and he tried to turn towards
the speaker of the word 'him'. Leena immediately stopped
him from exerting himself with a "No, Smarty, no!" and
asked the visitor to go around the bed to the other side.

The visitor finally came in Sukhlal's view and he
recognised her. Sushila!

6

LEENA wondered if this woman was here to visit Smarty or just to tour the hospital ward.

She had every reason to wonder. Sushila's eyes had yet to focus on Sukhlal directly. She would look at Sukhlal's face for a moment and then would nervously look all around and behind her as if to see if anyone had noticed it before returning to Sukhlal. Her behaviour was like that of a caged animal. She imagined every bed in the big ward to be occupied by familiar faces that were staring at her. She finally mustered all her courage to overcome that paranoia and managed to ask : "What happened to you?"

"Not a word, Smarty! Keep absolutely quiet!" Leena ordered before Sukhlal could even move his lips to answer. She sternly told Sushila, "Don't make him talk. I don't want him to start hemorrhaging again."

"Okay." Sushila smiled at this woman's authority over Sukhlal.

Leena came back with some medicine for Sukhlal and asked Sushila in Hindi : "What are you to Sukhlal? His employer? Aunt? Cousin? Where were you all these days? Are you from out of town?"

"Yes." Sushila did not elaborate.

"Now, listen," Leena carried on : "Don't take Smarty away from here any time soon. He has lost much blood and is still very weak. Keep him here and I will make him strong again."

Leena kept moving from bed to bed but made sure to stop at Sukhlal's bed to talk for a couple of minutes,

after visiting every other patient. It was as if the links
to all her other work went past Sukhlal's bed. She kept
a watchful eye on Sushila even from the distant beds
and yelled out at the slightest suspicion of Sushila's
attempt to talk : "Don't talk, Smarty! Don't answer her.
Careful now, Smarty."

After that, she would scold Sushila as she went by : "
You people from village just don't understand how
precious human life is! Don't you dare make him worse."

It was impossible for Leena to even suspect that an
obviously wealthy looking girl like Sushila could be
engaged to be married to the obviously poor Sukhlal
lying in that Charity Ward bed. From a distance, Leena
caught Sushila committing one more crime. Leena had
put some non-fragrant artificial flowers in a glass by
Sukhlal's bed that morning. She observed Sushila
replacing her flowers with some roses she must have
brought in her handkerchief. Sushila's state of trepidation
was evident as she fumbled through the motions of
arranging the roses. Only when she was rid of those
roses that she appeared to calm down a little.

Leena returned to Sukhlal's bed and tried, in vain, to
look stern. Sushila had already figured out that it was
not Leena's nature to show anger and any such attempt
actually made her laugh. Leena finally stopped laughing
and said : "You think you are verey smart, eh Miss! Or
is it Mrs.? I told you not to talk so you used the language
of the flowers! Listen, don't stay too long, okay? When
the Doctor comes around, he gets really nasty with
visitors during non-visiting hours. Understand?"

A half hour was gone before Sushila could exchange
even a word with Sukhlal. Finally when Leena looked at
Sukhlal, tears were running slowly down his cheeks but
his face still smiled.

"What's the matter, Smarty?" Leena wiped his tears
with a towel and caressed his forehead.

This was too much for Sushila to take. She was about to approach when Leena asked : "What did you say that made him cry like that? In all his days here, I have never seen tears in his eyes. You must have told him something behind my back. You people just don't know how to behave when visiting the sick. Don't you people have any sense at all? You people ..."

Leena's ranting about "you people" went on and on. Sushila had no idea how to deal with this woman gone berserk and just kept her silence—and fumed inside. This stranger, half-native and half-European woman— probably an untouchable Hindu-converted-Christian— had assumed total authority over her patient. Wouldn't even let me say a word! Who did she think she was? What right did she have to wipe Sukhlal's tears? Was she totally shameless? She would touch Sukhlal's face in my presence? But if she had any shame why would she be doing a nurse's job? Touching someone's foot or face was the same for them! Wasn't she ashamed of using the same hands that handled all the dirt and excrement to touch somebody's face? Sukhlal must hate that touch—or did he? If he did, why wouldn't he tell her so?

But, despite her own disapproval of Leena's actions, Sushila firmly grasped one fact from Leena's chatter that nobody had visited Sukhlal since he was hospitalised. She also agreed that after eight days of being the round-the-clock guardian, feeder and caretaker of the ailing Sukhlal, Leena was amply justified in objecting to this encroachment from an unknown like Sushila.

Leena didn't move from Sukhlal's bedside; her hands did not move from his forehead. Sukhlal's gaze moved between Leena and Sushila as if trying to establish a connection between the two. Finally Sushila broke the silence and asked Leena : "How is his health now?"

"Listen to her! After more than a week has gone by, the Princess wants to know how he is!" Leena was not ready to make peace just yet. "First, you tell me what you said to him that upset him so much."

"Nothing, I haven't even talked to him."

"Is that right, Smarty?"

Sukhlal nodded and smiled his weak but disarming smile.

"She is your employer, isn't she?"

The confused Sukhlal nodded again.

"You people," Leena turned on Sushila : "make your servants work like beasts of burden. And then you think your responsibility is over when you dump them in the hospital! Nobody brings any Eau de Cologne to sponge him with, no talc powder, no nothing! I brought everything from my home. See, all top of the line stuff!" She opened the side-table drawer to show the supplies.

"Lee...naa..." came the lilting call from the head nurse. "Coming, Matron." And Leena ran off with a "No talking, Smarty." caution for Sukhlal. Her quiet shoes glided gracefully as if on a ski-slope and her stocking-clad perfectly shaped legs moved causing her skirt to sway with them.

"Why were you crying?" Sushila asked quickly.

Once again, before Sukhlal could say a word, Sushila's surprised expression stopped him. Sushila stood facing the door of the ground floor ward opposite the stairs that lead upstairs to higher floors. A group of three people—Vijaychandra and two women—was on its way up the stairs. Sushila didn't know the women but her gaze met Vijaychandra's.

Sushila turned away before Vijaychandra could ask her who she was visiting.

Whether for being seen by Sushila in the company of the two women or for whatever reason, Vijaychandra, too, was taken aback for a second. He recovered his composure very quickly and was inwardly contemptuous of himself for his temporary discomfiture. The trio turned around on the stairs and entered the room to face Sushila.

"Who is sick?" Vijaychandra asked as he looked at the bed; he couldn't reconcile Sushila's presence at the sickbed of this contemptible creature. He didn't know Sukhlal well—and even if he did, the feeble Sukhlal was not very recognizable even to those who knew him.

At this point, Nurse Leena, the heretofore thorn in the side of Sushila, became her saviour. As if one visitor was not enough, the addition three more visitors for her Smarty—two women among them!—was more than Leena could take. Rushing back to Sukhlal's bed, she folded her hands in mockery and spoke with an angry smile : "So, they finally come out of the woodwork! What is going on here? Who are you people? What is my patient to you? And where were you all these days?"

None of the three had an answer as to their relationship with the patient, of course.

"Answer me!"

"Excuse me," Vijaychandra addressed her in English as he removed his hat and wiped his sweaty brow with his scented handkerchief, "but I was here to see this young lady." His eyes moved in the direction of Sushila.

Where the other people would have to use their hands to point, usually a slight move of his eyelashes was sufficient for Vijaychandra.

Leena's smile was filled with disdain : "Here in the hospital! Visiting the healthy rather than the sick! How appropriate! What is she to you?"

"An acquaintance." Vijaychandra had to pause before responding.

Leena used the opportunity provided by the "acquaintance" to caress Sukhlal's forehead.

Sukhlal remained a silent witness to this whole episode. He had seen Vijaychandra once and Pranajivan a.k.a. Praniya had repeatedly elbowed him while pointing out Vijaychandra to him : "See him, Sukhlal Sheth? Remember him well. It's good to know your competition." He had seen this man—responsible for those elbows in his ribs—at the picnic again. This was the third time. It was not easy to see him standing close to Sushila, talking to her with the familiarity of a longtime acquaintance, doffing his hat to show off his hair arrayed like the strings of an instrument, spreading fragrance from his scented handkerchief while ostensibly wiping his sweat!

You may perhaps ask : if Sukhlal was as sensible as I have tried to portray him, what was the reason for him to get so upset at that sight? How could a lowly worm like him have retained enough of his self-respect to be jealous of Vijaychandra? Some of you may even express the opinion that, in his place, openly confessing to your unworthiness of her hand and turning the beautiful Sushila over to her rightful mate, you would have proclaimed her as your 'adopted' sister and sent her your 'meagre gift' for *virpasali.*

But alas, Sukhlal, the worm, did not have that nobility of spirit in him! Lying in his bed, sickly as he was, he thought violent thoughts about Vijaychandra instead. After that close brush with death, what was he capable of but those thoughts? Such impotent jealousy!

He abruptly pushed Leena's hand away from his forehead. Leena was absolutely flabbergasted. In the eight day history of her Smarty's sick-world, being rejected like this was the first tremor that she had experienced.

Sushila had witnessed Sukhlal's gesture. She also noticed the tightening of his lips and decided it was time to get going. With a smile and an "Okay, then" to Leena, she started walking with Vijaychandra and the two women in tow like the coaches of a train.

"Would you care to join us?" Vijaychandra asked Sushila, "We can give you a ride home after visiting a patient here."

"I am not going home."

"We can take you wherever you want to go."

"I am not going far." And with that, Sushila started walking down the front steps of the hospital. Going up in the staff elevator at the invitation of a doctor friend, Vijaychandra was a little disappointed—not because Sushila had left, but because she left without witnessing this preferential treatment for him.

Sushila took a street car straight to her home. All the way home, she worried that her Mota Bapuji was going to find out about this visit. She knew that Vijaychandra went to the firm frequently. She was not all that naïve about whether these visits had something to do with business or were about the fulfilment of some secret personal desire of her Mota Bapuji's. When Vijaychandra visited their home, Mota Bapuji would suddenly develop this taste for fritters and ordered them made by Sushila. Not only that, when he would later call her out to discuss the recipe in the presence of Vijaychandra, she was old enough to understand the real purpose of that charade. Besides, if Vijaychandra was just one of Mota Bapuji's business associates or a friend, would there be any reason for him to look down in embarrassment and not say a word while the recipe was being discussed? Why would he sneak furtive glances at her?

What did that young man think of her now? Wouldn't he have to inform Mota Bapuji about today's visit? What will she tell Mota Bapuji about why she went to the hospital? Of course he would figure out who she went to see. Mota Bapuji had never even raised his voice at her. He loved her very much and that was why the old betrothal bothered him so very much. The extent of his hatred for Sukhlal caused by the picnic-day misunderstanding frightened her. Now she had been caught red-handed at the hospital. She shuddered to think of her own foolhardy step of taking flowers for Sukhlal. She could almost feel her mother's fury at the news. Sushila absolutely worshipped her Bhabhu. What would Bhabhu think of her? How would she face Bhabhu after this?

7

THE family car arrived just after dark and Sushila's heart started beating fast like the car's engine. She counted footsteps as her Mota Bapuji mounted the stairs. She heard the front door of their flat open and the shoes drop. When fifteen minutes went by and she didn't hear Mota Bapuji scream, she finally relaxed.

She was helping her mother in the kitchen but sensed the presence of a guest outside. Who could it be? Nobody bothered to tell Sushila. Her mother and Bhabhu held a whispered discussion about whether to cook a ceremonial sweet dish or not. The dinner was going to be served in the room at the far end of the flat instead of in the usual dining room adjacent to the kitchen. Sushila had not seen this happen for any guest, important or otherwise.

Sushila asked the servant and was told that the guest was some old man from the village. "Can you imagine wearing these on your feet?" the servant joked as he lifted and dropped the guest's shoes. The shoes were the real heavy and durable type, old and worn with a thick layer of dust attracted by the oil that was used to clean them. Sushila had never seen shoes that large.

Were they cooking the special sweet for the uncouth wearer of these shoes? What could he be discussing with Mota Bapuji behind closed doors? She got the definite impression that this man was not welcome here and was not worthy of respectful treatment.

From a crack in the door, Sushila observed the guest's behaviour. Except for a *choti*, his head must have been clean shaven but was now covered with a couple of weeks' fuzz obscuring the scalp. He had taken his shirt off displaying a lean torso. His body, showing evidence of years of abuse, was not muscular but hard and his skin was tanned and clean.

The guest ignored the plentiful supply of water available in the bathroom and very frugally washed his hands and face. For fear of dirtying the clean towel placed for his use or for whatever reason, he dried his face with his own coarse *dhoti*. With an invocation to the Lord, he sat down on the floor instead of on the *patlo* laid out for him. Mota Sheth took his place opposite the guest.

The 'uncouth' villager turned out to be a neat eater. He had the excess food removed from his plate. He only took what he was going to eat and did not wolf his food down. Sushila watched with interest the neatness with which he mixed the ceremonial *kansaar* with *ghee*. There was no greasy mess of unmixed *ghee* left anywhere on his plate when he was done.

Nobody noticed that Sushila was watching or listening to what was happening. Mota Sheth asked Bhabhu, his wife, to come out. Bhabhu paid her respects and spoke words of welcome for the guest, who reciprocated with his own courteous words. In answer to Bhabhu's query about his wife's health, he said :

"With God's grace and good wishes of friends like you, she is doing reasonably well. Physically she is very weak but mentally at peace. She shows no attachment, no complaint, no recrimination about anything; is very pleasant to the kids; and when the pain becomes unbearable, asks me to recite *Chattari Mangalam* to her."

Finally it dawned on Sushila : the guest was none other than Sukhlal's father from their native village of Thorewaad. She had not seen him since when she was a young girl of about ten.

So they were talking about Sukhlal's sick mother. Sushila's imagination conjured up the picture of a village home, a sick woman lying in a room, forsaking all medicine and medical care, depending on her 'Faith' to provide relief from her unbearable pain.

"Must be hard on you to run the household by yourself." Mota Shethani carried on with apparent sympathy.

"Thank heavens, it's not that bad," The guest answered with great ease. "Between the twelve year old girl and the seven year old son, the kitchen is well taken care of. They can even manage a few guests."

Mota Sheth showed not the slightest interest in this conversation. His ill-temper was displayed more than once by the bowl slammed to demand more vegetables. He yelled at the servant when he wanted some powdered pepper.

The guest wanted to return to the hospital after dinner. He had reached there right after Sushila left the hospital but Sukhlal had not mentioned her visit to him. He put his jacket back on to leave.

"Why don't you wait a few minutes? The chauffeur will drop you." Mota Sheth delayed the guest's departure and dragged him back into the unfinished conversation. "What do you plan to do about what I asked?"

"Please wait a little longer."

"How much longer?"

"How can I say, Sheth? My sick wife will not only not survive the shock; her soul will not find peace; I beg of you, please give me some time."

Mota Sheth's exhaled with unconcealed contempt.

"She is not going to live long, Sheth!" The villager spoke of his dying wife as if trying to harden his heart for the inevitable.

"How can I go by something that uncertain? And can you blame us? I am not about to condemn my educated and cultured girl to life in that hell."

The guest absorbed all these blows without saying a word. Assuming his silence to be a sign of weakness, Mota Sheth continued : "Look, let's settle this matter between the two of us. Take these two thousand rupees. Find a nice girl for your son and make your wife happy while you can. On the other hand, if you want to push your luck and try to blackmail me or take advantage of us, you will force me into going to the Elders of our caste. And Sheth, if you think that the Elders will not approve of breaking this engagement, you are kidding yourself. I have papers to prove that your son is impotent and medically unfit to marry."

That bombshell from Mota Sheth rendered Sukhlal's father utterly speechless.

8

"THINK it over, Sheth, and get back to me. Tomorrow, the day after, take your time. I don't like to play games nor do I like others to be dishonest with me. I badly wanted to have this talk face to face. Now, if you want to go to the hospital, the car is waiting for you downstairs."

With those final words, Mota Sheth leaned out from the window and issued orders to the chauffeur below and went to his own bedroom. His dejected younger brother, Nana Sheth was left sitting there.

Sukhlal's father walked right past the waiting car and kept walking. The chauffeur waited for the guest to emerge and after a half-an-hour or so, went in to ask about the guest. Mota Sheth was already asleep. Listening to the whole story, Sushila and Bhabhu were dismayed to realise that the guest had walked all the way back to the hospital.

"What a shame!" The gracious Bhabhu spoke in her soft voice, "Your Mota Bapuji, poor soul, should have walked the guest to the car."

"Please go to the hospital and find out if he arrived there safely." Sushila instructed the chauffeur. Sushila never gave any unnecessary orders and when she did ask for something, her orders were followed without question.

"She is right," Bhabhu concurred, "Please make sure he is all right. And while you are there, find out how our son-in-law is doing."

Bhabhu's words about 'our son-in-law' had come straight from her heart. For Sushila, those words instantly brought back images from that afternoon—of the supine and frail-looking Sukhlal, of the tears in his eyes ... and of Nurse Leena wiping those tears.

She asked Bhabhu : "Do you think the hospital provides sheets for the relatives who spend the night there?"

"Don't be silly, my girl. Of course they don't get sheets and even the mattresses have been slept on by hundreds of other people."

"Should we send some sheets and a pillow, Bhabhu?"

"Good thinking, girl but do it quietly. Don't wake your mother. She, poor soul, will not like it and will start raising her voice and wake up your Mota Bapuji. And he, poor soul, will not be able to control his temper."

Every creature, good or bad, was a 'poor soul' to the gentle Bhabhu. As she said her prayers with the prayer beads in her hand, Sushila got a freshly laundered sheet and a pillow with a new pillow case for her father-in-law. For his morning use, she cut, not one but two, fresh *daatun*s and then asked Bhabhu if she should send Bhabhu's snuffbox also.

The immediate answer was : "But of course, dear. Good thing you remembered! I saw him use some when we went to his father's funeral seven years ago. And get my better snuff box, the one cast from zinc. What will the poor soul think of us if we sent the tin one?"

All this was handed to the chauffeur to take to the hospital. Sushila reminded the man in a totally natural tone : "Don't forget to ask about his health. And also find out if the guest needs anything else."

"Nobody even told me about it!" Bhabhu lamented when Sushila sat down again. "Praniyo comes around with vegetables everyday. Poor soul must have forgotten to tell me about Sukhlal's hospitalisation. Even your Mota Bapuji, poor soul, comes home exhausted and it must have slipped his mind to inform me. Had I known, I would have gone to the hospital to visit him. A human being—and not just any one; our own person, no less—in the hospital! So far from home and no one to care for him! The hospital staff and the doctors-nurses, poor souls, can do only so much! Yes, I should have gone. Your case is different, girl! You can't go, not with the other thing hanging over our heads. At your age, it wouldn't take much to get a bad name. And the people, poor souls, blow things out of proportion without getting all the facts ..."

Sushila was about to blurt out "Bhabhu, I went to see him today" but swallowed the words. Then she thought : what if Bhabhu found out later? Then she would be a liar in Bhabhu's eyes. If she were to learn the truth now, at the most she would scold Sushila. Keeping something from Bhabhu was like cheating God himself.

The swallowed words returned to her lips : "Bhabhu, I want to confess something to you."

"I will beat you up anyway."

"Beat me all you want." Sushila grabbed Bhabhu's feet : "Beat me, scold me, don't give me any food for four days, if you wish. I will do whatever you ask me to, Bhabhu! But, for God's sake ..." Her voice broke and she couldn't go any further.

"Don't stop, go on!" But Sushila didn't say anything. In a few moments, Bhabhu felt warm tears on her feet.

Bhabhu quietly finished the rest of her prayers and put the beads away in their ivory box. When she tried to pat Sushila on the back, the girl seemed to be running a slight temperature. A touch on Sushila's forehead confirmed that. Shaking Sushila gently, she asked, "What were you going to tell me? Trust me, Sushila. No matter what happens, I won't betray your trust."

This fortyish and childless woman sounded like a bosom buddy to Sushila when she spoke those words. It was as if in the act of putting her beads away, she had shed her role as an elder and become a friend to share one's secrets with. She continued in that friendly tone :

"You don't have to worry as long as you don't stray from the path of virtue. The only time we women become totally helpless is when we step over the line we cannot come back from."

"It's not like that at all."

"Then what's the big deal?"

"Even if it's really not a big deal, it becomes big for me if you don't approve."

"Will you stop beating around the bush, you silly girl?"

"Bhabhu, I went to the hospital today."

"Oh my Lord!" Bhabhu pinched Sushila real hard in her fleshy back. "So that makes you a pariah! Who did you meet there? Did Sukhlal see you? He didn't bother you or say anything in presence of anyone, did he?"

"He was the one I went to see. I couldn't believe the conditions there, Bhabhu! How could Mota Bapuji send him there?" Sushila's voice shook. "To see him lying there like ... like a dog ..."

After a long silence, Bhabhu caressed her with love and asked : "You know how much your Mota Bapuji is concerned about you, don't you?"

"I know, but who can I talk to? Now I am talking to you."

"You don't have to tell me anything. Don't you think your elders understand what is good for you? I am the only one that's old-fashioned here and still attached to the old betrothal. All the others are going all out for what is right for you."

"But what if I don't want them to go out for me?"

"You, my good girl, will walk through fire if we ask you to. But your Mota Bapuji is not going to throw you to the wolves just like that."

"But Bhabhu," the harder she tried, Sushila was not able to convey her real thoughts and desires to Bhabhu and was confusing her even more : "Please tell everybody not to change my engagement."

"What are you worried about? Oh, I understand! So, you are in a big hurry to get married! And you think your Mota Bapuji is not?"

9

SUSHILA was exasperated that even her Bhabhu was not able to understand her. The darkness hid her facial expression, and that was just as well because she wouldn't dare show her irritation to Bhabhu.

What was surprising (was it really?) was that Sushila could have explained the whole matter very simply if she had said : 'Bhabhu, he is the one that I want to marry. Force me to marry someone else and you will destroy my life's happiness. Why is everyone bent on marrying me to this "sophisticate" against my wishes?'

Why couldn't an educated and Mumbai-bred modern girl like Sushila clear up a grave misunderstanding like this? This question is of the same puzzling category as the age old one : why would a bumblebee—capable of boring through thick hardwood tree-trunks—spend a whole night imprisoned in the closed but delicate petals of a lotus flower? Sushila herself wouldn't be able to answer that question. She had certainly seen the new age plays and movies with their modern heroines making defiant statements like "I will marry none but him" or "I will die rather than marry him". Had her Mota Bapuji trained her appropriately, Sushila would no doubt have delivered those lines at the designated time to the designated person or to the world. No courage nor an inner urge would have been required. On the contrary, the thin curtains of those rehearsed words would have barely shielded the leaping flames of her true feelings.

Sushila asked herself that night why she wouldn't come right out and speak her mind. But, alas, her inner self refused to provide any immediate answer. One voice from a remote corner of her heart even said on her : "Come down from your high horse, young lady! Even Vijaychandra is hiding here — right here among all your desires in your own heart."

Sushila was not very happy about being confronted by this deeply hidden secret. True, Vijaychandra had not been able to entice her to ride in his car. But also true was the strength of his unspoken but insistent claim : 'Sushila, you have to recognise that these two — not one, but two — young women didn't drive me to the smelling sick-house of that Hospital in their own car without a reason — without some attraction for me — without a motive.' He even looked like he had the right to the preferential treatment he received at the hospital. She couldn't deny the fact that Vijaychandra had scored points at every step — at the picnic and then during his various visits to the Sheth residence. He had the knack for winning people over and he most certainly had let that charm loose on Sushila. Sushila feared that she had not been immune from that charm. This deeply suppressed feeling had finally been brought out that night. Sushila had to admit that the reason for her inability to deliver a quick "Sukhlal is the only one for me" verdict was her ambivalence about Vijaychandra.

Sushila tried to stamp that ambivalent feeling into oblivion. Seeing her quiet, Bhabhu finally let out her first yawn of the night : "Go to sleep, girl, don't brood so much. Don't worry about us. We are not going to throw our only child to the wolves! So, relax and sleep well."

With that, Bhabhu stretched out in her bed alongside Sushila's bed. Before Sushila could lie down, Bhabhu asked : "Did you say your prayers?"

"Sorry, I forgot."

"It's wrong only to miss it on purpose. Go ahead. Prayers will help you sleep better too."

It was about three years since Bhabhu had given up her conjugal bed and started sleeping in the same room with Sushila. Since she was two years old, Sushila had been raised by Bhabhu. Until she was ten, she even slept in Bhabhu's and Mota Bapuji's bedroom. After that, Sushila's bed was moved to the hall outside their bedroom with the doors kept open. The practice continued until an incident spoiled that arrangement. Having come home late, Mota Bapuji closed the doors while he changed and then forgot to reopen them. When Bhabhu opened the doors in the morning, Sushila was already up and brushing her teeth.

The twelve year old girl standing there alone while the two pairs of adults — Sushila's parents and Bhabhu-Mota Bapuji — slept behind closed doors! The thought bothered Bhabhu no end and she couldn't face Sushila all day. How could I leave my girl all alone! What would she have imagined about the sleeping elders! What shameful reasons did she attribute to the closed doors? In the evening, her husband — uncharacteristically for him — couldn't help laughing when he heard Bhabhu's reason for her embarrassment and her dilemma.

But, blaming himself for not being able to give the gift of a child to his beautiful, wise and angelic wife, he had not been able to ridicule this apparently silly concern of hers. That night, he was not upset at the discovery that his wife's bed had been moved into another room. He had slept his usual sound sleep. This one virtue would have to be considered along with his other attributes when judging him.

Bhabhu had not considered this new sleeping arrangement a big deal. She had not mentioned the change even to Sushila's mother. In the morning, brushing her teeth and still trying to shake her sleep off, the mother had asked Sushila why Bhabhu had to go to Sushila that late the previous night. Only then had Sushila explained : "Bhabhu slept there all night."

"Bhabhiji!" Sushila's mother had pulled Bhabhu aside and asked : "We always lock the outside door and there is certainly no need to worry about Sushila being alone! Why, then ...?"

"Who said anything about her safety?"

"I keep the keys with me and check on Sushila at least twice every night. You shouldn't fret about her." The younger sister-in-law revealed the extent of her security-consciousness.

While laughing inside, Bhabhu responded : "I didn't mean to worry you, poor soul! I am not worried about her at all! It's just that your brother-in-law likes to keep the windows open and I can't take all that air. Not good for my arthritis, you know, and that's why I moved to the other room with Sushila. What fear? You, poor soul, worry about ..."

Only a woman would understand how keen a young girl's ears can be about certain matters like this. The reason is, many of those women have had this experience of being locked out of their parents' bedrooms and inside their homes. The following night, Sushila asked her mother for the keys : "Do you want me to lock the front door from inside?"

Her mother was slightly ruffled : "Do it only if Bhabhu wants you to."

Sushila's father was so embarrassed to hear about this, a few days later, that he found some excuse or the other to stay out of his bedroom that night. His wife had tried to argue with him : "Snap out of it , will you? What are you ashamed of when your elder Bhabhi is with her? I can't sleep alone. Bhabhi has moved out, I have not! We are not the only ones with a grown up daughter at home. Come in, now; I know how virtuous you are!" She had practically dragged him into their bedroom.

That was a couple of years ago. The 'younger' couple had a grown up daughter but in Bhabhu's universe they still counted as 'poor souls' and received all the care that she could bestow.

10

SUKHLAL's father did not return the next day. Sushila called the chauffeur upstairs and she and Bhabhu talked to him about the night before. The chauffeur gave the news about the *guest*. Pretending to be speaking for Bhabhu, Sushila asked if the *guest* had said anything.

Chauffeur Ahmed smiled : "Nothing much. All he kept saying was : 'What a girl! Bless that girl!' I couldn't tell whether he was happy or sad as he kept repeating those words."

"How did the patient look?"

"Fair. Mr. Sukhlal was in bed and this nurse was helping the guest with his bedroll and going on and on : 'No, Dad, not that way; that's much better; and listen, don't tell your son anything that makes him sad, okay!' The guest just listened, kept his hands folded and tried to talk—didn't know how but somehow managed in his broken Hindi—to the nurse about how grateful he was to her for saving his son's life, and how God would bless her for that, etc."

"Doesn't she go home for the night?" Sushila blurted out.

"Yes, she was just leaving at the end of her day shift." The chauffeur continued : "Told the guest that she was to go on the night shift from tomorrow and that she will make sure he has no problem. Told Mr. Sukhlal : 'Listen, Smarty, I am going to see a movie tonight and will not be back to wish you good night.' And then with 'good night, dad; bye, Smarty' and even wishing me good night she 'left. The guest just stood there frozen and stared at the nurse with his mouth open. All the patients and the hospital workers couldn't stop laughing at his sight."

Suddenly, the chauffeur remembered that the guest had given him something—a letter—for Sushila. Sushila handed the folded note to Bhabhu. It was written in a neat and flowing—if a little untrained—hand that the semi-literate Bhabhu could relate to. It was in the handwriting of a young village girl and seemed to be crafted by the help of a little stub of a pencil found somewhere. The letter read :

"May God bless my dear and loving sister-in-law Sushilabhabhi. Ba thinks of you all the time. We all think of you all the time. We very much want to see you. Ba says her soul will find peace if she can see your face once. But you live so far away, it will be difficult for us to meet you. Ba sends her blessings if she doesn't get to see you. We have sent some sweets made from fresh milk for you. Please take good care of your Bhabhu and your mother. If we do not meet, please forgive me for my faults. If Ba doesn't meet you, please say prayers for her for six months. Ba's fever is very high and she asks me to tell you this : 'I am leaving your little sisters-in-law and brother-in-law in your care; and I pray that your father-in-law gets the same loving care from you as he gave to me.' Bhabhi, can you send me a couple of books? Whatever old books you may have will be fine. I will be very careful with them and keep them with me until you come visiting. Bhabhi, we haven't ever seen you and don't know what you look like. I dream of you every night but can't remember your face in the morning. Bhabhi, please don't forget to write to me about how you dress; do you wear a regular *sari* over the skirt or a *chorso* like I do? *Bapa* got me a new *chorso* some time ago. There was a sticker on it with the picture of a beautiful woman. I call her Sushilabhabhi and keep her in my trunk." It was signed : Your little sister-in-law Sooraj.

Bhabhu read the letter aloud one word at a time as Sushila listened. Bhabhu handed the letter to Sushila : "Here, read this for yourself. What a nice letter your mother-in-law has dictated, the poor soul! Little does she know what's happened here. Who imagined this was to be? We have such little control over our destiny. Why can't I give up my outdated thoughts?"

Sushila read the letter over and over again. Meanwhile, her mother showed up from nowhere and learnt about the letter. "The stupid village folk! Bhabhi indeed! Bite your tongue before calling her your bhabhi!"

11

SUSHILA resented the 'bite your tongue …!' quip from her mother. She picked up the young girl's letter and quietly pocketed it when her mother left the room. In the privacy of the bathroom, two or three more readings still did not satisfy her. What was wrong with the address 'bhabhi' that annoyed her mother so much? To her, the letter seemed to overflow with deep love. She felt honoured to be called 'bhabhi'.

An only child herself, Sushila had not experienced the pleasure of addressing someone as 'bhabhi'. Sushila had no reason to believe there was anything despicable about being a sister-in-law to someone. It had not occurred to her that being this village girl's sister-in-law also required being married to the unsophisticated villager Sukhlal. Sukhlal never even entered the picture. A seriously ill woman wanted the benefit of Sushila's prayers; pined to see Sushila before dying; thought meeting Sushila would provide salvation for her soul. A young girl dreamt sweet dreams about Sushila and was apologetic even about borrowing Sushila's used books. Was all this not enough fertiliser for the blooming of an affectionate bond in the heart of a simple and loving girl like Sushila?

She turned the shower on and stepped under it. Suddenly, the touch of water felt more soothing than ever before. Somebody seemed to whisper 'Bhabhi, Bhabhi' in her ears; offered to soap her back where Sushila's hand could not reach; said : 'Bhabhi, let me help you wash your hair—how do you manage hair this long?'

Out of the shower, she looked in the mirror as she toweled herself. Her complexion seemed to look lighter. The drops of water from her wet hair seemed alive as they ran down her forehead, cheeks, bosom and stomach. A sudden thought struck her : did Vijaychandra have younger siblings? A mother? Something said no to both questions. The lines of his face somehow seemed to send the message : 'I am a free man; I belong to no one; nobody has any claim on me.' Sometimes when you enter a room, it speaks out to you : 'I am eight foot by eight foot; what you see is all there is.' Sushila thought some people had faces like that eight-by-eight room. Vijaychandra, she thought, had a face like that : what you saw on the face was all there was of him; there was nothing below the surface.

While toweling herself and later getting dressed, Sushila's mind unconsciously weighed Vijaychandra's candidacy for marriage, specifically in light of his not having any brothers and sisters. Lounging on a *hindolo* in the next room, her mother could be heard holding forth : "Absolutely no way is my Sushila marrying into a large family. Poor girl would be eaten alive! I am going to find an '*independent*' boy for her. She can keep house just for the two of them and have all the time for whatever she wants to do; that's the way to go. And there is no shortage of '*independent*' boys these days."

She didn't speak the word '*independent*', she chewed on it and relished the sweetness of it as if sucking on a piece of hard candy.

And then she counted off the names of all the '*independent*' couples she knew : "That Vanita from Jetpur, Kumud of the ... family from Peepalalag, Ramkorbai's Jaya ... all happy as can be. After giving the man his lunch and sending him off to work ... not a care in the world! Nobody to order them around or even to ask to move a chair. Why give up that '*independent*' life and get into a family of five? No way! Didn't realise what a mistake that engagement was until we settled down here in Mumbai."

Sushila chuckled listening to her mother's words. She knew the young '*independent*' women her mother had mentioned. She had gone to see them and had invariably found them gone. Even when she found one of them at home, she had never been able to spend much time with them; they had run out of things to talk about in less than thirty minutes.

With all the leisure time at their disposal, Sushila had seen two-day old piles of dirty dishes in these '*independent*' women's homes. When she asked, she was told : "The servants have not shown up for three days ... the idiots go crazy with the *Holi* celebrations. And damned if I am going to do the dishes myself! We have been eating out."

Sushila had not formed any hard opinions about these '*independent*' women but something in their lifestyles definitely bothered her.

"My, my! Look at her, Bhabhiji!" Sushila's mother looked at her freshly bathed daughter and beamed. "This girl is absolutely bursting with beauty. Can't you see what's happening to her? My girl is just glowing, Bhabhiji! What are we going to do with her? Don't you think we have to get her out of that old engagement?"

"Now, now; have you gone insane or something?" The smiling elder Shethani raised her eyes in mock rebuke. "You better go get busy. Don't let the girl get any ideas!"

"Hey, Sushila!" Bhabhu called the fresh looking Sushila : "Is the car here? Let's go and get some mangoes."

With Sushila in town, Bhabhu rode to the Bhuleshwar market, bought her mangoes and asked : "How far is the hospital from here? I think I will go pay a visit. You can just stay in the car. It won't be long.'

"As you say." Sushila dropped the end of her sari that had gone up to cover her hair. Her face betrayed no sign of unwillingness nor any excitement.

Bhabhu started walking and then came back : "Come and at least point the ward out to me."

"That door," Sushila pointed to the ground floor ward and started saying : "Right inside that door ..." and froze. The bed that Sukhlal had occupied was visible from where she stood; but ... why was it empty? Why was there no mattress on the cot? Why was the sanitation man cleaning the floor around the cot? And, above all, while she was worried to death, why were the nurses looking so happy and making so much noise?

The sight of that empty bed and the cleaning activity around it had the effect of an arrow shot through Sushila's heart. The expression of horror on her face that lasted only for a fraction of a second but was noticed. Bhabhu asked : "What's the matter Sushila?"

"It's nothing, Bhabhu. Come, I'll show you the way."

"Let's go. And, don't worry. You just stand on one side. Nobody is going to bite you!" Bhabhu pushed Sushila through the door.

Sushila trembled as she saw the strange sight in the middle of the ward. Nurse Leena sat in the matron's chair, surrounded by the ward staff. Four or five nurses, a couple of cleaning women and three ward boys were all poking fun at her.

"Hey, look at the long face of Leena!"

"She is about to cry, the poor baby."

"For Heaven's sake, Leena, what was this patient to you? Patients just come and go! What are you crying for? If you cared that much, you should have married and had children of your own!"

"Will you all please leave me alone? I said I was all right!" The frustrated Leena stamped her feet.

"Then why do you keep staring at that empty bed?"

"And why did you cheat the Doctor into keeping him here for the last eight days? You knew he was in perfect health while you kept plotting those fake peaks and valleys on his temperature and pulse charts!"

"Lies, all lies. Leave me alone, for God's sake!" The lines on Leena's face were getting deeper. She looked ready to cry any second.

"Did you get his address?"

"Why would I? What do I care?"

That was a lie. Leena, in fact, had tried very hard to get Sukhlal's address. Sukhlal's extremely limited English vocabulary and Leena's inability to spell names like Thorewaad and Peepalalag had finally caused her to concede defeat.

Sushila watched the show for a few minutes and then addressed the crowd : "Where is this patient?"

"Welcome to the group! That's what we are talking about too." One of the cleaning women told her.

"Where did he go?" Sushila asked the woman.

"He was discharged." The practically illiterate woman tried to be fancy and answered in broken Hindi.

Leena recognised Sushila and jumped up. Simultaneously, another nurse emerged from the House Surgeon's office and screamed with delight : "Leena, Leena, you are getting another — even more lovable — 'Smarty' for that vacant bed. Come, take a look."

All the other nurses ran off screaming "Come on, girls, let's have a peek!" They came back holding their handkerchiefs to their noses. Some whispered : "Poor, poor Leena. That horrible, old Marwaadi is moving into the vacant bed."

"Don't scare the poor girl like that."

"Why is she so upset about the young patient's discharge?"

"Don't you know? Leena is a widow; she looks twenty five but is actually about forty. Ever since her fifteen year old son died a couple of years ago, she becomes a mother to whichever young man comes here and is heart-broken when he leaves."

Meanwhile, Leena stood near Sushila. She assumed that her 'Smarty' must have gone home to this girl who had been the only person to visit him a couple of days ago. She hoped that this woman was sent by 'Smarty' to pick something up that he had left behind or to thank her, Leena.

"So, did he arrive home alright?" And, misinterpreting Sushila's startled response, Leena went on : "I begged Smarty to let me inform his pretty cousin. But no, he said he wanted to surprise everyone there. I wanted him to stay longer and get more rest, but the cruel, jealous doctors told on me and killed my whole strategy. Whenever non-paying patients show any sign of improvement, the heartless people here send them home. Now, tell me, does he remember me? Did he send any message for me? Didn't say a word of thanks when he left. Just said : 'Sister, read what you can in my eyes'."

Sushila didn't like any of that. Did Sukhlal really ask this Christian nurse to read his feelings from his eyes? Was he capable of saying such romantic things? Could his eyes talk? She thought of the face; thought about his eyes. She remembered the volumes those eyes had spoken to her from that very bed just the other day.

"And, please take good care of him, okay?" Leena had still not understood the reason for Sushila's silence : "Those young doctors don't know what they are talking about. They are just a bunch of inexperienced kids who can't make the correct diagnoses just yet."

"He didn't come to my place." Sushila's voice was dry and lifeless.

"What?" Leena was dumbfounded. "But nobody besides you ever came to see him. Where could he have gone?"

"Didn't his father tell you where they were going?"

"No! All he said was : '*Memsa'ab*, I will come back to
square things with you.'"

"What was that about?"

"This is what happened. It's customary to tell charity
ward patients to put whatever contribution they can
afford into the collection-box. He heard that and came
back and whispered to me : 'Memsa'ab, I don't have any
money right now but I promise I'll be back to take care
of this.' Poor fellow must have been terribly embarrassed
and left very quietly. What was there to be embarrassed
about? We see rich people come and use this charity
ward and then leave without tipping even the cleaning
women! And this poor man, when the cleaning women
and the ward-boys showed up, wouldn't even look up
while he packed and then left as if he had committed a
crime. He told me : '*Memsa'ab*, I will not leave town
before I come back here to give these folks their tips.' I
felt so bad, I gave those people a piece of my mind. And
then, I tipped them myself."

Bhabhu had quietly listened to this incessant flow of
words from Leena. Her impression was that of watching
an aerialist dancing gracefully across the span of a high
wire. She took five one-rupee coins from her pocket and
handed them to Sushila.

"And who is this?" Leena asked Sushila.

"My mother."

"How lucky to have such a beautiful mother! You,
indeed, are a very lucky person." Leena stepped closer
to Bhabhu.

"Give the money to her, Sushila, and tell her to use it
for tipping and for charity on Sukhlal's behalf." Bhabhu
instructed her.

"No, No," Leena had figured out what was being said :
"You don't need to; I already took care of it."

"You must accept it," Sushila grabbed Leena's hand
and insisted. "You absolutely must. He is... means ...

matters something to ..." and left the rest unsaid. What did she want to say? Perhaps it was something that she had never been able to say! What was it? What was her interest in Sukhlal? Was she happy to learn that Sukhlal was well? Was her sympathy for the poor hospital workers the symbol of her growing feelings for Sukhlal?

"No, no, absolutely not." Leena was equally emphatic, "We have feelings for him too, do you understand? Feelings!"

Before Leena could amplify on her 'feelings', she was summoned : "Leena, hurry up. Your new 'Smarty' is here; come and take charge."

Leena ran without accepting the money. The five coins bearing the imprint of George V fell to the floor with their silvery ring and started rolling. Sushila was immediately surrounded by the doorman, the cleaning women and the ward-boys and handed them the rupee coins she had picked up. At the mention of the name 'Smarty', her heart had skipped a beat and she looked at the new patient. She saw Leena with her arms around a pot-bellied, evil-smelling old man and she ran out of the ward. "Bhabhu," she said, "Let's go. Nobody here knows anything."

"Wait, wait just a second!" Leena came to the ward door : "Please forgive me for my behaviour the other day. I was being overprotective of him and didn't let you talk to him. I cannot explain but I ... I ... have this feeling for him ..." and she slipped back into the ward. Her back appeared to be overflowing with a huge swell of emotions.

"Where do you think they went? Back to the village? Why would the poor souls leave just like that? The nurse, poor soul, seemed to be a very loving person. Talked too much though, didn't she? The words came out of her mouth like popping corn; never stopped to even think. It felt really strange to see her touch your head and shoulders."

Sushila listened to Bhabhu's words without responding. Like a bird back in her nest for the night, a deep silence had entered Sushila's being and had settled in. In the manner of the male bird's song-notes going past the resting female bird's ears in the twilight hours, Sukhlal's memories had enveloped Sushila's heart.

12

THE stairs of the dark Hanuman Gali four-story tenement house were far from quiet when Sukhlal was brought there from the hospital. He was carried upstairs sitting in the locked arms of a couple of young *Vanik* men from *Kathiawaad* . Each of the men and their families occupied one-room dwellings on the fourth floor of the building. In a matter of minutes, one of the families vacated their own room and moved in with the another family. For the first time since his arrival in Mumbai, Sukhlal had a room to himself.

The two young men and their helpers lambasted Sukhlal's father while they worked on the move :

"You are something else, *Fua*! Sukhlal has been here for months and you didn't bother to tell us; and we find out about his sickness only when your horse carriage pulls up at our gate! You really are a piece of work!"

"You thought all of us in Mumbai were dead, didn't you, *Kaka*? How could you forget your friends so quickly?"

"Leave *Mama* alone, you guys! Somebody get a fan, Sukhlal needs some air." Another one came to Sukhlal's father's rescue.

Sukhlal had been made to lie down in a bed of double stacked mattresses. He tried to sit up, protesting : "I am not sick any more, please let me sit."

"No way," said the man who had addressed Sukhlal's father as *fua* : "Not without your doctor's permission." His name was Khushaal.

"He is right, son." Sukhlal's father agreed, "The nurse told you to rest."

"I don't believe this!" Sukhlal smiled : "She ruled over my life there, but here, too? Father has such a long list of instructions from her, I don't know when I am going to be a free man again!"

"But what are you going to do when you are free again? Go back to your father-in-law's?" Cousin Khushaal winked at his friends as he asked.

The joke's effect on Sukhlal's face was not pretty.

As the evening progressed, the stairs came alive with the heavy footsteps of neighbours and relatives transplanted from Thorewaad and the surrounding villages. All carried umbrellas with big sturdy handles. The new patches sewn on old umbrellas created an endless variety of eye-catching patterns. Long before the visitors arrived on the fourth floor, their steps announced that their footwear was not of the flimsy Mumbai variety but sturdy products of the *Kathiawaad* towns like Amreli, Jetpur, Junagadh and Rajkot. As each arrived, the shoes were removed and lined up in the narrow corridor that ran past the single-room tenements. The umbrellas were hung on the clothesline and water dripped down from them in silent testimony to the crazy Mumbai monsoon. The little room echoed with cries of "How are you, Grandpa?", "Look who's here!" and "How long has it been?" One after the other, each visitor greeted Sukhlal's father, some hugged him and then berated Sukhlal : "Hey there, you rich man's son-in-law! Do you know how many times we called and left messages for you, went to the office to see you? What have you been so busy with? Managing your mother-in-law's bankbook on the side or something?" "Or busy packing to go run your father-in-law's Singapore office?"

Sukhlal was in no condition to respond to those taunts. Whenever he tried to sit up, his father reminded him : "I wouldn't do that if I were you, son, the nurse said to ..."

Khushaal, the host, called the ranting relatives outside and quietly told them to go easy on Sukhlal : "Don't even mention his in-laws to him. Make him laugh, play cards, keep him amused some other way."

"But why?"

"I'll tell you later."

Khushaal's one comment changed the whole atmosphere. Out came the decks of playing cards and the 'in-laws' attacks ceased. Most of the 15-20 young and not-so-young men had borrowed the train-fare to Mumbai when they left their towns and villages. All had moved to Mumbai because their education had come to abrupt ends—not because they had lacked the smarts, but because their families couldn't afford to pay the fees. One's father's untimely death had confined his widowed mother to a *corner* for a couple of years. Another's father had become mentally unstable when his young daughter was widowed. Several's parents had been sent heavenwards by swift attacks of plague, cholera or meningitis in the manner of little chicks being snatched by birds of prey.

Some were married; some, after saving up for five years, were negotiating to get married; some were happy to be the targets of ridicule about their attempts to find brides; some complained about their futile attempts to find affordable housing while their wives waited back home to join them in Mumbai.

One of the visitors was a doctor who had been greeted with simultaneous cries of "What an honour!" That young man's arrival had put a stop to the frolicking. The only one that didn't seem to care was Khushaal, the host. Khushaal introduced the man to Sukhlal's father : "Fua, did you recognise the good doctor here?"

"No, do I know him?"

"Gulabchand, the son of Nenashi Doshi of Aambla."

"Oh, my! Gulab, son, you look very different. I thought you were in the cutlery business. I didn't know you were a doctor."

"He is a specialist."

"What kind?"

"Women's."

"Women's?"

"He is an expert on how to have more children, less children, how to conceive a male child or a female child. Gets his information all the way from Germany and America. Our doctor friend here has become a famous consultant for women."

"Must have studied and passed the exams."

"Oh no, he got his degree by mail from Germany."

"Is that so? I wish you all the success." The gullible old gentleman had not noticed that the other twenty or so visitors had their faces covered with their newspapers, books, etc. Everybody couldn't wait for the next phase of introductions to come from Khushaal. The young 'doctor' seemed to be eager to make an exit when Khushaal asked : "Why don't you check Sukhlal out?" Turning to Sukhlal's father, he continued :

"Fua, do you know of a nice girl?"

"What are you talking about?"

"Some eligible city girl from Rajkot, Jetpur or Jamnagar. Must be well versed in English. Has to be fair-skinned like a European. Must be a fashionable dresser — you know ... brooches for saris, sleeveless blouses and all! Someone who can carry on intelligent discussion with guests about merits of the current movies, you know!" Khushaal's ringing joviality was laced with heavy sarcasm that bit like a screeching saw.

"Please!" The doctor made a great show of examining Sukhlal's tongue, paleness of his fingernails and the dark circles around his eyes. He sat stiffly on a chair because, unlike the other guests, his fashionable pants would not allow him to sit cross-legged on the floor.

"Who is the candidate for marriage, Khushaal?" Sukhlal's unsuspecting father asked.

"The good doctor here, who else?"

"What? Isn't he married to our Dalichand's daughter?"

"Yes, he is, but ..."

"Please, can't we drop that ...?" So awesome was the host Khushaal's personality, that meek protest was all that the young doctor dared to voice.

The audience of twenty or so was getting its money's worth. The nephew Khushaal continued with his response to his *fua*'s question :

"...after ten years of marriage, our doctor friend suddenly discovered, that the missus is neither educated and smart nor good looking; and that there has to be a way around it! While he sold cutlery, he found nothing wrong with her. But, of course! As one gets smarter, goes from walking to owning an automobile, wouldn't he be able to see the shortcomings a lot better? It's never too late to make a new beginning, is it, *fua*?"

The doctor had just sent his wife of ten years to her father's on the grounds that she was too illiterate and stupid to live with.

Sukhlal's father remained silent. The group of twenty strained hard to suppress their laughter. The young doctor glared at Khushaal, his slightly older and therefore to be respected relative, with a strange expression of anger, misery and amusement for the subtle dressing down he had received. Khushaal was not one to talk back to. After a whole day of door-to-door selling of utensils, he was the one who spent his evenings looking after the families from his part of Kathiawaad. Travelers to Calcutta, Madras and other cities found a place to break journey at with him. He had earned the reputation of a 'bully-of-bullies' that got his friends and relatives sleeping room on trains, often getting into fist-fights for that and, occasionally, even at the cost of a bloody nose.

His upbringing, values, high-handed behaviour and way
of life were unique. Khushaal stood alone.
The young doctor got up and sought Khushaal's leave.
"Come on now, what's the big hurry, my friend?"
Khushaal practically grabbed the young man and sat
him down. As if by magic, tea and snacks arrived from
the room next door. Khushaal poured a cup of tea for the
doctor. A whole hour passed without any further mention
of the doctor's family life; the twenty men's behaviour
was likewise impeccable.

As the party broke up later, Khushaal talked to each
of his young guests :
"What do you say, Otabhai? How is the job going?
Anything you want me to tell your boss?"
"How is your wife doing? Have you set up the
appointment with Dr. Deshmukh yet? No! Let me take
care of it!"
"Listen, Bhana, Don't you dare have your wife deliver
her child here in Mumbai! Let her go to her father's
place. Hospitals in Mumbai are not for people like us."
"So long, Laghara. Are the Money Orders to your
mother going regularly? Don't make her go begging for
money in her old age, you hear?"
"Say, Monji, what have you decided about your sister?
Tarachand from Balapar is a real nice young man for
her. Of course, if you want a big shot attorney for her,
this Mumbai is wide open! Start visiting the college
hostels and boarding houses. Let the poor street cars
make some money!"
"Odhavji, someone had better talk to that good-for-
nothing Dhiru before I get him arrested for gambling. I
will personally take care of anyone giving us
Kathiawaadis, the reputation for being thieves, gamblers
or cheats. Don't tell me I didn't warn you."
One after the other, he bid everybody farewell and
then sat down to fan Sukhlal for a while. Seeing that

Sukhlal was asleep, he said : "*Fua*, let's go for a walk on the beach. Don't worry about Sukhlal; I'll have a couple of people sit and watch him." At the Marine Lines beach, he hailed a masseuse and got his *fua* a good massage. The old man felt very awkward at first but Khushaal explained : "*Fua*, look at the Chowpatty sands over there. The beach is full of people getting a massage. This city shows no mercy to anyone; the air here will suck you dry like a leech. You come here tired with aching joints, spend two bits on a massage and walk away straight and ready to go back to work. If you don't, you starve to death. Aching bones is an everyday matter. This Mumbai is a killer city, *fua*."

Later, he and *fua* sat on the backbay parapet and Khushaal started to piece things together : "If Sukhlal is not comfortable with his in-laws, let him work with me."

"I want to take him home with me. But he is dead set on staying here. Seems like he is addicted to this city."

"Addicted to Mumbai! That's a good one, ha-ha-ha!" Khushaalchand laughed, "Not addicted to anything, *fua*, he is possessed by the Witch of Worry. At his in-laws', no matter how well they look after him, a man like him will never open his heart about what bothers him." Khushaal said with a straight face.

"And they do take good care of him. After all, they are good people. But, Khushaal, I get the feeling something doesn't quite fit here."

"What doesn't fit?"

"*We* don't fit in the scene here. They are on their way up, while we are on the way down. Look at their child! And look at our boy! Tell me, Khushaal, is it right to hanker after this ill-fitting relationship? Honestly, what do you think?"

"Look, *fua*, there are plenty of other girls in this world. Her mother wasn't granted the monopoly on bearing girls. Our villages breed girls as good as Sushila. And it was only yesterday that that Santokdi roamed around the garbage dumps of Thorewaad. But, that's a small matter. What I cannot stomach is giving in to their blackmail and threats, *fua*."

"What can we do, my boy?"

"What *can* we do? I say, *fua*, we can kick the butts of their seven generations. You are going to let that son of a bitch break this engagement off—and, that too, by fraud? He is going to destroy a man by calling him unmanly and unfit for this world? I'll crack his head open before that, *fua*!"

"We can't take them on, Khushaal."

"Do you want to see what we can do, *fua*?"

"No, I don't. We lose both ways : we look bad and feel bad if we did that. And think about bringing the poor girl to our home against her will; would we want to be responsible for her broken heart?"

"You hit the nail on the head, *fua*. I am not that old-fashioned myself; dragging her in as a slave is not acceptable to me either. Therefore, the first priority is to find out what this girl, Santokdi, wants."

Khushaal was very aware of the Santok-to-Sushila name change and used the old name deliberately.

"There is nothing to find out. I know she is a good girl; but would you blame her if she didn't want to live in our poor house?"

"Then we forget about her. But we let them off the hook only after the big man apologises in writing. We crack heads if he tries to bully us."

13

IT was late at night before the two returned home. Khushaal's loud voice and the noisy heavy Jetpuri shoes turned silent as soon as they turned into his apartment building. A sound sleeper himself, Khushaal was extremely considerate of the others' need for a quiet rest. As the two mounted the stairs, they heard the sounds of the night : the ever-changing variety of sonorous snoring, the audible attempts to relieve the heat-caused discomforts with cardboard fans, the constant twisting and turning in beds turned into virtual hot compresses by the humid heat of Mumbai. The public urinals across the street added their own smells to the already heavy and oppressively humid air. The air was still as if the weight of that unbearable odour had broken the back of any breeze.

The air on the fourth floor seemed to be hiding after just barely escaping the clutches of the odour-producing urinals. Khushaal's one-room apartment had not remained totally immune from the malodorous hissing of the monster four floors below them. Sukhlal's gentle snoring testified to his being in a deep sleep. Khushaal read into the sounds made by Sukhlal his complete recovery and said : "*Fua*, this kid is one hundred percent well now."

In the morning, Sukhlal confirmed that he had slept that well for the first time since leaving Thorewaad six months ago.

"Get ready then, Sukha!" Khushaal exhorted.

"Ready for what?"

"To go out and sell brass and aluminum pots and pans with me. I'll pay you two rupees a day flat if you work for me. If you want to strike out on your own, I'll pay you a commission on what you sell. You don't answer to anyone when you come home in the evening. You sleep here for free until my wife returns after her delivery, not for twelve more months by my reckoning. She comes back to Mumbai only after I hear that she is healthy enough to ferry water from the Bhaadar river. Want to think about it?"

"I am ready right now." The prospect of earning two rupees a day had removed any apprehension from Sukhlal.

"This is not easy work, Sukha. You must know that you will have to walk several miles a day; but, if you stick it out, my boy, in a month, the roads will be just dirt under your feet!"

Sukhlal's father, listening from a few feet away, believed this to be no more than a joke. When he stepped away to wash his face, Sukhlal grabbed Khushaal's hand and asked : "You are not pulling my leg, are you, Khushaalbhai?"

"I am dead serious."

"Then convince my father not to take me back to Thorewaad for any reason whatsoever." Sukhlal's voice conveyed his fear of being weakened by his father's insistence, by the mental image of his dying mother's begging face, by his darling little sister's soft touch and a host of other emotions. Still holding on to Khushaal, he stood up. "I am not sick at all, I don't want to stay in bed any more. I beg of you, Khushaalbhai, take me to work with you!"

His father returned and saw him out of the bed and panicked : "Why are you up? What is going on here?"

"There's nothing wrong with me, father."

"Do you know that better than your nurse? Why do you think she asked for a complete bed rest for you?"

"Then let's go and ask her. I want to settle this once and for all." It was not clear what Sukhlal was really upset about. Was it his resentment of Leena? Or was it really his secret desire to see her again?

Khushaal decided to jump in : "Who is this super-nurse that is trying to run Sukhlal's life? Why does she think she is better than the doctors? I want to see her, too. Let me find out what her interest is in creating this scare."

Sukhlal's father said : "Let's go. I need to take care of something myself." He had a promise to keep.

The three of them took a horse-cart to the hospital to discover that Leena was not in. The ever present ward-boys and the cleaning women informed them that Leena had called in sick. The doorman told Sukhlal about the two women that had come to see him by car the day before; had wanted to know where he had gone; one of them had been here before and was young and slightly dark-skinned; the other was middle-aged and fairer; distributed five rupees in tips; Nurse Leena refused to even touch the money; ...

Sukhlal's eyes met his father's gaze. The thought of two women dangled from the thread that connected the two pairs of eyes. There was no need to discuss who the two women could have been. There was a good reason for this understanding between the two men. During his stay in the hospital, the father had asked many probing questions. In his son's answers, he had heard the delicate strumming of a lute. Reading between the lines, he had concluded that Sushila had visited the hospital to see Sukhlal. Any inquiry about Sushila had resulted in an embarrassed silence but the father had read in his son's eyes a clear expression of a stirring love, of hope, of warm affection.

"Two women in a car. Let me see, who could they be?" Khushaal, all smiles, wondered aloud.

"So we will not be able to see the nurse today?" Sukhlal's father asked the doorman who confirmed the improbability of that event.

"No problem. Let's go see the Ward Doctor." Khushaal pointed the way. During his many visits to drop off and pick up patients, Khushaal had gotten to know the hospital layout rather well. The Ward Doctor was emphatic : "There is absolutely nothing wrong with him. He is fit for full-time work."

"But the nurse ..."

The smiling Doctor interrupted Sukhlal's father : "You mean our Leena, don't you? That's just her way. She means well but don't be misled by her; she even beats up on us doctors here."

The old man knew he was beaten. He clutched at the last straw : "Doesn't he need a change of air? Clean air ..."

"All he needs is some work to keep him busy."

His defeat was complete. He left the hospital with a fallen face that complained bitterly about the grave injustice done to him by Khushaal, his own son and the doctor.

14

"WHY don't you boys go home? I want to make a quick trip to the market." Sukhlal's father lied, with one hand in his coat pocket. A little object in there reminded him of an unfinished task. He started walking towards Sushila's house.

Deep in thoughts and oblivious to the world around him, he made his way on foot; faltering, getting startled by the car horns, ignoring the ringing of trolley car bells till the very last second and thereby inviting the wrath of the conductors : "You stupid ass ...". But he was recognised for what he was only by the horse-drawn victoria drivers. Coming behind him, these smart people saw his distinguishing characteristic from their high perch and called out : "Move it, big-boots!"

And the truth was, his sturdy footwear did remind one of some old and dependent parents being dragged against their will behind their youthful offspring.

At the end of that long walk, tired but feeling good about having saved street car fare, he climbed the stairs of Sukhlal's in-laws' building. The elevator and the attendant were both available but the old man preferred to walk up because he was concerned that his shoes would dirty the elevator floor.

The two women, Bhabhu and Sushila, sat in the front room separating peas from their pods as the guest entered. Sushila respectfully covered her head and the side of her face with her sari; not in the manner of the old fashioned veil that would cover the head and face completely. The peacocks printed in the border of her sari hung as if enjoying the closeness to the dimples on her cheeks.

Bhabhu stood to welcome the guest : "Come in! Please come in, Kaka! Where have you been? Sushila's Mota Bapuji, poor soul, has been asking about you ever since ..."

The words were a blatant lie. But that lie was more innocent and holier than any truth could ever be. As she spoke, Bhabhu picked some clothes and keys lying on the nearby sofa to make room for the guest to sit.

Cutting off her well-intentioned falsehood, Bhabhu quickly switched to : "Sushila here, poor soul, has been worried stiff about her father-in-law and been asking why you hadn't returned and where you could have gone!"

Sushila had, meanwhile, slipped into the next room and stood there listening to this conversation.

Sukhlal's father removed his *paaghadi* and made a clumsy attempt at an explanation while he wiped the perspiration from his head : "You wouldn't believe it, but the relatives all showed up, grabbed us and took us to their house! I told myself I had to pay you a visit, if only to return this to you."

The right hand that had not left his pocket since leaving the hospital finally emerged. It held the expensive snuffbox Sushila had sent to the hospital for him.

"After all, it's a valuable item, inlaid pearls and all! I have kept it in my pocket all this time." He wiped the box with his *khes* and put it down.

"Really! Poor soul!" Bhabhu smiled broadly, "Did you hear that, Sushila? What kind of a man is he? He is here just to return the snuffbox—no other reason to visit us!"

"Not so! Lord take my soul even to think like that!"

"How is Sukhlal? Didn't you realise how worried we would be! We went to the hospital and got the shock of our lives when we found him gone! Sushila was absolutely dumbstruck. How could you do this? Not even a word from you!"

"I did telephone the office; but, I don't know how to talk and the other person didn't know what I was saying. Finally, he gave up and said something like where do people like you come from? My word, Gheliben, I couldn't stop laughing. One can be so nasty on the phone without realising who you are talking to! So I decided not to bother with the phone; I figured I would just drop in on you."

"But how is Sukhlal?"

"Thanks to you, he is doing very well. We just came back from the hospital. The doctor said he was one hundred percent; but this one nurse, God only knows why, had us running scared until this day!"

Sushila wanted to hear this conversation, but there was also another conversation taking place in the penthouse that was of vital interest to her. Sushila was unaware that while she was in the shower, someone had arrived and stealthily entered Mota Bapuji's sanctum. She recognised the voice : it was the smooth and modulated voice of Vijaychandra.

Sushila's ears were now trained on the penthouse conversation. Mota Bapuji was saying (he seemed to be begging) : "Grant me this one favour. Go and study abroad for five years as you wish, but do it after the wedding. I will do everything you say : I'll send Sushila to the school of your choice; she will learn English; she will take music lessons. We will train her every way you want; I'll hire five tutors for her if necessary."

The answer came in measured and slow yet authority-laden word steps : "In that case I can wait another year. I will want to see how her training goes before I commit to this marriage." The voice was Vijaychandra's.

"But why don't you give her all the training you desire after you marry her? My Sushila is no idiot! She is not a dumb village-bred girl who can't learn anything!"

"I am not willing to take any chances. As it is, I will have to forego some opportunities because of this one year delay."

"I know what you are giving up; I am not exactly stupid. But Sushila is my only heir. You will eventually run my whole business! I will arrange the opportunity for you to go to Japan, America, wherever you wish. Opportunities I have right here in my pocket. If you agree, this marriage could be over within a week's time."

"That's quite out of the question. In this day and age, you can't expect one to jump into a marriage without considering every angle."

"You will be able to cover all angles. Wait till you see how smart she really is."

"Can we do this?" Vijaychandra suggested an alternative, "Let her spend a couple of months with my friend's wife. If she approves, I'll consider what you want."

Sushila recoiled as if she had been slapped really hard. She could hear no more and had to lean on the stairway railing to prevent her knees from buckling.

15

U NABLE to take any more of that exchange, Sushila walked away from the penthouse. She picked up the threads of the conversation between Bhabhu and her father-in-law.

Bhabhu : "Wouldn't a change of air be good for Sukhlal? Why don't you take him back to the village for a few days?"

Father-in-law : "I have been begging him for that, but he wouldn't hear of it. Tells me, if he is going to die, he will die here in Mumbai; doesn't want to go back for health reasons."

Bhabhu : "He shouldn't talk such nonsense, poor soul! May he live a hundred years! It's just that Mumbai's climate is no good for the ailing."

Father-in-law : "He is obsessed by the thought of making it in Mumbai; doesn't want to show his face back home as a failure. Can you believe that! Who would even care? Ha-ha-ha!"

While Sukhlal's father was busy wrapping those words in his innocent laughter, Mota Sheth and Vijaychandra came down from the penthouse. Coming down the stairs behind Mota Sheth, Vijaychandra saw Sushila trying to hide from everybody's view. Immediately he took his hat off with characteristic flair, out came the famous silk handkerchief and he wiped his handsome forehead as if clearing a mirror in which Sushila could gaze at her fortune.

Sushila had routinely stolen a glance or two at Vijaychandra whenever he visited. That day, she pointedly left the room without once looking back. Vijaychandra read in that the natural reaction of someone whose time to be shy had arrived. The buds of bashfulness were about to bloom. The season had set when the eyes, unable to meet directly, start looking for screens, half open doors and cracks in the windows to hide behind. No question she was watching him from somewhere. But where! Where was she hiding! Vijaychandra took as much time as he dared in traversing the short distance to the front door, his eyes darting from corner to corner. His efforts to guess the vantage place from which Sushila had to be ogling him were fruitless.

On seeing Mota Sheth, Sukhlal's father got up immediately and just stood there with folded hands and the sympathy-seeking smile of an accused.

"I'll be back," was all that Mota Sheth said as he left to see Vijaychandra off. It was a long time before they heard the roar of the car engine coming to life. The conversation must have continued even after that. Sukhlal's father had difficulty suppressing the urge to ask who the young man was. The new son-in-law candidate mentioned by Khushaal? Did Sukhlal have a prayer against a handsome, smart and bright young man like that?

His simple thoughts raced along two different lines. One thought was of his son's impending defeat. For sure, his Sukhlal had lost the girl. Sukhlal couldn't possibly count for anything. Who would want Sukhlal when such a god-like son-in-law was available instead? Would the girl herself give Sukhlal a second thought after seeing that young man? Sukhlal had his expectations raised just because she went to the hospital to see him. The reason Sukhlal didn't want to leave Mumbai was the castles he had started building in the air. This would someday kill him. He wouldn't survive the news that Sushila was to marry someone else. The concerned father decided Sukhlal had to return home. Why did he ever send his son to Mumbai? He had consigned his son to a certain death!

The second line of thought concerned Sushila's future. Would she find happiness with his Sukhlal or with the young man he had just seen? Who was the obvious choice? Was she to blame if she picked the other over Sukhlal? No girl in her right mind would forego a candidate like that! Why hadn't he considered her happiness? He thought : 'Please, Lord, let Sushila, my would-be daughter-in-law, go where she chooses ... where she thinks she will be happy ...'

But the thought was shattered before it could reach its completion. It caused as much agony as walking on a sword's edge. Each step along that sharp edge had caused his heart unbelievable pain. The thought had drained all the blood from his face by the time Mota Sheth returned.

"You village folk do one thing very well ..." Mota Sheth spoke through clenched teeth with every ounce of vindictiveness he could muster : "Nobody can humiliate others as well as you country merchants can."

"I apologize, Sheth; I am indeed guilty." Sukhlal's father tried to blunt the attack with his meekness.

Mota Sheth had intended to ignore the guest and was about to walk right through the room but changed his mind when he heard the word 'guilty'. Turning around, he continued his tirade : "Oh no, I am the guilty party! I am your culprit, not once, but a million times over! I am fit to *lift your shoe with my teeth*. What I have done is unpardonable! I have put the noose around my daughter's neck ..."

"Don't say any more, Sheth, in God's name, please say no more!" Sukhlal's father approached Mota Sheth with his *paaghadi* in his hand in a gesture of begging for mercy : "I couldn't bring Sukhlal back here. Our relatives wouldn't listen when I told them that Sukhlal's father-in-law would be very upset and ..."

"Please feel free to take him wherever you please!" Mota Sheth steamed as he resumed walking to the sitting room : "If you have humiliated me enough in front of all of Mumbai, perhaps you will deem it appropriate to release this guilty party now!"

The trail of his voice led to the distant sitting room. Sukhlal's father followed in its wake asking for his forgiveness. Bhabhu froze with the vegetable peeler in her hand. Behind the door, Sushila's heart started beating faster. The only audible voice came from the kitchen. Sushila's mother was kneading the bread flour and venting her fury through her hands and her mouth.

"Serves him right. Guest indeed! Do we look good even talking to that ilk? How can we survive in this society if we don't know how to deal with them? We'll be taken to the cleaners by the sons-of- ..."

Sushila rushed into the kitchen before her mother could finish that epithet; she screamed : "Mother!"

Her voice broke. As she confronted her mother, her eyes glared and her lips quivered. She was more worked up then she had been at the picnic.

"You—you—mother, do you know what you are saying? Do you have any idea at all?"

The mother was shocked. It was the first time that Sushila had ever spoken to her like that. Those words carried the force of a whole attacking army. She had never had to raise her voice at Sushila; in fact, she constantly used the phrase 'meek as a lamb' to describe Sushila. She flinched and looked down after seeing Sushila so upset.

"He—what has he ever done to you?"

This was not the language Sushila was accustomed to using. Her lips felt heavy using these new and unfamiliar expressions. She experienced difficulty completing even one sentence. Her mother looked around seeking relief from Sushila's wrath.

She was rescued by her older sister-in-law. Bhabhu entered the kitchen as if for no other purpose than to deliver the peeled vegetables. Her unhurried steps and her expression were as natural as ever.

She asked very casually : "I had planned to roast the *karelas* but I think we better boil them. Better for the guest; his teeth have started bothering him, poor soul ..."

Leaving the kitchen, she quietly told Sushila : "Would you get me a couple of detergent soap cakes, my girl? I think I will wash the delicate clothes myself today."

She gave no hint that her real purpose in coming in was to prevent any further strain between mother and daughter. Her major concern was to avoid even a shadow of doubt that she was encouraging Sushila's disrespectful behaviour toward her mother. She smelled an air of discord blowing through their home for the first time.

Sushila worked on the soap bar. Bhabhu stood quietly in the doorway of the bathroom. The grumbling from the kitchen had ceased as if silenced by a collapsed wall. That quiet was broken only by the intimidating voice that could be heard from three rooms away. Bhabhu wondered if her husband's tongue-lashing was accompanied by some physical force as well; she was clearly worried but she could not see any good resulting from her intervention.

When Bhabhu applied the cake of soap to her wash, she tried to cover up her grief with that act. The only one who ever recognised her grieving was Sushila. Even Sushila had hardly ever seen Bhabhu crying or sad. Nobody had ever heard Bhabhu express any unhappiness or complain about anything. But Sushila always sensed Bhabhu's invisible crying when it occurred. The bracelets on Bhabhu's wrists were adorned with tiny gold bells. Sushila caught the sound of Bhabhu's grief from the ringing of those tiny bells. She sat down to help Bhabhu scrub the wash.

16

BHABHU and Sushila had been at it for quite some time in the bathroom, when Mota Bapuji's voice came through the opened door of the sitting room : "That does it, Sheth; our little dispute is over! And Sheth, we are still the friends we always were! That has not changed." That couldn't be Mota Bapuji'! There was not even a trace of harshness in his voice.

What could have happened? Why those words of satisfaction after such a long silence? Mota Bapuji and her father-in-law were up to something really hush-hush there. Coming close on the heels of Mota Bapuji's sweet words, what was that wailing sound? Who was crying? Was that her father-in-law? Had to be, because Mota Bapuji's sweet and consoling words sounded : "You must still think of her as your daughter, Sheth!"

And what could be the meaning of these words from Sukhlal's father? "I insist, Sheth! I beg of you : you will inform me about her wedding, won't you? I can't afford to give her an expensive gift, but I will be there with a *shreefal*."

"But, of course! You and I are not enemies!" Sweet words from Mota Bapuji again : "And remember, if Sukhlal needs a thousand or two to start his business, we will be more than happy to chip in."

Her father-in-law's voice had not recovered yet : "It will be a pleasure, Sheth; if he needs the money, I won't hesitate. But, you will do that other favour! Don't forget to write to me about Sushila's wedding ..."

Bhabhu gazed fixedly at the colours of the rainbow reflected in the soap bubbles, as if she was lost in a different world. Sushila asked Bhabhu with panic in her voice : "What's happening, Bhabhu?"

"What did you say?"

Sushila realised that Bhabhu's mind was elsewhere and she had not heard the conversation. Sushila was unable to explain the foreboding caused by the sitting room conversation. She herself had not heard everything clearly. And then, the voices and footsteps sounded approaching.

Bhabhu got up quickly, smoothed her attire and stepped out of the bathroom into the hall. Through the space between the half-open bathroom door and the jamb, Sushila saw her father-in-law's freshly washed face. His eyes appeared to be searching for someone. His feet seemed to have difficulty recognising their long-time companion shoes and were trying to get into Mota Bapuji's shoes.

"Where are you going, *Mama*?" Bhabhu asked the guest, "Why are you putting on your shoes?"

"I'll take your leave, Gheliben!" He folded his hands, "Please forgive me if I have offended you in any way."

"You can't leave just like that!" She had glanced at her husband out of a corner of her eye and, receiving the green light, proceeded : "You are not leaving without lunch; Sushila has had everything waiting for you."

"Sushila's wish is my command. If she has cooked for me, I'll be more than happy to stay for lunch." The guest removed his shoes. "I cannot turn Sushila down, can I, Sheth?" He looked at Mota Sheth.

Mota Sheth was all smiles : "Absolutely not, you must have lunch."

What Bhabhu and Sushila, from the bathroom, witnessed was unbelievable — Mota Sheth was embarrassed for not having thought of that himself. Until

a few moments ago, Mota Sheth had seemed to relish
every opportunity to put this country relative down, to
heap insults on him without cause and to drive him
away like a stray dog. What had caused this radical
softening of heart? Did the father-in-law's own mild
manners finally reach Mota Bapuji? This new accord
between the two was nothing short of a miracle!

The answers eluded her but Bhabhu seemed to feel
the dawning of a new life, of a new hope. The budding
of this happy feeling could only be sensed by Sushila.
The precise moment when green mangoes start turning
golden yellow and begin ripening is sensed only by
Mother Nature. Sushila sensed the lightening of
Bhabhu's heart in the manner of a lonely late night star
that hears the faint footsteps of that hue-change. Sushila,
after all, was the principal star in Bhabhu's life-sky.

But Sushila herself did not experience that same
feeling. She had heard what Bhabhu had not. What she
had heard was not very clear but definitely was
something mysterious. It was almost within her mental
reach and yet refused to be captured; a bird that came
and picked seeds from her hand and then flew away
before it could be caught. This unsolved mystery made
Sushila restless.

Mota Bapuji and her father-in-law sat down to eat.
Sushila helped Bhabhu in the kitchen but her ears were
trained on the jingling sound from the outside. The sound
was made by her father-in-law's silver-ringed finger's
rhythmic tapping on the metallic platter as he waited
for the food to be served. The continuous tapping notes
filled the room.

As she handed servings to Bhabhu, Sushila stole quick
glances at her father-in-law and saw again the clean
and shining skin of his bare upper body. She also got the
distinct impression of a pair of eyes darting around,
begging for one more look at her.

When he finished eating, the father-in-law exhibited the rare and rapidly disappearing village custom of swishing water in the plate that he had eaten from and drinking it. The underlying thought behind the custom was that not one grain of food was to be disrespectfully discarded; practiced by this village merchant, it represented the epitome of cleanliness and respect for the purity of the environment. On her father-in-law's first visit several nights ago, Sushila had not observed this unique behaviour as it was dark then.

The guest got up and folded his hands in a gesture of leave-taking. Both Bhabhu and Sushila felt he was showing unnatural haste to leave. He had appeared to struggle very hard to maintain his self-control during the meal. His last words were :

"Farewell, folks! I ask for your forgiveness. I offer my blessings to Sushila with all my heart. May I survive long enough to see her live the happiest of lives."

The guest and his words disappeared down the elevator shaft. Mota Sheth went along to see him off properly. The guest turned down Mota Sheth's insistent offers to take the car with the simple words "I can't digest the rich city food unless I walk it off."

Till last, his words remained free of rancour or sarcasm. Mota Sheth quickly went up the steps but the chauffeur's eyes stayed on the receding back of the guest. There are many whose backs are more expressive than their faces. When the back takes over the job of being the heart's mirror, its sight causes unbelievable pain. The chauffeur stared at the guest's back until it disappeared and then immediately sat down to write a postcard to his father living in a remote village in northern India.

The three women, now at lunch themselves, heard the sound of the safe in Mota Sheth's bedroom opening and closing. The three finished their meal in silence. Each had her own reason for being quiet. Sushila was still struggling to solve her mystery; her mother worried about the reason for the unwelcome truce between her brother-in-law and the guest—she still stood by the 'son-of...' description; Bhabhu's silence implied her incomplete understanding of the situation and an optimistic but tragic happiness.

"Has everyone finished eating?" Mota Sheth chirped. Showing this much pleasantness was a rarity for him!

Bhabhu answered : "Almost. What's happening?"

"Gluttons, all three of you!" Uncharacteristic joviality from the master of the house!

"Sushila, *tell your Mota Bapuji* that it's your mother and not Bhabhu who is a glutton." Sushila's mother spoke clearly enough for her brother-in-law to hear but with the respect due him.

Sushila had no desire to repeat those words, nor was there any need to. The rules of behaviour in the old-fashioned families very cleverly allowed for a show of respect and convenience to go hand in hand.

"The crying shame in my house is ..." Mota Sheth's voice from outside the room betrayed not a hint of the tragic : "... that the culprit goes scot-free and the blame is accepted by someone else. How can one tell who the real culprit is?"

Sushila's mother's head swelled a few sizes at the implied praise.

"All right," her brother-in-law said as he retreated to the sitting room : "When the three of you have finished stuffing yourselves, I want to talk to you about something."

The nervous Sushila couldn't eat a morsel after that. She choked trying to gulp a drink of water and started coughing to clear it from her windpipe.

On the way to the sitting room, they saw Mota Bapuji reading some document, smiling as he read, and then locking it away in the safe in his bedroom. The solution to Sushila's mystery, the document, was back in captivity and Mota Bapuji entered the sitting room. He started talking :

"I must say that I have to scold you two sisters-in-law. But I blame Sushila's mother far less than I blame her Bhabhu. Why don't I ever see any decent clothing on Sushila? What are you doing to this young girl who should be dressed for her age? Look at the designs and colours of her saris and blouses. Just because you two are in your thirties and forties, does she have to wear the same whites and lights as you do? Why does my only daughter look like a priestess in white?"

"Bapuji, it's not their fault." Sushila answered his questions, "I picked these myself because I like them." Sushila's tone did not reciprocate the affection flowing in the words of her elder. She sounded more like intoning "two fours are eight" in response to a teacher's command.

"You wouldn't know good stuff if it stared you in the face!" The elder continued, "Your Bhabhu, I am convinced, has killed off your taste. I am personally going to take you shopping today. Unlike your Bhabhu, I have not renounced the worldly pleasures yet. Get ready! You are going to buy things that please me, whether you like them or not; and you are not going to say a word! If you do, your Mota Bapuji won't talk to you anymore! What do you say?"

"But even if I don't want to?"

"Yes, even if you don't want to. Didn't I say I was not going to let you look like a nun?"

The loving uncle was trying to do what he thought would make Sushila happy. Sushila knew that she was going to have to make her Mota Bapuji happy by going along.

"Now the second thing that makes me unhappy." He felt special joy in this : "How many times must I talk to you two about this? Why have you buried this girl in cooking and laundry work? Are we training her to be a baker or a cleaning woman or something? Every time I go to *Khar-Santacruz* and hear the sounds of women singing and playing *harmonium* and *dilruba*, I long for the day I can hear my daughter sing and play like that! I would understand if our child was retarded or a total an idiot. But God has given us a smart, intelligent girl! What is our excuse for not letting her learn those arts? Why should she be any less than the girls from Khar and Santacruz? Sister-in-law, why have you also become lazy like Sushila's Bhabhu?"

"Ask your Bapuji, Sushila," the mother asked from behind her sari-veil, "why we need to train our daughter to sing and play, if we are going to bury her in a village after all."

No repetition was necessary; and Sushila wouldn't have done it anyway. There was nothing wrong with the brother-in-law's hearing. He replied :

"You want me to answer that? I will. Give me a minute." He started to get up, picked up the key to the safe but changed his mind and sat down again. "Never mind, not today. All in good time. When the time is right, sister-in-law, I will answer your question, I promise. I want you to know one thing, though; don't accuse me of such weakness again. And, don't lose sleep worrying about that either. I know why all of you walk around with long faces. I am not exactly stupid. I will do whatever is necessary when the time comes. For now, just trust me and work on making this home bright and cheerful. Don't make my little girl here worry about anything. I am going to take her to this place where she can be free, learn music, study, sew, knit, get around and ... just have fun!"

The words had not registered in Sushila's mind; she had been preoccupied with the thought of what object her Mota Bapuji was going to get from the safe. What was he going to answer her mother's sarcasm with? The document in the safe—was it going to explain the matter?

What was written on that piece of paper?

The answer to these questions hovered just outside Sushila's sphere of imagination and stubbornly refused to come inside. The darkness around her continued.

17

KHUSHAAL waited for his *fua's* return but eventually asked a neighbour to serve him lunch when he arrived and set out to initiate Sukhlal in his new business. Before entering his little shop, Khushaal touched the threshold and then his eyes three times and talked as he unlocked the door : "I owe everything I have to this little place. It accommodated me for a whole year before I could afford to rent my one room place. And even if I had the rent money, who was going to let a bachelor live next door to them? I slept and ate and lived right here."

The inside of the shop came in view as the words "I slept ..." left his mouth. While Khushaal was busy helping his hired help load the kitchen utensils into a carry-on-head basket, Sukhlal looked around. One look was enough to notice that there wasn't enough room to stretch out even for a short five-footer.

"You slept here?" Sukhlal was amazed.

"I could fit if I doubled up a little. The shop was twice broken into and I couldn't afford to sleep elsewhere even if someone invited me. Doubled up, you can't tell whether you are asleep or awake. When sleeping like that hurt, I would go and throw my two bits at the masseuse! In this city, that massage is like a mother to the people living alone."

"Now that you sleep at home, have there been any break-ins?"

"You better tell him, Tatya!" Khushaal winked at Sukhlal as he spoke to the helper.

The *Marathi*-speaking helper blushed like a little girl. All that Sukhlal could pick up from his mutterings was : "May *Vithoba* strike me blind before I steal from him again. He is the one that cared for me when I was hit by a truck. If it were not for him, I would go hungry today."

"Okay, okay, let's go!" Khushaal offered to help the guy lift the basket on top of his head.

"No, boss, that's too light. Put more stuff in it." The helper asked for ᵣ ore weight.

"Right, and I get the blame when you die under that weight! And anyway, we are going to take it easy today." Khushaal put the basket on his head and added the weighing scale and the weights to it.

They walked through different neighbourhoods, some of which inspired the feeling ɔf darkness even on a bright sunny day; some with people who looked more like inhabitants of distant even foreign lands than any Mumbaiites; some had not one familiar face and some neighborhoods were full of hostile faces. Oblivious to all this, Khushaalbhai led the way with his throat producing a clever mixture of sounds : "Degchi! Degchi! Utensils! Utensils!"

He addressed some as 'uncle', others with a more respectful 'Khansa'ab'. He saluted some with 'salaam aalekum' and ridiculed some with 'how are you *Miyan Then-tha-nen-then?*' He was greeted with much respect by his old customers with words like 'Khushaalbhai, where have you been?" and "Don't you come here any more?" Some of them, on their own, approached him with embarrassed faces : "I swear by my son, Khushaalbhai, I will pay up next month! If I don't, let my face be the target for your boots!"

"No problem, my friend, no problem at all," was his constant refrain.

Khushaal introduced Sukhlal to everyone : "This is my kid brother. He is taking over this route from me. When he comes around, you will buy from him, right?"

"There is one key to roaming around these neighbourhoods without a care, Sukha! Let me tell you what it is." And he pulled Sukhlal closer and whispered to him : "You must be absolutely blind towards the womenfolk here. If there is even a hint of a sidewise glance from you, you will not come out of here alive."

On their way back, Khushaal took the route that went through the neighbourhood occupied mostly by the half-caste Christians and Europeans. To Sukhlal's amazement, his calls and their tone had changed completely to "Degchi! Saucepans! Frying Pans!" Who would have thought that the throat that normally produced a harsh gravelly voice was also capable of making these highly inviting and musical sounds?

"Utensils, *Memsa'ab*! Best quality." Khushaal had stopped near the steps leading up to a building. A young looking fair-skinned woman in white came down the steps. She said "No, not today!" and then stopped in her tracks as she recognised Sukhlal. Her startled response was : "Is that you, Smarty?"

The speechless Sukhlal stared back. It was Nurse Leena.

"You little devil, you!" She ran down, taking two steps at a time—almost flew down.

Khushaal's face fell at this sight. His entire English vocabulary consisted of about ten words like 'utensil, saucepan, frying pan, best quality' and he obviously didn't understand what Leena was saying. For a second his thoughts ran to : What had happened? Was she going to hit Sukhlal? Did Sukhlal look at her the wrong way?

"I can't believe my eyes. Are you really here?" Leena stood there smiling, her eyes filled with tears of joy. She had switched to Hindi after the initial surprise had worn off.

"I am completely well, Nurse Baba!" Sukhlal had heard
the cleaning people at the hospital address Leena as
Baba but had never used that loving address himself.

"Pure stupidity!" She turned on Khushaal with a sad
and angry expression : "Who took him out of bed? Who
are you? What is he to you? Why is everybody so intent
on killing him? I will never forgive those damned doctors
for this."

"Memsa'ab, he is my little brother."

"So where were you when he lay there dying? And
why have you brought the kid out today?"

"For this, Memsa'ab!" Khushaal patted his own
stomach.

"How?"

"By selling utensils. Perhaps you should help him make
an auspicious start."

"Sure, sure! Come on up." Leena turned and ran up
the stairs, taking three steps in each stride. Behind her,
Khushaal grabbed the hesitant Sukhlal by the neck and
pushed him up the steps with the words "Move it, you
sissy! You don't turn easy business down ..." The basket-
carrying helper was next with Khushaal bringing up the
rear.

Leena unlocked her front door and entered; first thing
she did was to quickly cover up a photo displayed on a
desk.

The covered picture was overshadowed by a good-sized
clay statue of a sad-faced Virgin Mary with the child
Jesus in her lap. Nearby, a three-armed brass
candelabrum held three burning candles.

"Smarty, why don't you sit here." She pointed to a
chair right by the covered picture. The flickering flames
of the three candles were reflected off of Sukhlal's
forehead and the eyes like bathers in a swimming pool.
Sukhlal was lean in stature but his skin was almost
glass-like translucent.

Almost twenty, Sukhlal's face was still not ready for shaving. Following Leena as she moved around the room opening the windows, Sukhlal's face absorbed the emanations from the three flames and from that fourth human-luminary, and thereby became even more likable. Khushaal watched Sukhlal from afar like a protective bulldog and noticed the affection oozing out of his handsome eyes. Khushaal also watched Leena but he had not figured her out yet. His brain was still trying to understand her interest in Sukhlal.

Leena finally sat down on a worn out cane chair and asked : "First of all, explain to me what the situation with Sukhlal is. I am totally lost here."

It had not taken Khushaal long to realize that Leena was like a watermelon ripe enough to slice easily. He set the stage : "Sukhlal is my cousin and has joined me in my utensil business. He makes a commission out of all sales. I am with him only to get him acquainted with the territory. With help from people like you, he will make it·big in no time! We are working on getting him married soon, too."

"Okay, let's see what you have, Smarty. I'll take this, and this and these three here."

"And this too, *Memsa'ab*, is of superior quality; to help Sukhlal." Khushaal added a couple more pieces on his own and reached for the scale to *weigh** the purchase.

"No need to do that; what do I need to know the weight for? Just guess the total—here, take this." And she handed a ten Rupee note to Khushaal.

"She probably doesn't need all that—give her just what she wants ..." In Khushaal's awe, but also embarrassed by his utter nerve, Sukhlal whispered to him.

---

*   Even today, many shops price kitchen utensils by weight rather than by piece.

The cool and collected Khushaal prepared the receipt for the sale and spoke through his teeth : "Don't be silly! That's not the way to sell! Are we cheating her? She knows what she is buying. And if she is trying to help you, don't you deserve it?"

And he tore the cash receipt that showed a total of nine rupees and two *annas*. "I'll get the change for you, Memsa'ab."

"Don't worry about the change; Smarty will keep it. Come here again; I know a lot of people around here. I will take you to them, Smarty."

"We went to the hospital to see you this morning." Khushaal mentioned.

"I didn't feel like going to work today." She looked at the lit candles and then at Sukhlal. Then she remembered the previous day's episode : "Oh Smarty! After you were gone yesterday, that girl—who was she, your cousin? or your employer?—showed up in the afternoon. There was an older lady with her. She—the young one—almost took my ears off : 'Where did the patient go? Did he go back to his village? Who took him from here? Didn't he leave an address?' And the older lady—she was the most beautiful mother I've ever seen—wanted to give me money! You know what for? Told me in Gujarati : 'Nurse Madam, you made Sukhlal well. Spend this on charity.' Ha-ha-ha-ha-..." That long laughter terminated her attempt to speak Gujarati slowly and with emphasis on each word.

Who could those two women have been? One he placed immediately and a huge tidal wave of feelings spread through his heart. Had to be Sushila. Who else would care to ask for his whereabouts? But who did she have with her? Her mother? Couldn't be. Sukhlal had seen her, even gotten to know her a little. Leena's description of the motherly beauty—and also the generosity to spend for charity—did not fit Sushila's biological mother. Had to be the older mother-in-law. The handsome image of that embodiment of civility immediately appeared on the young man's mental screen.

Sukhlal was silent a long time after they left Leena's home. He showed no joy about the wonderful first sale of his life. At last, Khushaalbhai broke the silence : "That was a very auspicious beginning, Sukha! You are on your way. The butterflies in your stomach will be gone in no time flat. Just remember one golden rule : if you keep your eyes where they belong, the world cannot touch you."

Those words were a reflection of Khushaal's one big fear. He believed that an unmarried, white, young woman nurse whose business it was to deal with human body and all its frailty was someone to fear. But his old-fashioned thinking was healthy. What he taught Sukhlal was to keep his eyes where they belonged. He did not talk about the deceptions thrown his way by other people nor did he broach the subject of wiles that could be used by seductive women. The attractive aspect of this logic was that it emphasized one's own careful behavior; its followers never hid behind the weak excuses of the seductive charms of certain women ...

"Who did she say came to the hospital, Sukha?" The bashful look on Sukhlal's face prompted Khushaal to probe further. "Your bride, was it?"

"Sounded like my older mother-in-law was there too."

Sukhlal felt a new thrill in answering that question. Without the slightest contact, without having touched, met or properly seen a girl, one can refer to her as one's 'bride' and actually believe it! This was enough to make even the mousiest of men feel like a winner.

"Now that you are well again, why don't you go and ask for her blessings? You don't expect her to come looking for you, do you?" Khushaal joked.

Sukhlal chose to let that pass. He had no doubt that his ill-treatment at the hands of his in-laws was public knowledge. He had no intention of trying to hide it from anyone. But, the civility of not wanting to talk about the indignities he had suffered came naturally to Sukhlal. He was not among the people who sought sympathy by crying on the shoulders of true well-wishers or those pretending to be sympathetic. That was a trait inherited from his simple village parents. This kind of a natural response was not something that could be consciously learnt or taught.

"The initial rumor was," Khushaal continued the thread, "that Sushila was a girl out of control, wore western clothing and walked around like a modern woman. The recent reports have been very favorable, though."

"Those were all lies ..." Sukhlal stopped there. He wondered why he was defending someone that he had no call on. The immediate extention of that thought was : why was he trying to save the good name of the girl who was going to belong to that villain Vijaychandra? If he knew that Sushila was never going to be his, what was it in him that kept repeating that she was his; his and his alone!

"Why has your father given up?"

"Given up?"

"Yes, he has been talking about an annulment of your betrothal."

"Annulment my foot!"

Khushaal had to look squarely at Sukhlal to assure himself that those were Sukhlal's words. Sukhlal was still muttering to himself : "Out of the question!" Red hot blood had rushed to his face.

"That's my man, Sukha!" With those words Khushaal lapsed into silence. Fearful of causing a premature and ill-considered action from Sukhlal, he refrained from further stoking the fire of that newly surfaced courage. As they neared his shop, he asked Sukhlal : "Who is this Vijaychandra person?"

"How would I know!"

"Why does he go to your in-laws' place so often?"

"Ask him."

"He is asking for trouble! Even thinking about him, I swear, I get the urge to slap him around."

It was just as well that Sukhlal didn't say what he felt like doing about it. Khushaalbhai would undoubtedly have acted on it.

Khushaal continued his tirade as he arranged the unsold items back in their places in the shop. Then he took some money out of his pocket and paid the helper a rupee for the day. "And this is what you have earned today, Sukh... He said as he offered five rupees to Sukhlal.

"Later. I have to talk to Bapaji first."

"Later, nothing; there is nothing to ask Bapaji about. Take this, and keep plugging!" Khushaal forced the money into Sukhlal's shirt pocket.

When they reached home, Khushaal saw Sukhlal's father and cried out : "Watch out, *Fua*, your son has already earned enough to pay for your cremation on his first day! His first shot at business and he's ready to put you out to pasture, *Fua!*"

"A good cremation is all I ask for, my boy!" Sukhlal's father laughed generously : "I'll be happy if the vultures don't get to my body!"

"What are you all dressed up for, *Fua*? Why don't you relax?"

"I'll relax on the train."

"What?"

"I am leaving now."

"That is madness, *Fua!*"

"There is nothing more to do here and I don't feel good here in Mumbai, Khushaal! I want to get out of here."

"If that is how you feel, by all means. I will not try to keep you. Go without worrying about your Sukhlal. He has started earning from today. Have you had your supper yet?"

"I have no room for any food in my stomach, Khushaal!" And he let out a loud belch. The talent of producing a belch at will helps keep face—one's own as well as the others'. It is as useful as the talent to yawn—when wide awake—that gets rid of a long-winded visitor at one's home.

"Sukhlal's in-laws forced me to eat a big lunch. And you know about my custom of cleaning the plate—I ended up stuffing myself." Another belch followed.

"Great, must have been quite a feast! You must have settled on a wedding date. I was afraid they might decide to be difficult. But looks like you got it done! I will go get a horse-cart to get you to the railway station."

Khushaal left quickly. The father sat his son down close to him and said : "I want you to go home with me."

"I don't want to go. My work has just started."

"You will be better off back home, trust me. You will not be able to concentrate on business here."

"Oh? Why not?"

"Brace yourself and listen to what I have to say. Remember that I am your father, not your enemy and that I love you. That is why I was forced to sign the annulment today."

"What annulment? Who made you sign it?"

"Your betrothal's annulment; I gave it to the Sheth family."

Sukhlal was in a shock. His father explained further : "I have done this quietly because they were prepared to start a scandal if I didn't. Did they ever have you checked by a doctor?"

"No!" Sukhlal was dumbfounded.

"Then he was lying till the end. He has a doctor's certificate testifying to your impotence. He showed me the document and gave me the choice : I sign the voluntary annulment or he would drop the bombshell on our community. I saw your whole life being destroyed, son, and decided to put my signature on the annulment. I didn't want to be in the shadow of that house after that, but ended up staying for lunch. What I swallowed were not morsels of food, but hot embers of coal."

The father paused here for a while. Sukhlal didn't look up from his stare fixed at the floor. His father continued after his pain let up a little : "Look, we are not rich but we have a good family name! We will look for a girl from a poor family. I already have a couple of prospects in mind. If you go with me, finding a girl will be a snap. I will not rest until I see you settled."

"I will not go, not like that." Sukhlal was breathing fire.

"At least come back long enough to see a girl or two!"

"I don't even want to think about it."

"But I have to start looking ..."

"Please don't."

"If not now, when?"

"Not before I am ready and able."

"You don't understand, son! These things become impossible once the rumours start flying."

"Don't fret about that. Please go and don't worry about me. Give me time to get settled here."

"What you say scares me!"

"Don't be afraid. Let me see what I can do with my own arms."

His fists were clenched. His father had never seen this persona of his son emerge before.

18

THE vision of Sukhlal's clenched fists scared his father out of his wits. He had reason to be scared. Rupaawati, Sukhlal's little hometown on the outskirts of the Gir forest, had a majority population of the feudal landowners of the *Kaathhi Garaasiya* ruler class. Their rowdy presence had not made for a smooth and trouble-free life for Sukhlal, especially during his teenage years. The normally good-natured and mild Sukhlal turned into a vicious animal when the limits of his tolerance were exceeded. Even when buried under a pile of his adversaries and overwhelmed by their savage beatings, Sukhlal had fought back silently and even drawn blood with his bites. Not a few Kaathhi boys carried his bite marks for the rest of their lives.

When he couldn't save his belongings from his attackers, he had managed to render them useless rather than surrendering them to the would-be-robbers. There were numerous instances of his being waylaid by the *Garaasiya* youth when walking to his school in the neighbouring town of Devalpur; every single time he had managed to throw his lunch in the dirt before it fell in the hands of the rampaging boys. The resulting fist-fights had left their marks on him but he had never complained to his parents about those. His horrified mother would discover the stains left by the homemade yellow turmeric salve on his clothing the next day and finally get the story out from him.

In his later teens, he had helped his father out at their little provision store. For refusing to give free dates and roasted betel nuts to the Kaathhi revenue collectors, Sukhlal had received threats and had not been able to venture out after dark but had never sought his father's intervention.

Intimately familiar with these traits, his father saw the fearsome face of his son in place of the meek and bed-ridden Sukhlal in Nurse Leena's embrace or the Sukhlal in love and blushing at the mention of Sushila. Legitimately worried, the father said : "Please, son! You are in hostile territory, so take it easy and don't even step in their direction."

"The roads here are not anybody's private property." Sukhlal's look was trained out the door.

"That's not the point. Why would you even want to see their faces?"

"So, this is what they invited you to their house for, to shame you!" Sukhlal's words were slow and deliberate.

"Just get them out of your mind! Time will take care of everything. But, for God's sake, learn to control yourself, son! Don't make us, back home, worry about you."

"I will try." Sukhlal was not sure what he was agreeing to.

"So, what are the father and son talking about controlling here?" Khushaal entered the room. He handed a basket to Sukhlal's father : "Fua, this is for you to take home."

The father and son stared at the basket tightly packed with various kinds of nuts, dry fruit and toys.

"What are you staring at it for? Hurry up, we don't want to miss the train!"

"But ... this is too much ..."

"What kind of father will make the children cry like that? How can you even think of returning home empty-handed?" Khushaal spoke with his endearing bluntness as he tied a rope around the basket of gifts.

Sukhlal was filled with shame at the mention of his siblings. Lying in his hospital bed, he had read his little sister Sooraj's letter to Sushila. He could picture an eager Sooraj looking at her father's bag of clothes when he arrived home. The younger children may not want anything else after stuffing themselves with the nuts and fruit; the bashful Sooraj, on the other hand, after waiting in vain for her father to give her a message from her sister-in-law, would finally ask him about it. What answer would she get to her anxious inquiry about whether Sushilabhabhi had sent anything—old and used books if nothing else—for her? A smart girl like her was certainly going to find out about the annulment even if her parents tried to keep it from her. How would she react? Her hungry heart's refrain of the word *bhabhi* had cried out from every sentence of her letter. What kind of horrible mental images would the little sister have of the disdainful rejection of her sentiments by the woman who was not a sister-in-law even in name anymore?

It would be nice if she did not know for a while longer. He should have sent her an *odhani* from the money he had earned that day with a note that said 'This is from your sister-in-law.' But now there was no time for anything like that.

The three men went downstairs with the baggage. At the railway station, Khushaal got into an argument with other passengers about the good seat he grabbed for his *fua*. Intimidated by his bullying, the others finally gave up the fight. Khushaal had saved some of the fruit and nuts for Sukhlal and himself to enjoy sitting on the Marine Lines lawn later; instead, he turned them over to the children of the families he had fought with. The train departed without *fua* saying a word or betraying an expression on his face that would tip Khushaal off about the terrible thing that had happened during the day.

On the way back, Khushaal thought Sukhlal was sad about parting from his father. To perk him up, Khushaal talked about his own tearful and brave separation from home and added : "Give yourself six months and you'll have a place of your own to call your family over to live in with you. If your in-laws play along, we will have a wedding right here in Mumbai, my friend. Once you are married, your older father-in-law and your mother-in-law can scream and holler all they want. The important thing, Sukha, is for you to find out the will of your Santokdi—excuse me, Sushila. And the last thing you want to do is to bring home an unwilling woman, my friend! Someone like that will make life a living hell for herself and for the entire family. If she is unwilling to marry you, who cares where they marry her? There are hundreds of other eligible girls waiting out there. All you need is to save up a couple of thousand rupees to get established. And you will get there, Sukha! We have taken care of about fifty of our brothers over here. There is strength in numbers, you know! But, you better understand one thing! If you think once you are married you two lovebirds are going to move out to the suburbs— you can forget it right now! That is not going to happen even if you move heaven and earth!"

Sukhlal remained a listener all the way home. He resented even the forceful pep talk because it included the unthinkable suggestion of giving up on Sushila. Every ounce of his being protested that thought.

'Sushila's will!' He laid in bed and thought : 'All right, I'll drop her if that is what she wants. But no, wait, how can I let her go even then? I don't dare; how can I do that? A sinking man clutches at straws to save himself! But why am I thinking these thoughts? I am the one who has been dropped already. Do I have the choice of keeping or releasing Sushila? I wonder who dropped me! If Sushila wanted to reject me, why did she talk to me at the picnic? Why did she sneak to the hospital that day to visit me? And why did she return to ask Leena where I was?

'That's what I will do; I will go ask Leena. She will describe to me what Sushila looked like and talked like that day. I'll ask if she showed any emotion when she asked those questions. Did her eyes radiate any sweet desire? Did she mention me by name? Come to think of it, that will be the real test. Facial expressions and the eyes are difficult to read and can deceive one.

'The only dependable test is : did the girl mention me by name? A Hindu girl would not mention one name— name of the one closest to her heart, her would-be-husband. All I need is the answer to that one question. After that, we will see what I am made of—we'll see how willing, able and brave I am.'

That settled, the young man finally fell asleep.

19

IF some prying eyes had seen Leena after Sukhlal and Khushaal left, alone and behind closed doors, she would have easily passed for someone else. The cover had come off the framed photo by the statue of Mother Mary and she had the picture pressed to her closed eyes. The face in the picture was of a young boy of about fifteen.

Her words were almost conversational : "You would have been his age today. He wants to save money so that he can marry soon. You would have been of the marrigeable age; maybe not, perhaps a couple of years away! But his wife will live with his parents, will look after his little brothers and sisters. You would have left me to myself after getting married, right? You would send me to a hospital if I were to take ill; if disabled or too weak to look after myself, I would go into a nursing home, wouldn't I? Would I have left you to fend for yourself if the same thing happened to you? I would have come running to help out when your wife gave birth. Even old and weak, I would have cared for your children. But you didn't stick around for any of that! Do you know that everything I do is with the thought that you are watching me from the Holy Mother's lap and that you would approve? I bought all those utensils from this young man; did I need any of that? What I did I did in the hope that if you were alone and helpless like him, some mother would do the same for you. I am glad he came here when he did—it was as if you had sent him!

I was going to spend that money on an opera today; I was dying to have a good dinner at The Cornelia later. But then the wonderful thing happened! I felt so good— like I would have being your old mother! Everyone thinks of me as the young Leena. I would rather be an old woman, but privately only! I cannot afford to flaunt my old age in the public yet. You know why? The old have difficulty finding employment. I have to make false declarations about my age even when I know that you don't like it. You didn't like falsehoods when you were alive; you certainly don't like them now, sitting there with the Virgin Mother. Had you been around—with your wife—and kept me with you like the Hindu and Muslim sons do, I wouldn't have to tell lies, would I? I wouldn't need to go through this charade, would I?"

Overcome with grief, Leena pulled out her full set of false teeth and held them out as if showing them to her son. The hollowness in her cheek would have made it impossible for anyone to recognize her. She had lost her teeth not due to old age but to some other malady; but the toothless face certainly ratted on the fortyish age of the attractive Nurse Leena that moved around the hospital looking much younger.

About the same time three days later she heard the call from the street : 'Utensils! Aluminum utensils! Durable and quality utensils!'

The voice was not experienced but sounded mellow and sweet.

Leena peeked out of her balcony and saw Sukhlal with the helper carrying the basket of utensils. Her hand immediately covered the front of her face. The sweet notes of 'U..ten..si..' were cut short at the sight of Leena. The voice melted back into Sukhlal's throat the same way a lump of sugar dissolves in a glass of water.

The noise-free neighbourhood inspired quietness even among the talkers. Sukhlal's hawking tones had automatically lowered to suit. The quiet appeared to frame his silhouette in cool and diffused hues.

"Come on up, Smarty!" Leena quickly went inside and donned her false teeth. 'You must have known I was thinking of you!' She whispered as she covered her son's picture. The Catholic are no less superstitious than the Hindus. Their beliefs about the dead and the afterlife seem to go a lot farther than the Hindu 'superstition'.

Sukhlal went up to her apartment alone. He was still trying to set in words what he wanted to ask her, when he was left speechless by Leena's attack : "In all those days in the hospital, you never let on that you were so devious, so cunning! I am very angry with you." He tried to think of what devious and cunning behaviour he was being credited with?

"Why didn't you let me in on it?"

"On what, Nurse Baba?"

"Your treacherous scheme." Leena's tone was harsh and she scared Sukhlal. Had she called him in to insult him before throwing him out? The young man, a stranger to that life-terrain, regretted his rash decision to venture out there and started praying for a way out.

"That afternoon, I asked you over and over again, Smarty, why you were crying; when that woman showed up, why you had tears in your eyes. You pretended to be in pain. You gave me not a hint about who that woman was, what she was to you!"

Now Sukhlal was really lost. The matter he wanted to ask her and inform her about had already escalated to a fearsome level.

"I discovered the truth only yesterday when she came to the hospital again. I now know that she is your fiancee—your wife to be. Please forgive me, son!" Her voice mellowed : "I had assumed you were one of her servants. I didn't allow a word of conversation between you two. But, why haven't you kept in touch with her?

Why does she keep asking me of your whereabouts? What am I to you that she is so irritated with me? I have not kept you in hiding! Sit down, relax and talk to me. Have you had a fight with her? Don't you like her? Why did she say that her misfortune was that she was born in a rich family? Why was she so upset yesterday? She looked so terribly hurt yesterday!"

Coming from someone else, this would have sounded like a monstrous joke, a farce. A person, desperately thrashing around in the ocean, may suspect the sudden feel of the ground beneath his feet as the back of a man-eating shark. Sukhlal experienced the same feeling of terror at what should have pleased him.

"What did you tell her about me?" He timidly asked. He prayed that Leena had not told Sushila about his new occupation. Sushila might change her mind if she knew that he had become a mere hawker of utensils!

"I told her everything about you. Told her you were working very hard because you wanted to get married soon. I could tell that she was very concerned about that and was deep in thought about something. Then she asked me with much hesitation : 'Is he saving up for his marriage? With whom? Is he going to marry someone else?' What was I going to tell her? What was I to you that I would know every little detail about your life? How stupid can you be! How strange! Where do I figure in this matter between you and her?" She could not stop laughing.

"Did she sound happy about my new business?" The question came out as slowly and painfully as the *meend* from a sitar's string.

"She asked if you knew how to make a sale. I told her you didn't know the first thing about selling. But he will so endear himself to the customers that they will not be able to take advantage of him."

Sukhlal's did not look up. After a pause, he asked :
"Where can I see her?"

"Where she lives! Where else did you think?"

"Are you going to see her?"

"Only if she is sick and I am called in. But she won't
ask for me because she knows that I am a tough nurse
and demand total discipline. And, why would a healthy
girl like her fall sick anyway?"

Sukhlal knew that she was having fun now.

"Then again, anything is possible!" Leena quickly
followed with : "Sickness comes in many forms; we know
one of them as 'love fever'. If you stay away from her for
a while and if I tell her that you are going to marry
another girl, I may have a chance at treating her. That
would mean you helped me earn some money and I will
pay you back by helping you sell utensils to my friends.
Is that a deal?"

Sukhlal was in no mood to enjoy that levity. His
thoughts were racing in a different direction : 'What a
mix up! Isn't Sushila the one that wants to leave me?
What is this about my leaving her? Is she unaware of
the annulment signed by my father? Does she consider
my father guilty of fraud? Has her Mota Bapuji planted
that seed of distrust in her mind? How can we meet to
untangle this mess?"

The words 'Can you help us meet here?' almost came
out of his mouth but he stopped himself. No, it wouldn't
be proper to ask her. Besides, a respectable woman like
her could lose face by allowing a tryst at her residence.
What would happen if someone found out?

How about sending a message for Sushila through
her? He immediately discarded that idea, too. Secret
messages, secret meetings, secret negotiations are just
not in some people's makeup. Doing anything with
secrecy seems like conspiring or cheating to them.

Sukhlal loathed the very idea of secrecy. That inherited loathing made Sukhlal mindful of Leena's good name. He wouldn't consider anything that might hurt her. 'If Leena wanted us to meet like that, would she not suggest it herself?' he argued with himself.

"Something the matter, Smarty? Why the furrows on your forehead, darling?" Leena asked.

"I want to see her."

"Where will you meet her?"

"Didn't you suggest her home?"

"That's my boy, Smarty."

Sukhlal thanked her and rose to leave. Leena didn't stop him but called down to him : "Doesn't look like you have sold anything today."

"Oh yes, I have. This is my second trip today."

"Come, let me take you to my neighbours."

"Some other day."

"Wait then, I need some more things. My friends took what I bought the other day."

Sukhlal did not believe her. He said : "Why don't I come back tomorrow?"

"I won't be here tomorrow; I am on the day shift from tomorrow on. Wait."

Sukhlal hesitated.

"You idiot! No guts, no glory! Your associate knew how to sell; he would make people buy one way or another, and you dilly-dally when the customer wants to buy!" She was downstairs in a flash and picked out a few things. "Write me a bill while I get the money."

Sukhlal started writing in the bill-book. When Leena went upstairs, he told the helper to get going, that he would catch up. He himself left before Leena arrived with her money. He left the items selected by Leena right there on the sidewalk; the receipt inside just read : 'With *pranaam* from your humble Smarty.' His village education had taught him just enough English for that note.

When Leena came down with the money and saw the note, the biggest confusion in her mind was created by the word *pranaam*.

20

AFTER dinner, when Sukhlal put his shoes on, Khushaal asked : "Where to?"

"Just going for a stroll."

"Of course. Lock one of the doors from the outside and take the key with you, just in case I am asleep when you return."

Sukhlal left; Khushaal followed him down a minute later. He stayed far enough behind so Sukhlal wouldn't notice.

Khushaal was deeply concerned for a couple of reasons. One: the young man was left in Khushaal's care by his father. Two: his and Khushaal's prestige were tightly linked; that unblemished character was the strength on which Khushaal and the other poor Kathiawadi men survived and earned their livelihood in Mumbai. If Sukhlal—still a kid in Khushaal's mind—strayed from the straight and narrow and got into gambling or women, all would be lost. But warning him about it would only serve to point him in the wrong direction. Better to keep an eye on him.

Perhaps the kid was just confused and really needed some fresh air, but something did seem to bother him today. What was even more worrisome was, the kid was not easy to read and kept everything bottled up within himself. Gambling was an unlikely habit because he deposited all his money with Khushaal; didn't keep even two *annas* for a drink of coconut milk. Even at that time of the night, he had avoided taking a street car. He was not headed in the direction of the houses of ill repute, nor towards the beach. So where was he going? Just turned on the Sandhurst Road; so, the Romeo was going to his in-laws' place!

Khushaal had heard rumours about the engagement with Sushila being off; but, nobody had been able to provide a confirmation. Was the idiot going there to sign the annulment papers?

At that exact moment, all hell had broken loose in Sushila's home. Mota Sheth's bedroom was a volcano ready to erupt. Mota Bapuji sat on his bed and cracked his cold verbal whip at his wife who stood there with a guilty expression on her face. The reason for his anger was Sushila's refusal to go to the house of Vijaychandra's 'adopted sister'.

"So tell me why the girl stopped going there."

"How can I tell what is really on her mind? She just says she doesn't like it there."

"Do they beat her, abuse her, call her names? What is it that she doesn't like there?"

"I don't know for sure but they did get into an argument the first time she was there. No poor soul was going to beat her!"

"Had an argument already? Couldn't hold her tongue even for a couple of days? I guess she does not deserve a prize catch like Vijaychandra! All my hard work is to go down the drain. Does she have any idea how many proposals I have managed to have turned down, what unmentionable games I have played so that we come out ahead? But if she is destined to have a ..."

"Please don't say it. We should only wish her well. After all, she is our own flesh and blood."

"Ah yes! Our ... own ... flesh ... and ... blood!" The husband let out a big sigh of disappointment : "The tragedy of my life is that we were not able to produce even a dead rock!"

That last cruel strike hurt Sushila's Bhabhu as nothing else had in her life. Her life's emptiness, failure, lowliness, unworthiness and the lack of the very right to live were all driven home like simultaneous stabs into her heart. She absorbed that immeasurable and unbearable pain with no more than one backward glance. Her hidden and silent prayer rose skyward on the back of one heavy sigh : 'As you are my witness, Lord, didn't I try hard to get him to marry again? Wasn't he the one that adamantly refused?'

"Will someone tell me what big argument she had?" The irritated Mota Sheth asked : "Until yesterday, you couldn't get her to open her mouth. So what made her lose her cool ? And over there of all the places?"

Bhabhu had no answer for him.

"Has the cat got your tongue?"

"What can I say? I don't understand the whole thing myself. They asked her questions like : 'Do you want children or not? Why do you observe those outdated menstrual cycle practices? Are you going to trust your husband implicitly? ... After the marriage, you will have to forget the old-fashioned lifestyle taught by your Bhabhu; you will have to do what I say. Vijaychandra is more than a blood brother to me; if he must, he will leave you but will not give up his relationship with me. ... And why do you go and visit that hospital nurse so often? Do you have some kind of disease that we do not know about? We are going to have you examined by a lady doctor and ...'"

"And what?"

"She asked Sushila in Vijaychandra's presence : 'What kind of dowry is your father going to pay? Is he going to keep his word and pay for Vijaychandra's study abroad or not? Do you know that he can have his pick from among several other girls but your Mota Bapuji is holding us by repeatedly begging him to marry you?' Sushila couldn't take that last thing that woman said and must have said something."

"Like what?"

"That 'If my Mota Bapuji chose to beg, that was his choice; I didn't come here to beg. I didn't know I was going to have to answer questions like that. I thought I was going to study and train with you.' So the woman told her not to be so cocky; that educated men like Vijaychandra didn't grow on trees."

"And then?"

"That was it! Sushila got up and tried to leave without finishing her tea. Vijaychandra tried to stop her and spilled the tea on his clothes. He told Sushila that she will have to come back and wash those stains off his clothes. Sushila hit back with strong words of her own."

"What strong words?"

"That he should ask his 'sister' or whoever she was to wash his clothes."

"Okay, so the girl has botched it up really well! Who is this nurse that she has been seeing?"

"She and I went to the hospital once—to see Sukhlal."

"Didn't I ask you not to mention his name to me?"

"But the poor soul ..."

"Knock off the poor soul bit! Keep your compassion to yourself! I am warning you, I don't want him anywhere near our house and I will tear off the tongue of anyone that utters his name in my house!"

"But what has he done to us? Let him go his way and we will go our way."

"How stupid can you be? Don't I know that he has paid off the hospital nurses to get a hold on Sushila? What do you take me for? Even the two-bit chauffeur is not blind like you."

"But why do you want to force Sushila into something she doesn't like? What is the problem with doing what she likes?" The wife spoke clearly for the first time.

"Shut your trap!" Mota Sheth reached for the slipper dangling from his foot.

"Don't get excited ..."

Those words accompanied by a strained smile and the slipper leaving Mota Sheth's hand happened without an instant's gap between them. The slipper struck Bhabhu in the chest, bounced off and flew through the door to land on the balcony outside.

The doorbell rang. Someone was at the door. Sushila opened the door and saw Sukhlal outside. Sukhlal waited for Sushila to step aside so that he could enter. Instead of moving aside, Sushila stepped out and closed the door behind her.

"Why are you here at this hour? Please leave."

Her facial expression didn't match the request 'Please leave!', there was no contempt on her face. Sukhlal was puzzled by this dichotomy between the words and the evident lack of intent.

Speaking to her only for the second time, long after the meeting at the picnic, the good-looking young man, the guest, the traveler she had gone crazy looking for was standing at her doorstep; and she had just asked him to 'Please leave!'.

The brightly lit elevator slid past them several times. The upward and downward bound occupants noticed them standing in the corner and wondered. The elevator operator stopped at their floor several times, expecting one or both of them to go with him. He would leave after a fruitless wait and they would hear comments like : "The poor kids are not done talking yet!"

"Please leave quickly!" Sushila repeated to the quiet and worshipfully staring Sukhlal.

"I want to have one last talk—ask him about something."

"Not now."

"What is the matter? Isn't your Mota Bapuji home? I want to see him."

"You don't want to see him now."

"Why not?"

His answer came loud and clear all the way from Mota Sheth's bedroom inside : "Just go back to the village. I don't need you here."

How loud must that have sounded inside if it was heard that clearly through the closed doors! Sushila's ears and heart were inside. Bhabhu had been hit with a slipper. What was her state? She quickly told Sukhlal : "Please leave right now and come back in the morning. I will not let you see him now."

"Hold it!" She commanded the passing elevator to stop.

21

WHAT Sushila didn't think of was that the elevators don't respond to voice commands like 'hold it'. The descending elevator had to go all the way down before returning to their floor. The two were forced to wait near the elevator shaft. A highly nervous and scared Sushila kept looking at the front door of their apartment and asked : "Why do you want to talk to him?"

"Because you people keep complaining to people all over." Sukhlal didn't look up.

"Tell me what I have done wrong and then please go. Tell me quickly, the elevator is almost here." Sushila looked at the moving elevator cables and down the dark and deep shaft.

"You people forced my father into signing those papers; and now you are blaming poor me for it!"

"You seem very proud about trumpeting your poverty but show no desire to rescue your woman from her peril! Why don't you ask the person that got your father to sign the papers?"

"That's what I am here for."

"This is not a good time to see Mota Bapuji. He has blown his top and is beating up on my poor Bhabhu. You must leave here right now; I fear for your safety. Thank heavens the elevator is finally here."

The elevator came to a stop and the attendant dumped his entire day's frustration on Sushila by noisily opening the doors.

"Wait, wait just a minute!" The words appeared to come from the stairwell right next to where they were.

The two were joined by a third person walking with a long and firm stride, of a solid build and slightly crossed eyes. Khushaal carried a long stick and had apparently taken two steps at a time on his way up. He walked straight up to the elevator attendant and told him : "Carry on, my man!"

"Make up your mind, you people!" The attendant slammed the door shut and took the elevator down quickly like someone that couldn't stand another second of this love-charade.

"There is no need to worry about me," Khushaal assured the startled Sushila : "I am what you can think of as your older brother-in-law." Before the words were out of his mouth, Sushila had turned away, her annoyance for an aggressive stranger transformed into a shy and respectful demeanour. Khushaal quickly added : "On the other hand, I also happen to be a distant uncle of yours, Santok, my dear!"

Among the Kathiawadi *Vanik* families, the seemingly tangled threads of mutual relationships reveal a very intricate and beautiful pattern. Each new thread adds a new variation to the pattern. The bonds generated by this pervasive pattern often help alleviate the stiffness and the distance separating the newly connected families. A bride does not forget her ties with a distant *mama* when he becomes her father-in-law. There are numerous cases of aunt-niece pairs that married two brothers and became sisters-in-law. The flow of this weave has stagnated considerably but it still flows lively in certain enclaves.

The address 'Santok, my dear', immediately evoked a feeling of closeness in Sushila's heart; it revealed to her Khushaal's tender heart hidden under a coarse exterior.

Before Sukhlal could recover from the shock of seeing Khushaal there, Sushila started for the door to her residence. In her hurry to keep Sukhlal out, she had pulled the door shut behind her when she came out. It would now have to be opened by someone from within. As she pushed the door-bell, both Khushaal and Sukhlal observed her bared right forearm. Each saw different things in the sight. Sukhlal's eyes started plucking at the veins on that forearm like the strings of an instrument. Khushaal muttered to himself : 'That's the arm of a girl that works around the house. She doesn't look like a piece of your typical, delicate and fragile, Mumbai-ware.'

Khushaal had never stopped examining women the way one would evaluate houseware or furnishings. He constantly poked fun at some 'modern' Kathiawadi men who called their wives 'goddesses' or 'life-partners' : "This is the third 'goddess', isn't she? What you look for are these 'goddess' types that last for two or three years before dying of malnutrition; what I want is the sturdy stuff that would wear and last for ever. Look at this 'Roscop' pocket-watch I inherited from my grandfather : hasn't stopped working yet; I also have owned this 'Rajesh' knife for twenty years. For me, a wife is someone to care for and to preserve forever, my friend! You look after her, don't ignore her, don't let her wither away and don't show her off but treat her right. If you do all that, then describing her as a 'ware' is not putting her down! And if you don't do those things, calling her a 'goddess' is not doing her any favour."

Khushaal continued to examine Sushila from that angle. He looked at her head. 'Not a flat head; the round head will have difficulty carrying an *indhoni* and pitchers of water. Not to worry; if steel flattens out under load, her soft head will, too.'

These thoughts were soon interrupted. Bhabhu opened the door and saw the curazing sight. She had no idea Sushila had gone out! And who was this? She had last seen Sukhlal at the picnic as a pale, sickly and humiliated man, totally devoid of any vitality. At first, she did not recognize the free, confident, buoyant youth standing there, his face glowing with determination. She offered the customary welcome of : "Won't you come in?" before the recognition finally dawned on her, helped a little bit by Sushila's quiet and respectful stance. "Oh my God, where have you been? Come in, come in; how do you feel now?"

When she noticed the third person there, her confusion returned. Fearful that Bhabhu might throw him out with a 'who are you and what do you want?', Khushaal stepped through the door and disarmed her : "You will not recognize me, Gheliben, but you were at my sister Hemi's *diksha* ceremony ..."

The memory of that occasion came very easily : "But of course, you are her brother Ghoghabhai!"

"You did remember my name; I am impressed, Gheliben!"

Their use of the old nicknames became the means to resurrect the almost extinct memories of that old acquaintance.

"Come in, please make yourself comfortable." She simply buried the agony and anguish of the slipper thrown at her deep into her heart and attended to the guests. On her way to the kitchen to get glasses of water, she closed her husband's bedroom door without attracting any attention from the guests.

Khushaal watched Bhabhu's saintly face as she returned from the kitchen. His words conveyed genuine affection : "I remember how good friends you two were and how much you wanted to take the renunciation vows with Hemiben! But you were younger and the family didn't let you. Hemiben shined in her ascetic life and you, Gheliben, have lived an exemplary worldly life. I have been wanting to pay you a visit but never got around to it until today. Seeing you is like meeting my own Hemiben ..."

Khushaal was unable to continue. He pretended to be wiping the sweat off his brows as he wiped the corners of his eyes; then trying to emphasize that he had not been crying, he looked at the incandescent lamp overhead and added : "These bright lights bother my eyes."

One could hear the water flowing down Khushaal's throat as he drank from the water glass without touching it to his lips. Khushaal felt no embarrassment in the way he gulped water down. Bhabhu offered the other glass to Sukhlal and simply said : "I could hardly tell it was you. It's good that you, poor soul, have adjusted well to this Mumbai life."

"Learnt to stand on his own two feet, Gheliben; why wouldn't he look good?"

"On his own! In business for himself?"

"Absolutely. And doing well too! Sends a few bucks to his father; puts some aside for himself; he is on his way! With your blessings, he will have no problem earning his keep."

This was no attempt at small talk. Khushaal's clear motive was to solidify Sukhlal's claim on Sushila's hand.

The formality of offering water to the guests over, Sushila's Bhabhu kept standing. She was anxious to send them on their way as quickly as she politely could. Her heart was beating fast. Her husband was not asleep; he had kept staring at her as she stood without moving after being hit with his slipper. His angry eyes had followed her when she had left the room. Her quiet return and placing the thrown slipper in its place had shattered his self-respect. Hating himself, he had tried to find refuge in solitude and turned on his side away from her like a wounded snake coiling up in his basket. Sukhlal, just the mention of whose name had caused him to explode with such vehemence, was here in person. She shuddered at the thought of what her husband would do if he saw Sukhlal now! She mentally rehearsed her good-byes, worried that her habitual behaviour would force her to ask them to stay even if the guests wanted to leave.

But her anxiety to see the visitors off did not bear fruit. Her secret prayers went unheeded. Every second crawled as if weighted down by lead in its feet. Khushaal was trying to catch Sukhlal's eye but Sukhlal's attention was focused elsewhere. He had been watching another person's behaviour.

That person was Sushila's mother. She had entered and left the room two or three times without saying even a word of welcome. He could hear some angry words being exchanged between Sushila and her mother in the inner room. Her mother's words to Sushila were quite audible : "What are you watching through the cracks for? Why don't you just go and join them? What is he to you that this affection is oozing out of you? Do you know that your old man will tear him to shreds if he wakes up? Didn't you see what he just did to his old woman? Let him wake up! We should set the police on that idiot! Only that will teach him to leave us alone."

This art that some women are born with—addressing one when you want someone else to hear—was having its desired effect on Sukhlal. His heart started beating fast like the war drum during a battle; his sensitivity was under attack; he felt like he was being skinned alive. Those words were draining away any desire to leave this place peacefully.

In an attempt to drown out her sister-in-law's voice, Bhabhu turned talkative and started firing questions at Sukhlal : "Have you heard from your father yet? How is your mother's health? What do you do about your meals? One has to be careful or this Mumbai life can turn on you in no time!"

It fell on Khushaal to answer all those questions. Sukhlal's entire being was concentrated on his sense of hearing. He had felt Sushila's mother's every word strike him like sparks flying from a hot ember; he heard the daughter's short reply :

"Tell me whatever you wish; I am warning you one last time, mother, you are not going to utter a word about anybody else."

Khushaal, meanwhile, had been busy with his own plans. He had asked casually about the Mota Sheth's whereabouts and was told that he was home but asleep.

Khushaal's voice started getting louder, loud enough to cause the ear drums of a sleeping person to tingle. His boisterous laugh sounded like the clang of pots and pans knocked off from a high shelf by a cat. This residence had never experienced anything approaching this man's nerve. Mota Sheth squirmed in his bed like a patient trying to suppress his stomach cramps. What he resented the most was his wife's easy conversation with this wretched visitor. The strong itch in his hands to use that slipper repeatedly on her leaked away from his finger-tips.

"It's time to formally bring Sukhlal into your family, Gheliben! That will relieve us of our responsibility too."

Bhabhu did not respond to Khushaal's words, but the pillow-covered Mota Sheth's ears still allowed the words to get through and the resulting pain in his skull was unbearable. The bed felt like it was afire. He sat up and his feet entered the perfectly positioned slippers, a humiliating reminder of his wife's forgiving behaviour. Her words rang in his ears : 'You shouldn't get upset like that, poor soul! You are not going to do anything hasty now, are you?'

For the second time that day, he crushed that heart-softening word-touch under his feet and banged open the door that his wife had closed so gently.

If looks could have killed, the entire assembly in the outer room would have been decimated right there from the intense glare he aimed at them.

"Greetings, Champakbhai! Greetings! So, our racket disturbed you too! Good for us because we would have missed you otherwise."

Khushaal had trained himself from his early school days never to be nonplussed under any circumstance. He had learnt that teachers liked the pupil who gave an immediate answer—right answer or wrong did not matter; the slightest hesitation and the game was lost. It was no different in real life. The one that snapped right back without worrying about being right or wrong invariably came out ahead of the others.

Khushaal, the master practitioner of that principle, had managed to blunt Mota Sheth's attack before the arrogant man had the time to say an insulting word.

"Welcome to my home." It killed Mota Sheth but the words just slipped out of him.

"Isn't this something?" Khushaal was not about to let his advantage slip. "Your elders' good deeds and your own ability and hard work were rewarded by the Lord. With our luck, we have to toil all day to make ends meet. I have often thought about calling ahead and coming out to meet you but it just never worked out. Today, I said to myself, come what may I was going to meet Champakbhai. I never had a chance to really see you since coming to Mumbai—except when we once sat next to each other during a community feast; you had liked our lemon pickle very much, if you recall. Well, I finally got my courage together and got Sukhlal here to go with me ..."

"What can I do for you? I have this bad headache." Mota Sheth, whose original name Chanpshi had become Champaklal since arriving in Mumbai, had reached the limit of his civility.

"Oh, nothing much really. I was telling Gheliben here that Sukhlal has settled down comfortably. Everyone will feel relieved when he becomes a son in your house here. People start a thousand rumours in this town. Nobody will dare to tell you, Champakbhai, but we have no choice but to listen to the talk out there!"

"I don't want to talk about it. That matter has been settled."

"Settled?" Khushaal expressed surprise.

"Yes, with his father."

"That is what I have come here to talk about. " Sukhlal finally spoke his first words of the evening : "I want to know what agreement you have reached with my father."

The words hit Mota Sheth like a crack of thunder. Were these the words of the sickly, half dead, wretched Sukhlal he had known? Was that possible?

The women had withdrawn to the inside room. Bhabhu and Sushila were together, wearing concerned and worried but controlled expressions in spite of the tempest raging in the outer room. Sushila was understandably jittery and started every so often.

Just then, the elevator stopped on their floor. The doors were heard opening and closing and then the doorbell rang. Bhabhu opened the door and saw a police officer standing there and accompanied by two policemen. The sight of policemen at their door frightened Bhabhu.

"Is Champak Sheth in?" The officer asked with some authority.

"Why?"

"I need to see him." The officer entered the residence.

Bhabhu went in and informed her husband : "The police are here to see you."

In a businessman's life, two of the most frightening events are the arrivals of Income Tax and Police officials. Mota Sheth rose and showed the policemen the meekest face possible for him.

The officer asked him : "Does a young man named Vijaychandra Dalapat visit here frequently?"

"Er...er... why?" The shrewd businessman avoided answering the question.

"Is it true that he is your future son-in-law?"

The hemming and hawing was repeated. The police officer continued : "When was he last here?"

"I—I can't remember—don't remember ..."

"Is your daughter home?"

"Yes."

"I would like to ask her a few questions."

"Sushila—" Mota Sheth's voice cracked. Sukhlal stepped in : "What kind of questions do you intend to ask her? On what grounds?"

"You, sir, frighten us by asking for Sushila." Now Khushaal interjected mildly : "Why don't you ask us whatever questions you have? What is this about Vijaychandra?"

The two young men's stand made the police officer hesitate just a bit. He recovered quickly and spoke with the arrogance befitting his power : "And may I know who you are?"

"If you really want to know who I am, let me accompany you to the Commissioner's office. You will find out my real identity then." Khushaal knew how to put others at disadvantage.

The police officer was convinced he was dealing with someone with influential connections. To reinforce his impression, Khushaal added : "If you are here on official business, let's hear what it is." Somewhat humbled, the police officer asked : "May I sit down? Let me explain what we are trying to do."

"Certainly!" That one word, delivered with some authority, established Khushaal's temporary command of the situation. The officer was ushered into the living room. Mota Sheth saw Khushaal as a god-sent helper. Sukhlal lit his own candle of courage from Khushaalbhai's glowing flame of fearlessness and joined them. Everybody else sat on chairs; Khushaal alone graced the silk-covered sofa with his muscular bulk.

"Now, tell us what all this is about, Raosaheb!" Khushaal's words carried the ring of authority that went with the ownership of the house. Mota Sheth's state of mind being what it was, he would have gladly played the part of Khushaal's servant at that point!

22

THE police officer's story went something like :
"A college graduate named Vijaychandra has been
enticing girls from good families with the prospects of
marriage. He extracts promises of financing his education
abroad from the unsuspecting parents of these 'brides'.
Under the pretense of educating them, the girls are
invited to the home of a woman friend one at a time.
The woman is a well-educated widow and goes through
the motions of tutoring the girls."

"That means ..." Before Champak Sheth could say
any more, Khushaal jumped in to stop him from talking :
"Doesn't surprise me a bit. Mumbai is a city with a big
heart. It has room for everyone, Raosaheb!"

As he spoke, Khushaal slapped his flattened cap on
the sofa. He wanted to mute Champak Sheth's tongue
at any cost.

All blood had drained from Champak Sheth's face.
The police officer continued his narration :

"This Vijaychandra had laid an elaborate scheme with
the promise of Civil Marriage to a Marathi girl from an
affluent family. The girl was already betrothed to another
man. Her widowed mother knew nothing of what was
going on. Last night, this Vijaychandra and his 'sister'
took the girl and all her jewelry and ran. They were
apprehended earlier this evening. I came here because
I had heard that the scoundrel is engaged to your
daughter. Our information was that the stolen jewelry
was to be used as wedding gifts for your daughter. The
other girl's deceased father was my good friend."

"There you go, Raosaheb!" Khushaal's mocking laughter was delivered without even looking at the target : "Another perfect example of how ineffective the Mumbai Police has become." The officer was now sure that Khushaal had inside and intimate knowledge of his department. He had no idea that Khushaal had affected his carefree attitude only to avoid the officer's eyes; the image of a VIP was complete.

"What makes you say that, sir?" The officer was well aware of the rot in his organization and asked with evident humility.

"I was referring to your ill-considered and hasty arrival here based on totally false information. Such monstrous gaffes would never happen if only someone had the sense to put some Kathiawadis in your department."

"I don't understand."

"My older cousin here will explain. Tell him, Champakbhai," Khushaal turned to the incredulous Mota Sheth : "How long has Sushila been engaged, about ten years?"

Mota Sheth squirmed like a snake caught in a pair of pincers : "Almost eleven."

"And isn't the young Sukhlal—sitting right here—your future son-in-law?"

"He's the one." Champak Sheth almost bit his tongue. Less than an hour ago, he had slammed a slipper on this Sukhlal's name, vowed never to let him even near the house, was going to report Sukhlal to the police to have him removed from his life like a thorn from his path and was unwilling to even see his face again. And here he was, admitting to the police Sukhlal's ten-year old status as his future son-in-law!

"Good." Khushaal was thoroughly relishing his practice of this 'worldly law' : "Champakbhai, now clarify a few things for the Raosaheb here. Did you invite your future son-in-law to Mumbai or not? Did you put him to work and set him up with a business or not? And did you invite him here tonight to discuss the final details or not?"

Just then, the telephone rang in the next room. Sushila got up from her seat next to Bhabhu—from where she had heard Khushaal's every word—and went to get the phone. Her defiant words resonated through the room :

"Who are you? ... He is busy right now. You can tell me what you want. ... Never mind who I am, he will get your message. ... Stop it, stop this nonsense right now! Don't call here again. Do you have no shame? Such nerve!"

Sushila hung up with those last words.

The phone rang again and continued to ring. Sushila picked up the phone once but hung up on hearing the same voice without saying a word. She returned to Bhabhu and sat down.

Who was the caller that Sushila spoke with like that? The surprised Bhabhu asked : "Who was it?"

"That scum!"

"Who?" Sushila was known for her controlled speech. It bothered Bhabhu to hear the scorn in her voice.

"Vijaychandra!"

"What did he want?"

"Said he wanted to speak to Mota Bapuji at once, that he was in trouble. The bully tried to order me around even on the phone, the scoundrel!"

The phone bell started its strident ringing again.

Champak Sheth had gone virtually deaf. The police investigation was delving deep into sensitive and dangerous areas. The inevitable police station interrogation was already screaming like a banshee in his ears. He was oblivious to the ringing of his own phone. Before Mota Sheth recovered from his reverie, Khushaal directed Sukhlal :

"Why don't you go see who is calling?"

Like a courtier trying to control his stomach cramps in mid-court, Champak Sheth sat and tolerated these two trespassers who had taken control of his world. His attempt to get up was thwarted by Khushaal : "Why don't you stay? We don't want the Raosaheb here to think that we are trying to cover something up."

Sukhlal approached the phone in the hall outside just as Sushila was taking it off the hook and quieting its noise. Bhabhu was in the inner room.

Sushila thought Sukhlal was there to make a phone call of his own. When he was close enough, she said : "Please don't pick it up yet."

"Why?"

"It's kind of hot!" Sushila joked. Not getting it, the embarrassed Sukhlal asked :

"Who was it? Mota Sheth wants to know."

"It was nobody important, just a girl-friend of mine." Sushila's dimples got even deeper. "Please don't try to answer the phone. This friend will bore you to death." She started walking back towards Bhabhu.

"The police officer is going to summon you soon." Sukhlal tried to frighten her.

"I guess the men are not able to take care of the business ..." Sushila fired back as she returned to Bhabhu and started listening to the living room conversation.

The policemen left a few minutes later. Khushaal walked the officer back to the elevator. Upon his return, he asked for Mota Sheth's leave : "Well, Champakbhai, we'll take care of our original business later."

"But I want to take care of it right now." Sukhlal moved closer to Mota Sheth. "I have come to ask for two things. First, I want the annulment paper that was signed by my father. In return I am willing to sign one myself. And the second, I want to see the medical certificate about my condition that you have somehow obtained."

Both those items were news to Khushaal.

"Please relax, Champakbhai. Sit down, Sukhlal, and calm down, please." After making sure the two were seated, he asked :

"Annulment of what? And what certificate are we talking about?"

"What certificate? Why don't you ask him, Khushaalbhai? He has arranged for a doctor's certificate attesting to my impotence, my lack of manhood! I have come to tear that paper to shreds or to get the name of the doctor that signed it."

"Impotence? Certificate of your impotence? A medical certificate?" Khushaal turned his gaze on Champak Sheth : "And the annulment?"

"Of my betrothal! My father was abused and threatened with that certificate's use into signing that annulment." Sukhlal's lips quivered as he spoke.

"Be calm, Sukha!"

"How can I be calm? I have lost all patience after learning about this. Is this what my father was tortured and made to cry for? Working me like a dog and putting me in the hospital was not enough!"

This was not the Sukhlal that everybody knew. A humiliated and beaten Champak Sheth looked down with shame. The desperate agitation in Sukhlal's voice worried Bhabhu enough for her to come and stand in the doorway.

Sukhlal broke into sobs and then started crying. Intense rage causes tears in the young and dead quiet in the elders.

"Where are these documents, Champakbhai? We don't want any public scandal about them, do we, Sheth?" With that Khushaal grabbed Sukhlal's hand and told him : "Get hold of yourself, my friend. Sheth is going to produce those documents. You rip them up with your own hands. After that, if the Sheth still wants an annulment, you can write one out yourself."

"Whether anybody wants it or not, I want it. I want to release them and I want to be released from this bondage." Sukhlal's throat overflowed with pain and hurt.

"You said it , Sukha! A happy marriage cannot result from a mismatch of one's upbringing and the station in life. You are wise beyond your years, kid! Champakbhai, let's get this thing over with. This will remain between the three of us only. Not another soul will know that those documents ever existed. Please go get them."

Champak Sheth just stared back with extreme embarrassment but made no move to produce the fraudulent documents.

"No matter; there is no urgency about it," Khushaal straightened his hair, put his cap on and then adjusting it with a flair to one side of his head in the manner of a street bully, added : "We'll be back tomorrow night. That should give you enough time to think this through. Let's go, Sukha. How long can these nice people tolerate a person of my ill repute in their respectable home?"

Bhabhu intercepted them as they made to leave. She said : "Oh no, poor souls, you shouldn't talk like that! It's late now; why don't you two stay here for the night?"

"No Gheliben, I won't lie to you," Khushaal's cap was back on straight in its most civilized mode. "You don't know, Gheliben! How can you have any idea that your friend Hemibai Saadhvi's brother Khushaal has the reputation of a Mumbai bully? I don't belong in a respectable household at night. And there is nothing amazing about it, Gheliben! A snake's venom is its source of power; likewise, some people derive their power from their reputation for being 'bad'. How else can you explain a police officer feeling intimidated by a simple Kathiawadi villager? So excuse us, Gheliben! It looks like I will have to come back tomorrow. There is no choice but to wrap this thing up tomorrow, Ben!"

While Khushaal was held up talking to Bhabhu, Sukhlal was already at the stairs outside. When Khushaal finally caught up with him, he heard Sushila's parting words to Sukhlal : "Tear up the papers—but, for heaven's sake, don't tear up some poor girl's heart!"

Before she could cover the side of her face in deference to Khushaal, Khushaal's observant eye had read the frustration on Sushila's face. Quickly she side-stepped him and entered her home through the door.

The serpentine staircase carried them towards terra firma. Taking two steps at a time, Khushaal held forth : "Can't let her go, Sukha! I can tell : this girl will make a perfect bride for you. A Mumbai brat would have given herself away. Did you see her cover her face for me? She gave me respect; me—a worthless nobody! A spoilt Mumbaiite would have endlessly parroted some inane chatter. We were in this house for two hours and never even knew what her voice sounded like. A perfect match for you, I tell you, Sukha. And she, too, seems to be caught between a rock and a hard place!"

The hooves of the hired victoria's horse tapped the wet pavement with a steady cadence; consciously or not, Khushaal's words kept perfect pace with the horse-provided rhythm.

* * *

When the aunt-niece pair finally laid down in their beds, the sickly looking Champak Sheth stood near his wall-safe. Feeling as weak as a patient coming out of a six-month bed-confining sickness, his hand shook in trying to turn the key. The two documents—the annulment from Sukhlal's father and the fraudulent medical certificate—fluttered in his hands. His eyes roamed from one to the other, stopping to read each over and over again.

The rustling noise of repeatedly unfolded and refolded documents started a huge competition between Sushila's ears and eyes. What were those papers that kept going in and out of the safe? Sukhlal's anguished utterances had solved the mystery of what had caused her father-in-law's heart-breaking crying in the living room the other day and the secret weapon that had emboldened Mota Bapuji to work on a new candidate for marriage for her. If the demon *Hiranyakashyap's* sins could cause a red hot iron pillar to explode, she wondered why her Mota Bapuji's sin-filled safe was still intact. What was to happen when Sukhlal showed up tomorrow night? She had no courage to speak her mind to Mota Bapuji. What was she going to do if the visit turned violent?

"Bhabhu," she called out. That mild-mannered and gentle woman had put all her agitation out of her mind with a simple recitation of her faith's five-line *Navkaar* chant and was fast asleep. She was the living proof of the belief that layers upon layers of mental distress can be swept away with a little bit of water. If those five phrases from the Jain scriptures, repeated chanting of a hymn or a bedtime *tasbi* are capable of quieting a tortured mind and sending it into a dreamless sleep, isn't that worldly utility alone enough justification for one's faith in the Supreme?

Just a touch was enough to awake Bhabhu from her sleep. Her composed response betrayed no sign of being awakened from sleep : "Yes, my girl? Did you say something?"

"Yes, I want to ask you something."

"I am listening."

"I want your promise that nobody will take me away from you against my will. Promise me that you will not abandon me even if everybody else does."

"You think you need a promise from me, girl? Haven't I been with you all this time, even at the exclusion of the others?"

"And Bhabhu," something reminded Sushila, "if you decide to take the vows of renunciation like your friend Hemiben, I will too. What do you say to that?"

"Have you gone mad? Renunciation! If you keep your emotions and desires in control, no vows are necessary. And remember one thing, girl, there is no bigger place of worship than your home. Stop worrying and get some sleep now."

Wonders never cease, but in no more than two minutes the two city women were sleeping like newborns.

But the sleep that had blessed these two simple-hearted women had not sent even a wink to the adjoining bedroom. Mota Sheth's head crawled with thoughts like a basketful of slithering snakes. And to top it all, a new terror had raised its ugly head. The phone rang : "This is Vijaychandra speaking. What is going on, Sheth? I have dialed your number until my fingers ached. I finally found someone else to post my bail. You are going to have to help me; I have passed up a lot of lucrative offers in your favour; I will be over to see you at ten in the morning ..."

His voice had carried the unmistakable tone of a command.

Mota Sheth was scared out of his wits. What if Vijaychandra dragged him and Sushila into court to testify in his behalf? Sushila in a court of law? His Sushila to appear in a criminal proceeding? His girl there to face a thousand stabbing eyes ... his darling Sushila?

His ego had been shattered. Sitting atop the dump of that self-image, his empty and lonely heart was still trying to effect some semblance of the old arrogance. But the thought of Sushila being dragged into a courtroom by Vijaychandra roamed the expanse of his mind with the terrifying effect of a black venomous snake crawling in the rafters of one's bedroom.

The night was ticking away. Even the breathing sounds reminded him of hissing snakes. He turned the blue night light on and walked into his wife's room, bent over her and whispered : "Are you awake?"

He didn't notice her eyes opening. The words "I will be right there" sounded not the least bit sleepy but full of the nightly fragrance of the Queen of the Night blossoms. Taking care not to disturb Sushila's sleep, she quietly went and stood by her husband's bed.

Was it the husband that pulled her to him or was it his touch that made her move to him? Only the blue night-light knows—we will never know.

'The poor soul!' The phrase that her heart felt and she uttered for every living person, stayed unsaid but reverberated through the dome of soul; her hand caressed her husband's body ... how many years had it been?

The husband asked : "Can you and Sushila leave for the village by the morning train?"

What a difference : earlier, a thrown slipper had preceded that barked wish! This time around, her husband's loving hands had formed a garland around her neck.

23

WITH a genuine feeling for her husband's 'poor soul' state, the wife felt her head giving in to his pull after a gap of many years. The touch of their foreheads burnt her; his felt like a frying-pan full of boiling oil cooking on the flames of his many frustrations. His embrace conveyed neither the cool comfort of a man at peace with himself nor the warmth of a fulfilled love.

"Shhh..., Sushila might wake up...." She pulled her head away gently.

"Can you be ready for the morning train?"

"Certainly, if that is what you want ..."

"My reason for asking you to go is different this time. I think it will be best if Sushila were not here for some time. Why don't you two go and spend some time in Thorewaad? I will send a telegram to our Jetpur office and ask our man to get the Thorewaad house cleaned up for you today."

"Fine."

"You may want to start packing now."

"We'll be ready. We don't need much besides our clothing."

The new residence—built only three years ago—had been equipped by Champak Sheth's orders with everything ranging from a spatula to a thermometer. There really was no need to carry anything from Mumbai.

"Do your brother and Sushila's mother know about this?"

"We'll tell them in the morning. And Nano went to bed early this evening. Poor fellow doesn't know the difference between night and day."

"Will you take good care of yourself?"

"I will be okay."

"May I say something?"

"No, we are not going to talk about it. My decision is irreversible. My daughter will not marry into that beggar's hut as long as I am alive. What that boy said to me tonight was like molten lead poured into my ears. I am telling you there are thousands of good *families* in places like Rajkot and Junagadh. I want you to keep your eyes and ears open. I'll do the same from here."

The wife's hands were on the soles of his feet. She leaned and slowly rested her head on her husband's feet. If his forehead was aflame, there was no reason for his feet to be cool. Her gesture of reverence went unnoticed. His heart showed no sign of softening. His hurt pride, like the temporarily limped hood of an injured cobra, was upright again. Finally, defeated, disappointed and saying silent prayers for quenching of the raging fire of his wounded ego, she returned to her room. Her mind asked : 'Is this our last meeting? Am I ever coming back here?'

Upon arising, when Sushila heard about her planned departure with Bhabhu, her heart resurrected the memories of a river-bank when she was a seven-year old. She was packed and ready to go in half-an-hour. To her, leaving Mumbai seemed like being released from the stranglehold of a python. Why did she had to leave, where she was going, for how long—none of that mattered. Even a prisoner being transferred from one jail to another finds some sweet relief in the change.

The car left for the station at 7:30 in the morning. Mota Bapuji went to the station to see them off. Her own father, in the stern presence of his older brother, was not able to say even a loving 'take care of yourself'. The departing daughter's eyes were wet at her father's watery plight. She realized for the first time how lonely and miserable her father was. The father and daughter had never been able to talk or spend any time together. When a tree loses its bark, the bark is usually torn from it. Sushila left her father's life in the same manner, torn from it.

Just three minutes before the train's departure time, Sushila saw a young man enter the station platform. No, that couldn't be Vijaychandra! His customary firm steps were missing from the man's walk. The jacket was wrinkled. Loose strands of hair peeked from under his cap and ratted on his loss of balance. The silk handkerchief had been used to wipe the perspiration off his face and looked like a dusting rag's kin.

But Sushila's eyes were not fooled. At his sight, she gave a start, faced away and arranged her sari around herself.

It was Vijaychandra. He was to be at their residence at ten o'clock, but got impatient and had arrived there much earlier. Sushila's father, being unaware of the previous night's happenings, had told him where to find them and Vijaychandra had rushed to the station in a cab.

"This is great!" He was still out of breath, "Why wasn't I informed?"

"Who told you?" A disconcerted Champak Sheth asked.

"Nana Sheth."

Champak Sheth was so upset at his idiot younger brother that he wanted to go home and slap his face for this stupidity.

"What was the big hurry?" Vijaychandra pressed.

"Not keeping well lately; the change of air will be good for her."

"But there is no shortage of good doctors here! Why risk breathing in all that dust! I should have been consulted about this. I think this is a mistake. There is still time to get them off at Dadar." His statements flowed like a deluge. Every word bit Sushila like a scorpion's sting. She felt like repeating, for the sixth time, the adjective 'shameless' she had used five times on the phone the night before : 'you still think you own me; do you have no shame?'

"And she also has to go on this pilgrimage we had pledged." Champak Sheth added to his defense arguments.

In that one minute, Vijaychandra had tried to peek through the window of the coach but failed to catch even a glimpse of Sushila's face. And Champak Sheth, who prided himself for being fearless, was not able to say a word to scold the young man's nerve.

The whistle blew and the train shuddered into motion. Simultaneously, Vijaychandra opened the door to the coach saying "I have some business in Dadar ..." and boarded the train. The surprised Champak Sheth stood on the platform with a droped face for a while and then left.

Vijaychandra worked quickly to regain his lost composure. He looked for a seat in the compartment occupied by Bhabhu and Sushila. The two berths were completely covered with the women's bedding. Neither Sushila nor Bhabhu even looked at him. When he was about to lower himself into one corner of the stretched bedding, Bhabhu told him : "Young man, it will be better if you sat in the next compartment."

In that hard line taken by Bhabhu, Sushila saw a clear signal approving the declaration of war and the clarion call to get her loud and clear flowing.

Meanwhile, Vijaychandra had moved into the next compartment with only the wooden partition that served as the back rest separating him from Bhabhu. Sensing this, Bhabhu shrank away from the backrest to put some distance between them and started chatting with Sushila like she was a close friend. It didn't take Sushila long to understand Bhabhu's motive behind the loud and free spirited conversation on just about anything that came to her mind. The whole idea was to put Vijaychandra in his place and to keep him away until Dadar, the next stop. Realizing for the first time how clever her Bhabhu really was, Sushila herself was energised up. Hidden behind the petals of Bhabhu's healthy and self-developed attributes of simplicity, civility, gravity and uncommon grace was this cache of fragrant sense of humour.

By the time Dadar arrived, the ignored Vijaychandra had lost the courage to show his face and quietly left from the other side. The two ladies heaved a sigh of relief and went quiet again.

The whole journey was a source of wonder for Sushila. Bhabhu's keen eyes observed Sushila's every gesture, every move minutely. Their day train stopped at many stations with a variety of people boarding and getting down each. These passengers talked about their lives, littered the coach with their rubbish, fed and played with their children, occasionally even dished out physical punishment. Sushila made no attempt to keep away from them; she tried to help out with the children; helped some parents rig a temporary hammock to put the babies in; asked each mother about how old the baby was, what it was fed, why the baby's father wasn't with them, what their livelihood came from, what medical care they were able to get for the baby, etc.

Seeing her niece interested in talking to the village folk on the kind of old fashioned topics shunned by most city girls, Bhabhu thought she was more a 'country' person than a Mumbai girl. She didn't seem the least bit conscious about her own, albeit home-tutored, years of English language education. Bhabhu had also noticed with interest that Sushila had not brought any book— novel or poetry—to read on the train.

"What will you do when you get bored, Sushila?" had been answered by : "Bhabhu, for some reason, I wonder why I never knew there were so many people in this world of ours! Why was that, Bhabhu?"

"Listen to this girl! Back in Mumbai, you refused to leave home as if you couldn't stand the smell of the people!"

"I cannot tell you why, but here on this train, I like the smell of the people. The suckling babies smell so sweet to me."

At every stop, Sushila helped the detraining women : "Why don't you get off first and let me hand you your son! ... Be careful as you step down, grandma; there now, let me help you with your bundle of clothing."

Helping people became her pastime for the entire train ride. And it was pleasure and not pity that inspired her behaviour. Not once did she utter anything like 'poor folks'. She was going at it as if she had been starved of any contact with such a mass of humanity!

About nine o'clock in the evening, when the train crossed the Sabarmati river into Kathiawaad, Sushila woke up with a start and looked all around her : "Bhabhu!" was all that she was able to say.

"What's the matter, my girl!"

"Nothing."

"So, you still want to keep secrets from me! Speak up, girl! If you keep it bottled up, you will not be able to sleep. You should not torture your mind at this tender age, my dear!"

"Bhabhu, I thought about my Mota Bapuji and what may be happening at home right now."

"What do you think is happening?"

"Weren't those two going to come calling?" The words came so softly that they seemed to slide off the end of her sari that covered her face.

It was not Bhabhu's nature to show her surprise or to express any alarm. When startled, all that showed on her face was the hint of a flitting dark shadow. The two women just sat there, staring at each other and thinking the same thought : why doesn't the train just turn around and return to Mumbai!

But the dark cloud on Bhabhu's face dissipated quickly. Blood rushed to her face as if her soul was inscribing something in red one letter at a time : the words of the early morning hours of that day : the words cried out by her heart when her husband's feet were on her forehead : 'Will I ever return to this house! Could these be my last moments with him!'

"Oh, get some sleep. What is there to worry about?" And then, Bhabhu added with a slight smile : "You just don't know your Mota Bapuji very well. Do you think he is not ready for those two? He probably has the police waiting to take them away in shackles if they come and cause any trouble—do you understand?"

Sushila closed her eyes for a while. Bhabhu's word-picture worried her more than it comforted her. Bhabhu's eyes seemed to be insinuating : 'You, girl, are something else! You talk about your Bapuji's welfare but deep inside, your real sympathy is with the enemy, isn't it?"

When she opened her eyes, Bhabhu's firm voice continued : "And your mother is not one to sit around and watch those two attack your Bapuji! She will rush in with a bottle full of acid. Do you know what a splash of that acid can do to you? That Sukhlal's face will carry those etch marks for ever. And if it got into his eyes ..."

Sushila got up and covered Bhabhu's mouth with her hands : "Please, Bhabhu, must you keep talking like that!"

"Why, what's the matter?"

"What you say scares me!"

"What is so scary about it? All I want is your Mota Bapuji to be safe. And let someone try and lay even a

finger on him! He will let the whole neighbourhood know
that the pair of them tried to murder him. Even if it
costs him fifty thousand, he will put that Sukhlal in jail
for a few years. So, girl, don't you worry about your
Mota Bapuji's safety!"

Chewing on finely shredded betel nut, enjoying its
taste one drop at a time, flashing the light red tint of
her teeth from a now years old dye-job, Bhabhu continued
to paint—seeming to enjoy every second of it—such a
vivid word-picture of Sukhlal's acid-treatment and his
incarceration that Sushila almost hated her for it. Blood
rushed to her face and she turned away from Bhabhu
and just sat there fuming. Bhabhu asked :

"Still worried about your Mota Bapuji?"

When Sushila kept facing away, Bhabhu continued to
tease her : "I am sure your Mota Bapuji played it safe
and alerted the police. He must have told them he
suspects that two criminal types were going to be at our
house at a certain time and must have asked for police
protection. And right now, that charming Sukhlo is
probably behind bars begging for your Mota Bapuji's
forgiveness."

With her face turned away from Bhabhu, Sushila's
ear was even closer to Bhabhu and Bhabhu further
helped her hearing by raising her voice a little. She
continued to add colour to her picture :

"And you just watch; he is going to shed tears on your
Bapuji's feet and ask for his pardon. He will write out
whatever kind of annulment your Bapuji asks for. They
will know that your Mota Bapuji is not to be trifled
with; that nobody plays him for a fool! He is going to
teach Sukhlal such a lesson that the boy will not want
to as much as look in the direction of Mumbai again."

Bhabhu swallowed the last of the betel nut in her
mouth and replenished that with a fresh supply of beetle-
nut shavings made with the help of a *soodi*. Some people

find the smacking sound of betel nut chewing as painful as a stab in their ears. Sushila's ears experienced the doubled pain of being stabbed by that smacking sound and the scenarios painted by Bhabhu. She had never spoken out of turn to Bhabhu and, in her present state, was afraid that she might lose control and do just that. To avoid that, Sushila covered herself with a sheet and enduring the oppressive August heat and her own internal unrest, laid down and tried to get some sleep. In that, Bhabhu saw the scope to further exercise her sarcasm and she raised her intensity one more notch. Moving her mouth closer to Sushila, she continued :

"It was just as well that Sukhlal did not lay a hand on you by the elevator—I am sure he was there to get you to elope with him in a car waiting downstairs. The sophisticated crook Vijaychandra and this innocent looking Sukhlal have one thing in common : both are interested in victimizing unsuspecting girls. If it were not for your Mota Bapuji's foresight and savvy ..."

Flinging her sheet aside, Sushila sat up and just said : "Does torturing me make you happy?" Huge teardrops fell from her eyes like a deluge.

"Torturing you?" Bhabhu acted surprised : "My girl, I was only trying to stop you from worrying, to reassure you."

"You are a lot of help ..." Sushila's tear filled eyes glared at Bhabhu.

"Wasn't I trying to help? Your Mota Bapuji ..."

"I don't want to hear about it."

"All right, all right! You were the one that was worrying!"

"I was, but ... oh, forget it, you wouldn't understand anyway!"

"How was I to know, girl, that while you talked about your Mota Bapuji's safety, you were really concerned about someone else's."

The betel nut smacking sound coming from Bhabhu's mouth had not ceased. There was a twinkle in her eyes and a mysterious smile on her face. These sights and sounds puzzled Sushila. Her voice choked and then cracked. She tried to stifle her cries by burying her face in Bhabhu's lap. Bhabhu stroked her back gently and said :

"There's something strange about the Kathiawaad air; one feel of it and the children turn sly like you wouldn't believe! So tell me, whose welfare did you really have in mind : your Mota bapuji's or someone else's? Come on, touch your heart and tell me!"

"And you ... you are the big compassionate type! Talking about sprinkling acid on people and turning them over to the police really suits you well!"

"Then you should have been more direct and told me it was Sukhlal you were worrying about, my girl. I cannot read your mind!"

"When will you stop torturing me?"

"Not until you come clean with me."

When Sushila did not respond, Bhabhu asked :

"Do you know the real reason why you are going to Kathiawaad?"

"Why?"

"To find another groom for you."

"I will see how you are going to do that!"

"What will you do?"

"Whatever comes to my mind at the time."

"Your Mota Bapuji wants you to be in a well-to-do family."

"What he cares about is to enhance his status."

"Is he wrong to desire a family consistent with his own station in life?"

"Bhabhu, all I want you to know is : don't try to find anyone for me and don't bring anyone to see me either."

"And what if we do?"

"Then I will act deaf, mute and lame; or else I'll raise such a ruckus ... that will chase them away."

"What do you really want?"

"As if you don't know!"

"Sukhlal ...?"

Sushila said nothing. Bhabhu's hand resting on Sushila's bosom read her clear answer from the pace of her heartbeats. Sushila chewed on the loose end of her sari and finally said :

"You always want to know how I feel. Why don't you ever tell me what you are hiding inside of you?"

"Why does it matter what I think? Is it going to change your decision?"

"If I didn't care about your opinion, would I still be waiting?"

"So you have been waiting for my word?"

"Who said anything about waiting for you? You are stuck with me forever."

"Meaning?"

"Meaning if you don't approve, I want to be with you for the rest of my life."

"Fine. Give me four days. I will tell you what I think exactly four days from today onwards."

"I am afraid of only one thing."

"Tell me."

"You are so devoted to my Mota Bapuji that ..."

"That I will betray you and turn you over to him, right?"

Bhabhu's hand felt the answer provided by the full-body shudder and the fast beating heart of the young woman.

"If I was going to do that, I wouldn't have waited all these days. Nor would I have taken that thrown ..." The fresh memory of being hit with that slipper rose to her lips and returned as quickly to a corner of her heart. "Try to relax and catch some sleep now. There is no need

to worry about the situation back in Mumbai. Your Mota
Bapuji was going to take the afternoon train to Nasik.
No straight thinking man wants to wait around to pick
a fight with someone, my girl!"

24

THEIR train reached the Tejpur station at about eight in the morning. An employee from the local office picked them up, gave them lunch at his home and set them up with a bullock cart to ride to their house in Thorewaad. The man tried to explain : "It will be better to travel later in the day when it's cooler. The house is ready, and the servants and cook are already there." Bhabhu just said : "The sooner we get there the better" and took his leave.

Once on the way, Bhabhu asked the escort that accompanied the cart : "Is Rupaawati village on our way?"

At the mention of Rupaawati, Sushila sat up straight.

"No more than a mile out of our way," replied the escort.

"Do you know Deepchand Sheth there?"

"Who doesn't? The family may be in their leaner days now, but their good name is as good as it ever was!"

"His wife has been sick for a while. Do you know how is she doing?"

"Still the same. She sees a couple of good days and then slips back into a few bad days. Deepchand Sheth personally looks after her. Nobody but Deepa Sheth can care for a sick wife like that."

"Let's go that way then. We would like to stop in at Deepa Sheth's place."

"Sure thing, Ba! Just in time ... this here is the turnoff for Rupaawati."

The cart turned east. Sushila sat up and straightened her clothing around herself. The realization of her first visit to her in-laws' place had quietly dawned on her. And, although not watching her directly, Bhabhu had seen it all.

On the way to Rupaawati, Sushila's eyes gazed, for no apparent reason, at the outlying mass of land lining both sides of the cart path. Bhabhu's indirect vision followed everything Sushila looked at. Sushila's every gesture, every facial expression became an entry in Bhabhu's mental notebook.

Diwali was just around the corner. The bright afternoon sun beating down on the millet crop was a totally new sight for Sushila. Surely these delicate plants did not deserve to be the targets of such a fiery onslaught!

"Tell me, Bhabhu," she asked : "Do these poor plants not burn out in this heat?"

"No, they don't. Without this heat the grain will not be ready for the harvest."

The landscape spread on both sides of them showed inconsistently cultivated farms—some with sickly looking millet and some looking overly rich with cotton, sparsely filled ears of grain, an occasional uncultivated plot of land reminding one of a lazy beggar among hardworking poor people. The only humanity they saw was a rare caretaker or two.

Watching all this, Sushila asked a few questions but showed no sign of being bored nor did she utter even one condescending expression like 'oh my God' that one would expect from a Mumbai-bred girl. Bhabhu's secret notebook entries continued non-stop.

Sushila was still trying to digest their escort's words about 'Deepa Sheth ... nobody can care for sick like he does ...' when their cart crossed the river into the Rupaawati village borders. The sands of the riverbank seemed to want to consume the large cart-wheels.

"Here we are, *ben*, this here is Rupaawati." Before the words were out of the escort's mouth, Sushila stopped looking around and pulled her sari around her, covering herself even more carefully. The end of her sari modestly hid half of her forehead.

"Will you stay here in the cart, Sushila?" Bhabhu asked : "I want to make a quick stop and look in on your mother-in-..." and then catching herself in mid-sentence, continued with "I want to see how Sukhlal's mother is doing."

"Can I go with you?" There was just a slight hesitation in Sushila's words.

"How can I take you there?"

"I won't do a thing." The words, by themselves, were quite meaningless, but the intent behind them was to express the feeling that "I will be on my best behaviour".

"That is a house with a very serious illness. Won't you feel stifled?"

Sushila answered those words of doubt or sarcasm with a strange smile : "Really!"

With that 'really', the niece took all wind out of Bhabhu's sails and without waiting for any further words of reproach from her, Bhabhu directed the cart-driver to take them into the village.

Immediately upon entering the village limits, they were greeted by the snorting and kicking of a raging bull, flaunting its own freedom and showing its contempt for the servile bullocks pulling the cart. Other than that they found the market section of the town to be quiet and deserted. As their cart went by the muddy and dirty centre of the town, Sushila heard the senseless wisecracks exchanged between a couple of lazy watchmen and a few landowner Kaathhi young men.

Bhabhu observed that Sushila was neither disgusted with nor did she show any fear of that environment. Quite accustomed to the late night drunks and the trash-talking toughs that regularly walked by their Mumbai residence, Sushila found the idle chitchat of the village-folk no cause for any outburst like "How sad!"

The escort had gone ahead to get the word of their arrival to Deepchand Sheth—Sukhlal's father who came out to meet them. Sushila paid her respects and then deferentially looked away. He was bare-chested but his *paaghadi* covered his head. He rubbed his hands together as if trying to shake some white powdery substance off of them. The escort ran ahead to inform Bhabhu : "He was busy cooking when I got there."

"Oh boy, the poor soul!" Bhabhu now understood what the white substance was : "That was flour on his hands. Cooking this late?"

"Yes," the escort said : "The wife is bedridden and the older girl Sooraj is running a fever. Probably got delayed getting their medicine and running errands."

Sooraj! Sushila heard the name and the memories came back : that was the name of the sister-in-law that had written to her. Sushila had not acknowledged or replied to that letter. The same Sooraj who had asked for Sushila's old books and she had not sent any. That Sooraj ...

At that point, Deepchand Sheth arrived at the cart and greeted Bhabhu with folded hands : his tanned face glowed like a slightly dulled copper vessel.

"Ben! Gheliben! How wonderful to see you here!"

"Here I am, *kaka*!" Bhabhu reciprocated with fondness : "And not alone, either. I have brought your daughter with me."

"It feels so good to see you, my daughter! May you live for a hundred years!" He was well aware that he had no call any more on this girl who would have been his daughter-in-law. She was now probably betrothed to someone like Vijaychandra, and the words 'your daughter' were meant to convey that message.

Sushila's sari covered her face even lower than earlier but her gaze was riveted on the flour-smeared hands of Deepa Sheth. In all her years in Mumbai, she had never seen any man cook. She knew of men who left their sick or menstruating wives at their neighbours' mercy to stuff themselves with restaurant food*; at her own house, she did not recall either of the Sheth brothers showing the slightest inclination to cook. And here was this gentle person not embarrassed to greet his guests with flour-covered hands!

The cart stopped outside the gate of the house and the two women went inside. The oxen were unhitched from the cart and Deepa Sheth told the cart-driver to come in and get a bale of dry fodder for the animals. He, then, quickly laid a cot in the front porch, spread a blanket over it and invited the two guests to sit on it.

"Where is my *kaki*?" Bhabhu inquired.

"Why don't you rest for a couple of minutes? What is the hurry?"

"We can sit with her, *kaka*!"

"It's better that you sit here."

"But, why?"

"The sickness has gotten worse and the air in there is not fit ..."

"Oh come on, *kaka*!" Bhabhu got up and started for the inside with Sushila in tow.

"Please, Gheliben, give me a minute and I will take you to her. Please, I'll be right back!" Deepa Sheth ran to another room, put a glowing coal on an earthen roof tile and sprinkled some incense on it and took it to the sick room. He quickly broke the news to his wife : "Champak Sheth's wife is here; Sushila is also here. I didn't want to tell you this, but now I have to : in

---

* Orthodox Hindu tradition forbidding women in their periods from touching anyone or anything.

Mumbai, I signed an annulment of Sushila's betrothal with Sukhlal. Keep that in your mind when you talk to them."

After that caution for his wife, he went out and escorted the two women inside and spread a blanket on the floor for them. Then he strode to a room at the other end of the house. There, he instructed his daughter, lying in a feverish daze : "Sooraj, my dear! We have a guest and she will be here to see you shortly. Be a good girl and don't address her as '*bhabhi*', please! She may not like to be called that, OK!"

"OK. But, who is here? Bhabhi? Sushilabhabhi, Bapa?" Sooraj struggled to open her eyelids weighed down by her fever and asked.

"Oh boy! Chhuchhilabhabhi ijh hiyal!" A six year old boy, sitting by Sooraj's bed and applying cold compresses on her forehead, cried out. He turned to his two year old sister sitting next to him and started : "Did you hiyal that, Poti! Chhuchhi..."

"Oh please! Have you all gone crazy?" The father tried to control his children : "Listen, if you promise that you will not call her 'bhabhi', I will treat you to some *gol* and *rotli* later."

The children went quiet without understanding the reason for their father's rebuke. He left for the other side of the house. He took a load of hay from the shed and stacked it outside. When he was about to enter the kitchen, he saw someone sitting by the burning *chulo* and kneading the dough left half-done by him.

"Oh no, no!" was all he could say before he walked out of the kitchen. He ran into his wife's room extremely distressed and asked : "Is that Sushila at the stove? Who sent her there?"

"No ... no ..., would ... I ... do ... that ...? Don't... I ... know ... better ... than ... that ...!"

"I am telling you I just saw her kneading the dough for *rotli*!" Unable to stand the strain, Deepa Sheth went into the courtyard. He walked to the shed and stood stroking the neck of the calf tied there. The motherless calf raised its head and looked at Deepa Sheth as he scratched its head; whether the calf could see and feel the significance of the tears in the man's eyes is something we feel unqualified to comment on.

In the past several months, Deepa Sheth had many occasions to sit at that stove and cook. He had visions about the daughter-in-law that would one day be here to relieve him of cooking and other chores; but all that had ended with his last Mumbai visit. He used to tell his ailing wife while cooking in the kitchen : "We cannot possibly subject our daughter-in-law to the smoke from these primitive *chhaanas*! I am going to order a sack of coal and a charcoal stove from Tejpur. Sushila is not going to spend her life trying to get these rain-damped *chhaana* to burn."

His wife would suggest : "You should get bales of dry twigs; those will burn clean like oil."

"Don't be silly!" The husband would answer : "Those twigs burn up too quickly. Is the poor girl going to sit here and cook or keep feeding that stove with fresh twigs? And listen, we are going to have to get a window in this kitchen. Mumbai-raised people need air and sunlight. The delicate child would suffocate in this closed up kitchen of ours."

"I don't understand why you worry so much!" The wife would say : "Wouldn't the Lord give me my health back when Sushila arrives? If I am up and about, you think I am going to let the new bride even step into the kitchen? No way! I don't want the luxury of having someone cook for me. You and I know that we have too many relatives; and we live right here on the main drag. Having five guests arrive unannounced is nothing unusual for us;

we don't want to scare the young bride by having to cook
for all those people. I want her to sit and sew or knit or
whatever. But here I am, completely laid up and it burns
me up to think that I am going to have to stick the poor
young kid in the kitchen as soon as she arrives."

"Now you are being silly again and worrying without
reason!" The husband would slip into tall talk : "You are
laid up, I am not! I am not going to let her do much of
anything. She is going to hear from me if she tries! Our
Sooraj will help out a little and I will make everyone
believe it is the daughter-in-law that is cooking while I
take care of cooking for five, ten or even twenty-five
people in no time flat. Don't you lose any weight worrying
about your daughter-in-law! I am not exactly a cripple
myself, you know! Do you think you value having a
daughter-in-law and I don't? Haven't I seen Dungarshi's
family line end with his seven sons dying bachelors?
Right here among us are the Ghelani brothers who at
the ages of sixty and fifty have to repeatedly beg at the
Shukals' house to have a *rotlo* made for them; don't you
think I have noticed how, semi-blind and all, they walk
to scrounge some buttermilk from the neighbours?"

"And the sacks of money didn't do them any good," the
invalid wife would chime in : "Don't I know?"

"The bride that comes for money will leave with it.
That's why the two Ghelani brothers didn't spend their
money on getting married."

"Remember Dulo Bhabho? Obsessed with finding a
bride, he went around with a bundle of money; told
everybody he would marry any woman—scatterbrain,
lame, one-eyed, mute, middle-aged were no problem; he
got taken by scams and lost most of his bundle; finally
married a supposedly insane woman who turned sane
and absconded with the rest of his money."

"A daughter-in-law is the most precious gift from God;
my son was betrothed with good omens. I worry a lot

about how we will accommodate our daughter-in-law in this house.

Chatting like that with his wife in the sickroom across from the kitchen, Deepa Sheth would breeze through his cooking chores by the late morning and then would sit on the verandah outside his wife's room and brush his teeth and gums with tobacco. The calf's mother was alive then and would be out grazing at that time of the day. The little she-calf would jump around the stake where her mother was usually tied and call out for her; when her mooing got much too noisy, the man of the house would threaten the calf : "When my daughter-in-law is here, she will straighten you out!"

But all those were only memories now. After returning from Mumbai, his cook-time chats had not touched the subject of the daughter-in-law to be. If the topic of wedding with Sushila ever came up, he cut the discussion short with "Our son's business is going to keep him in Mumbai. She is an only child. Eventually she is going to be in our family anyway and five years will make no difference to us. Our daughter-in-law is still somebody's daughter! Sushila is no less to her parents than Sooraj is to us."

He had revealed no more to his wife. He had told Sooraj that Sushila had given a bundle of books for her but he had forgotten to bring them back.

And he had constantly steeled his own self : "Watch it, Deepchand, don't you rush into telling your dying wife about this and spoil her last moments. She has only a few days to live."

25

THE she-calf was the only witness to the torrent of warm tears gushing from the courageous gentleman's eyes. He was bewildered by what was happening around him. For what was this rich woman trying to punish him by bringing here the girl that was once engaged to his son! Who were these people that were trying to ransack his already plundered nest? What did he ever do, who did he ever wrong that these women must so witness his disgrace? This girl would have been his daughter-in-law by now. She would have cooked for him and gladly served him hot meals; instead, there she was, cooking in the kitchen, but under radically different circumstances. Her presence in the kitchen was a fact and yet a fantasy; a reality and yet a horrible delusion. Someone was playing a terrible trick on him! Fate had delivered such a slap to his face! Had the Lord kept his wife alive to witness this day? Why did he rush in and disillusion her? If he had not blurted out the news of the annulment, she would have died a happy woman. Instead, he had destroyed that one chance of happiness and spoilt her last moments.

Deepchand Sheth didn't even notice the calf sucking at his finger as if she was feeding at her mother's breast. He was engrossed in his thoughts like a hopelessly lost traveller when Bhabhu's voice brought him back :

"How about some food, *kaka*? Your lunch is waiting for you."

The old man stared at her. Ghelibai's laughter was like a dagger in his heart but he concealed his hurt and managed a smile. He answered with "Already! We put you to work as soon as you arrived, didn't we?"

"Sushila has been looking forward to cooking for you."

"The pleasure will be all mine. It will be no small treat to taste her cooking!"

The bare-chested Deepa Sheth sat down on the raised open porch outside the kitchen and rested his knee on a wooden knee-support. He caressed his forehead as if attempting to decipher the future written in its wrinkles and doing his best to conceal internal unrest. He was served a couple of small *rotla*.

Gheliben (Bhabhu) commented : "Isn't this something? This young generation has taken all the art out of making *rotla* by patting them out on a flat surface. Gone are the days when a rotlo was sculpted between two palms, carving intricate designs into its surface. What a shame!"

"Come on now, Gheliben! I see nothing wrong with these *rotla*. In fact, they look pretty good to me!"

"But of course you wouldn't see anything wrong with them! That, however, is not going to make your Sushila stay and cook for you everyday!"

"Even a strange dog doesn't forget you if you feed it once. How can I not feel good about it?"

After serving him once, Bhabhu continued to watch Deepa Sheth's plate as Sushila came out of the other kitchen door on the far side. She carried a plate and a bowl. Her sari didn't completely conceal her face but was left hanging modestly on the side of her face in deference to Deepa Sheth.

"She's over there," Bhabhu pointed to a room across the courtyard.

"Who is ... what is going on here?" Deepa Sheth asked.

"Sushila has made some porridge for Sooraj."

Unsure of what havoc the children would wreak in dealing with Sushila, the old man almost panicked.

Since her father's warning, Sooraj had tried to fight her feverish daze and to keep her drowsy eyes open.

'Sushila-*bhabhi* is here' had barely registered in her fever-dulled consciousness. The six-year old brother, helping bring her fever down by putting cold salt-water compresses on her forehead, was familiar with the name 'Chhuchhilabhabhi' as he pronounced it. Unable to contain his curiosity, he had visited the kitchen once pretending to get fresh water for his sister's compresses. After a quick glance, he had returned to his assigned chore. He had come back with the imprint of a sweet face that had filled his little eyes; his little heart and his coconut-sized head. "Chhuchhilabhabhi" that had once been only a name, now had become a person to him. He had tried to shake Sooraj out of her trance : "Wake up, hully! Chhi ijh going to be hiyal soon. I could shmell hul in the kitchen, Chhi even looked at me and shmiled. Only at me! Not at you, Poti, chhi ... chhi ... won't talk to you ..."

Listening to his ecstatic chatter, the two-year old sister Poti's face fell and she started crying, immediately causing him to back off : "OK, OK, chhi will ... I'll tell hul to talk to you, OK?"

With fifteen minutes of furious effort at the salt-water compresses, the little boy brought Sooraj's temperature and drowsiness down. She opened her eyes and looked around her. Her glance settled on the stickers of pretty women and goddesses—taken from the rolls of cloth in her father's shop—adorning her trunk next to her. She struggled to pull the cover over her and started her wait for the guest. In pain, she tried hard to keep a smile on her face for the benefit of the guest. She was puzzled by one thing : Why did her father advise her not to address Sushila as 'bhabhi'? Was it considered rude in Mumbai to call a brother's betrothed 'bhabhi'? Since she had practiced the 'Sushilabhabhi' address a million times over, what would happen if it slipped out of her? Would Sushilabhabhi walk out of here? What if she cannot

stand the smell of her perspiration? Would she touch
Sushila? If not 'bhabhi', what would she like to be called?

In spite of these thoughts clouding her mind, she had
readied herself with a great effort for this first meeting
when Sushila walked in with the porridge. One look at
her and Sooraj forgot everything she had worked on.
The hands that were going to touch Sushila's feet froze.
Words of greeting were all forgotten. All she could do
was stare at Sushila. Stared and smiled ... and then
tears welled up in her eyes.

"I got your letter," Sushila spoke as she sat and tried
to get the porridge to cool down. "Much as I tried, I
couldn't write as well as you did and shamed by that, I
couldn't bring myself to write at all."

Sooraj's intense stare on Sushila was more than
matched by the intensity with which Sushila's eyes were
watching Sooraj's face. The same exact eyes ... the same
patient expression ... as if shaped by the same mould.
She wondered which Mumbai footpath the other sibling
of that shape was walking on at that moment. She also
worried about him being in jail, put there by her uncle.

"The books you sent me ..." Sooraj finally got a partial
sentence out of her mouth. Even that had gone through
an untold layers of filters.

"I forgot to send them." Sushila suspected sarcasm in
Sooraj's utterance.

"No, no! Father told me that he was the one that
forgot to bring the bundle of books you gave him."

Sushila was moved by yet another example of her
father-in-law's nobility. She said : "I will get you more.
I am going to be around for a while."

"Here?"

"Not far from here. In Thorewaad."

"I've been there."

"Been there? How?"

Sooraj was embarrassed but finally said : "We were
out picking up cow-dung and ended up there."

"When was this?"

"A couple of months back. It got dark by the time we returned."

"Your parents ask you to go?" Sushila was thinking of a twelve-year old girl's vulnerability.

"What else can we do?" Sooraj hinted at the economic necessity of gathering cow-dung for fuel.

"Aren't you afraid?"

"Only if I am alone. Accompanied by even a child, I wouldn't be afraid of anyone. Nobody would dare lay a hand."

"Do you know girls your age?"

"No, there is no one here of my age."

"Then who goes with you?"

"My little brother here."

Sushila took a long look at the boy. As she looked, she could feel her compassion for him growing. The child was repeating to himself "Chhuchhila bha-bhi, Chhuchhila bha-bhi" and felt tremendously shy when he felt their gaze upon him. Sushila asked him : "You look pretty busy there, little brother. What are you up to?"

"Putting cold compleshis on my shishtel's folehead." His baby-talk sounded so sweet.

In the manner of cold water springs bursting forth in midsummer's burning heat, Sushila felt a surge of sympathy growing in her heart. The thought of what these young children were going through kept hammering at her conscience.

The six-year old boy's smiling but meek face was radiant with love. Without a conscious thought, Sushila's hand caressed the little boy's head.

When you scratch an animal on the head, it voluntarily moves closer to you. Children exhibit the same trusting behaviour. Like a little calf, the trusting child crept closer to Sushila but, afraid to dirty her clean and fragrant body, stopped short of snuggling up to her. He kept his head under Sushila's palm.

"Are these the beautiful pictures you wrote to me about?" Sushila was looking at the stickers on Sooraj's metal trunk.

Sooraj was too embarrassed to reply and looked down.

"You are disappointed, aren't you?"

"In what?"

"That I am not as pretty as you thought."

Sooraj looked down again and simply said : "You are."

With her head resting on her knees, Sooraj's eyes moved back and forth between Sushila's face and the pictures. If her moving eyelids could talk, their unending chatter would sound something like "You are as pretty; you are, you are, you are ..."

The weak Sooraj finally tired of sitting up. Her feverish face flushed redder and the eyelids became heavier. She asked Sushila if she could lie down.

"Let me help you."

"Will you be able to touch my feverish body?"

"What are you talking about!" With that, Sushila gently helped Sooraj lie back. Sooraj tried to rush through the process so as to minimize the clean, pleasant smelling sister-in-law's contact with her own feverish, perspiring, smelly body. This feeling was nothing new for Sooraj; even when putting on clean clothes, she felt she was degrading something.

Sushila's attention now turned to the two-year old girl that the boy had addressed as 'Poti'. Mucus from Poti's running nose had attracted so many flies that her face was beginning to look like a beehive. Poti just quietly endured the buzzing flies that seemed intent on digging up her face.

On first look, Sushila was disgusted with this sight. She asked the brother : "Doesn't anyone wipe your sister's face?"

"*Bapa* does."

"Does anyone bathe her?"

"Yes, everyday. Bapa was busy helping Ba bathe today and didn't get to Poti."

The boy got a rag and started wiping his sister's face; Sushila was ashamed of herself. She thought of the hospital in Mumbai. She recalled nurse Leena sponging off Sukhlal's dirty body and shuddered at the memory of the nurse cleaning the neighbouring old invalid's disgusting body. She even remembered seeing some college-girls playing the stage-roles of caring for the sick. She quickly got up and cleaned Poti's face. Poti's unchanged facial expression gave no hint as to whether she considered this good or bad. She stopped smiling perhaps because of the disruption this act had caused in the play of the flies.

"Did you see Ba today, Ben?"

"Ba wantchh Poti to shtay away flom hul." The little boy interjected.

Sushila looked at Sooraj for an explanation.

Sooraj had to struggle hard to even open her eyes. Her brother's words had vaguely reached her consciousness through the fog of her stupor. Trying to prevent any wrong impression in Sushila's mind about her mother, she explained : "Ba has been sick for two years. She stopped nursing Poti when Poti was six months old. She doesn't even let us near her bed. Says children catch infections easily." The drained Sooraj's droopy eyes closed with that.

The silence was shattered by a cry of anguish from the room across the courtyard. Before the startled Sushila could get up, Bhabhu was already with her. Her usuall serene face looked extremely disturbed.

"What are you doing, Sushila?"

"I was getting to know the children."

Encouraged by her answer, Bhabhu decided to take the next step. She said : "Your mother-in-law's condition has suddenly turned serious."

"What happened?"

"She just found out about the annulment. She is not going to survive the shock. Oh God, what are we going to do!"

Sushila's face turned red. "Who told her that?"

"Your father-in-law did."

"She heard wrong! I want to talk to her."

"Would you? God bless you!"

Sushila hurried after Bhabhu and entered her dying mother-in-law's room.

The sight she saw was something unimaginable and unheard of.

The supposedly unsophisticated husband is kneeling on the floor in front of his wife's bed. His hands are folded in a gesture of veneration. Bare-chested, he looks like an ascetic. There is a smile on his face and his sweet words are urging his wife : "Peace, depart in peace."

His wife's hands are folded, too. Her breath is racing like that of a galloping horse. Her words are few and barely understandable :

"I... will... go... in... peace... but... once... just... once... let... me... see... Sushila... please... just... once..."

"Why have even that much attachment?" The smiling husband continues. "Immortal soul! Free yourself! Sever all ties! Don't cling to anything, don't stop for anyone, o itinerant soul!"

"Once... please... just... once... and... I... will... go..."

"Here, here is your Sushila." Bhabhu pushed Sushila into the room.

"Oh God, please, no!" The gentle father-in-law protested. "This is no place for that delicate child right now!"

"Please don't worry, *kaka*! Sushila, pay your respects and bid her farewell. Here, give her this spoon of water in her mouth; and tell her what you wanted to tell her."

Sushila offered the spoonful of water to the rapidly sinking mother-in-law. The dying woman folded her hands in a thankful gesture and stared at Sushila : "*My... daughter...in... law...! The... mother... to... my... children ...*"

"You must not call her that," her husband scolded her for that forbidden utterance.

"*I am... sorry... Won't... happen... again... Your... per..mi..ssion... to... leave... now...*"

Her words penetrated Sushila's heart to its core. A few minutes ago she had been with three mother-deprived children. Just before that she had seen her father-in-law's flour-smeared hands. And now she had heard the heart-rending cry of 'my daughter-in-law'. The womanless home called out to her ... she heard Mother Earth bellowing like a cow for attention.

She gathered her courage, put the spoon between her mother-in-law's lips and said : "What you have heard is a lie! Nobody will dare take me away from here! This is my home." Overwelmed with emotion, she could say no more.

"That's my girl!" Bhabhu lowered her head. Her eyes were brimming with tears.

The husband and wife had their eyes closed. The man appeared to be in deep contemplation. A little teardrop sparkled in each of the woman's eye-wells.

Sushila broke down and started crying, too.

A serene, deep, slow chant emerged from the father-in-law's throat : "*Namo Arihan...tanam, Namo Siddhanam...*"

A mere semi-literate villager, he sang with an uncommon depth of clarity and belief. Their remote village was not important enough to be a stop on the Jain Godmen's itineraries, causing his religious beliefs to be self-developed and to remain more refined. He believed that each moment before death was precious and, losing all sense of his surroundings, immersed his whole being in reciting the holy words.

The only break in this detachment from the world was one lone haunting voice : "This is my home." To him, the voice seemed to call across the ages, from the other side of the river of time!

The chanting done, his voice resumed its earthly tone. He opened his eyes and looked at his wife. Her life-beat was still strong, the light in her eyes still bright. Sushila stood on one side with folded hands. Bhabhu was on the other side, whispering a prayer with her hand covering her mouth.

Deepa Sheth addressed his wife : "Our life's companionship of twenty-five years ends today. You have never raised your voice at me. You protected my honour all these years. All I pray for is that in my next life I be born from your womb..."

Sushila listened with amazement. This husband of today seeks to be the child of this woman in the next life; how much must he love her? Their attachment must go across life-spans!

The husband broke his pause : "Do not be concerned about the children. They will be your keepsakes under our care. Wherever you are, be assured that I will never cause them any pain."

He continued : "I can't afford to give much to charity in your name, but I promise to do this in your memory : I will care for the sick and the lonely in our town who have nobody else to care for them. May the Lord grant you eternal peace."

The dying body made three convulsive movements. The old man said : "Sushila, child, please leave now."

Bhabhu escorted the hysterically sobbing Sushila out of the room and instructed her : "Wipe your tears and pull yourself together. You have three little children to care for now."

26

IT was one of the smaller post offices in Mumbai that accepted registered mail. Sukhlal was the only one standing in line with an envelope in hand and with his back towards the door. And it had become a back to look at, getting broader by the day, causing the once loose-hanging shirt to lose most of its folds.

He waited patiently for quite some time but the post office clerk took no notice of his presence.

Sukhlal finally tried to draw his attention by tapping his envelope on the wooden ledge of the window. The clerk looked up with annoyance in his eyes and indicated his full awareness of Sukhlal's presence : "If you are in a rush, Mister, why don't you come back later?"

"I am in a rush because I can't afford to come back," Sukhlal snapped back.

"Really! Come back tomorrow, then."

"Why would I do that?"

"Because we have other things to do besides taking care of your business."

It was just before Diwali and the utensils were selling like hot cakes. With great difficulty, Sukhlal had found the time to go to the post office to send fifty rupees to his father and the clerk's behaviour dampened his enthusiasm no end. It had been a matter of great shame to Sukhlal that in the six months since leaving home, he had not been able to send home even a rupee. The clerk could not possibly have known Sukhlal's ardent desire to wipe out some of that embarrassment with this remittance.

It had become an obsession with him to get the fifty rupees to his mother's sick-bed. He wanted to convince his mother before she closed her eyes for good that he could earn his keep, that he was in fact earning his keep, and that he would earn enough to support his aging father and his younger siblings with ease. Having depended on his father for food and clothing for twenty-two years of his life, the young man could not rest easy until he could make it on his own. It was as if the envelope with his first remittance, symbolic of his manly courage, determination and vigour, was yearning to reach his dying mother. Standing there at the post office window, Sukhlal had a glorious vision of the delivery of his envelope four days later by the mailman from the Tejpur post office, amid raves from the populace of Roopawati.

The clerk had no idea what a blow he was delivering on the young man's face raised high with such ardent hopes. Hurt badly, Sukhlal was unable to hold back and said : "Do you understand civility, Mister?"

"Shut up," the clerk closed his register with a bang and snapped. But Sukhlal had learnt at the feet of Khushaal, the master psychologist and used one of his tricks. He raised his voice and started a tirade : "Do we have a senior manager present? Why is my registered mail being denied? Do you people think we have nothing to do but wait here? Do the working people come to Mumbai to waste their time? You think of us as ignorant villagers and treat us like dirt... "

His ranting quickly gathered a crowd. The Post Master arrived, quieted Sukhlal and instructed the clerk to take care of his business. As the clerk grumbled and finally started on the registration procedure, a man stood behind Sukhlal and quietly witnessed the entire incident. He had seen the envelope in Sukhlal's hand and had his eyes especially drawn to the notation underlined in red :

'Insured for Rs. 50'. The familiar name and address of a resident of Rupaawati on the envelope had pleased the man. He decided to wait there especially after he read and recognized the neatly written sender's name.

The boiling water in a pan continues to simmer even after the heat is turned off. The same rule applies to human minds—certainly to the minds of post office clerks. The fuming clerk kept firing instructions like "That will be eight annas", "Here's your stamp", "Paste this on the envelope" and Sukhlal answered, emphasizing every word, with : "Yes, sir", "Here's the money", "With pleasure, sir", "may I use your pen?", etc. The respectful tone was music to the ears of the low-ranking clerk and helped cool him off considerably. Processing the registration, he complained about how overworked he was. Sukhlal responded with his own carefully measured and soft words : "My problem is I have a sick mother; my father cannot meet the expenses; I have been stuck here for six months; have three younger siblings at home; if the money reaches home quickly, it will make my mother happy, and who knows, she may even survive..."

His voice faltered and he could not continue past that. The clerk was embarrassed at the thought of the anguish his behaviour had caused. He tried to lighten the atmosphere with : "And to top all that you must be married, with children perhaps?"

"Oh no! I have escaped that calamity, but just barely."

"What, no noose around the neck yet?"

"It was almost there, but I slipped through."

"I wish you good luck!" said the clerk as he handed Sukhlal his receipt. Sukhlal pocketed the receipt and said : "I was upset and lost my temper. Please forgive me."

"Happens," the clerk waved the apology off and continued : "I have a widowed mother back in my village. Just got a letter from my married but unhappy sister and I was upset myself."

It was Sukhlal's turn at being embarrassed about taking his frustration out on a fellow sufferer. Without saying another word, he turned around to leave and came face-to-face with the man who had stood quietly all that time. The man hesitated and then stammered as he addressed Sukhlal : "How are you now, healthy and all?"

"I am all right."

It was Nana Sheth, Sushila's biological father. His face resembled Sushila's so much that one expected Sushila to step out of him any moment.

Much as he wanted to, Sukhlal could not get angry with the man who had Sushila's face and all he could manage was the "I am all right" reply. Even more than that, he felt uneasy about how long Nana Sheth had been standing behind him. Sukhlal also knew Nana Sheth could not possibly have enjoyed the scene and his utterances.

"Would you join me in a cup of tea?" Nana Sheth looked at Sukhlal softly as he spoke.

The eyes that looked at Sukhlal were Sushila's father's. Sukhlal's gaze fixed at those eyes for the first time ever. What he perceived in those eyes were hands reaching out in supplication.

"I will be happy to," said Sukhlal as they started walking. On the way, Nana Sheth delivered a monologue on the subject of his appetite : "Lately I feel ravenously hungry. I have stopped riding in the car—I have been walking to work and back home everyday. I eat before I leave for work but by this time of the late morning, I find my stomach growling with hunger. I don't like to order food brought in and to eat alone in my office. So I slip out of the office and go to a restaurant. How is your appetite? Nothing like the appetite one feels back in the village, is there? What can I say about being there? The big difference is, there is no such thing as winter here in Mumbai. Have you ever seen any steam coming out of anyone's mouth here? Never. Mumbai's heat can cook the bones of even the elephants."

Holding forth like that, Nana Sheth displayed the childlike simplicity of his nature as they walked to a small restaurant in an alley. Mounting the steps of that restaurant, Nana Sheth suddenly stopped and supported himself on Sukhlal's shoulder. He didn't move for a few seconds. Sukhlal noticed that his eyes were closed. Finally he opened his eyes and told Sukhlal with a smile : "It's OK now. I have been experiencing these lately."

"Experiencing what?" Sukhlal felt the first signs of compassion for the man.

"Nothing much; slight attacks of dizziness. Never happened before but started two or three days ago. I have been feeling very lonely lately."

The thought raced through Sukhlal's mind : Sushila had been gone for two or three days.

27

"NO matter how good the home-cooking, nothing satisfies your hunger like a restaurant meal, don't you think?" Nana Sheth was obviously relishing his snack.

"I really can't say. I don't eat out much." There was no warmth in Sukhlal's words. He found this man's stupidity growing by the minute; but, for some reason, one look at his face was sufficient to forgive him for that. Sukhlal could not take his eyes off that face as he ate. He compared that face with Sushila's and found a hundred faults in the way Sushila looked; internally, he ground his teeth and asked if anybody would think of Sushila as being beautiful; certainly not him, no way!

"You wouldn't believe this but when you were hospitalized, I wanted to come and visit, I swear!" Nana Sheth's expression belied his childlike stupidity more than any deceit.

Sukhlal didn't pursue that line of inquiry; his mind was occupied with other things—he was too busy trying to scratch and unearth Sushila's face buried under this man's. He didn't ask but Nana Sheth told him any way :

"You will ask 'then why didn't I'? I will tell you why. I didn't go because I was helpless. *Motabhai* has very strong views about some matters. Even at my age, if I want to go to a movie or a play or a restaurant, he stops me with : 'Nana, movies are not good for your eyes... restaurant food is not good for you... this is not good for you... that is not good...'."

Lord, how stupid can you be? Visiting me in the hospital and going to the movies seemed at the same level of importance to this man! How did I get stuck with him today? Is he a thirty-eight year old father of a girl of twenty or is he a toddler taking his first steps holding the hand of his older brother? Sukhlal was disgusted one moment... and then couldn't help but feel sorry for the man.

Having disposed off the snack, Nana Sheth made the two-fingered sign on his lips and asked Sukhlal if he would mind.

"I don't smoke." Sukhlal read his intention.

"I don't much, either. Only since I started getting those dizzy spells, I have been coming here and smoking one cigarette, never more than one a day. Motabhai hates the thing. He caught me once when I was very young and beat me up real bad. Helps me take my mind off some things that have been bothering me—are you sure you don't mind?"

"I don't mind."

"Good—well, thank you." Smiling a childish smile, he got the waiter to bring him a cigarette and lit it. Sukhlal excused himself to go to the washroom, returned and sat down. The two got up to leave a few minutes later. Nana Sheth reached for his pocket as they approached the cashier; Sukhlal said : "Let's go."

"As soon as I pay the check."

"It's all taken care of."

The *Irani* sitting at the counter was laughing as Nana Sheth looked up. Open wallet and a five rupee note in his hands, he froze and didn't say anything for a few seconds. Feeling very inadequate, he very slowly descended the restaurant steps and just managed to say : "That was not right, you cheated me. Sushila always tells me : 'Father, you are so gullible, it would be a snap for anyone to take advantage of you!' You proved her right!"

Only after the words came out of his mouth did he realize that he had mentioned Sushila's name to the wrong person. There would be hell to pay if his brother ever found out! When they parted, Nana Sheth asked Sukhlal where he lived, etc. He also mentioned : "This is the only restaurant I go to, and always at this time. I don't like to change my routine. If possible, I sit in the same booth at the back where we sat today."

When Sukhlal did not respond, he added : "I would like very much if you would join me here once in a while. I avoid other people's company. I get a headache when someone talks a lot. You and I are quiet people and the two of us can sit and have a few moments of peace and relief. There is no need for anyone else to know. I guess I don't need to tell you about my brother's temper!"

Sukhlal heard the 'you and I are quiet people' and with much difficulty kept himself from laughing. He had understood the real reason behind the invitation— the idiot needed a patient ear to listen to his senseless chatter. It was pointless to expect any refined sensitivity from this crude person. Why would he have any soft feelings for Sukhlal? He was just hungry for some companionship.

"I will try," Sukhlal told him and started walking.

"Listen," Nana Sheth stopped him and approached him again, his eyes darting in all directions. He asked : "If you need any capital for your business, would you let me know?"

"I will." Sukhlal walked away disgusted.

But his contempt for the man was accompanied by a good deal of pity. Having been at the receiving end of much pity in his own life, Sukhlal had never experienced the feeling of "poor fellow" for someone else. He found those words coming to his lips for his 'would-have-been' father-in-law.

And then, another very annoying chain of thought came to him : 'Was Sushila ever going to learn about my entertaining her father? How did she behave with my father when he visited here? Didn't my father leave their house scorned and broken-hearted? Did Sushila participate in that demeaning treatment? Even if she didn't, I had a perfect opportunity to get even with that family. I should not have wasted it. I should have put him down; I should have used such choice words that Nana Sheth would have gone back and cried to his brother about. The big brother that promised to turn the papers over the following night—and then packed his family off to the village and then left town himself—ran with his tail between his legs and had not returned. I not only squandered the chance to hit him back but was stupid enough to pay the restaurant tab!

'Who was the real idiot—Sushila's father or I?

'No matter. There is still tomorrow. The man said he ate at that same restaurant everyday. I can even bring Khushaalbhai with me. His presence would get a rise out of me.

'What I cannot understand is how this childish and cowardly man's daughter could turn out to be so fearless! She certainly did not appear to be stupid. On the contrary! Didn't she tell me that night, 'we'll talk more tomorrow'? What happened overnight that, come morning, she had to run and hide in her Bhabhu's lap? Deep, real deep, is this girl! Does she really have feelings for me or is it all just a show? Even if real, one mention of the inheritance from Mota Sheth would be enough to freeze out her heart's feelings. I would feel avenged when that schemer Vijaychandra finally got what he wants. Then let her sit and enjoy the mountains of wealth from her Mota Bapuji!'

And thus, in his state of abstract musing, Sukhlal places Sushila on the heap of her inherited riches and

then adds Vijaychandra right next to her. But then what?
He cannot bear to think of what would have to transpire
between the two to punish Sushila adequately. Thinking
realistically, he is disappointed because Sushila's father
may be an idiot but her Mota Bapuji is not. He will not
be as naïve as to turn all his belongings over to
Vijaychandra and then roll over and play dead! In the
worst scenario, she may not get along with Vijaychandra;
in that case, she would just return to her father's place
and live in the lap of luxury for the rest of her life. What
good would that do for Sukhlal?

And Sukhlal's thoughts finally returned to the reality
of his existence. 'It's better I forget all this talk of revenge
and jump back into the business of selling utensils. I
can call myself a real man only if I send another
registered envelope next month with Rs. 50 in it. I can
take on the world if my mother gets a psychological
boost from this and pulls through her illness. If she dies
yearning for a daughter-in-law, whether Sushila suffers
or not would make no difference.'

28

MOTA Sheth, who had disappeared the day Bhabhu and Sushila left for Tejpur, had neither returned nor had sent any word on when that might be. Nana Sheth returned to the office and appeared totally relaxed in his brother's absence. Gone was the loneliness that had ruled his heart until an hour ago. The contented heart seemed to be addressing the stomach below it : 'See, Ms. Tummy, until yesterday, you returned from the restaurant stuffed and ready to burst and teased me because I came back as empty as ever! But look at me today—I am as happy and overflowing with joy as I can be. And, you know what, Ms. Tummy? From now on, I am going to be as full as this every day. If Sukhlal shows up at the restaurant everyday, I will have no reason to bury this poor Nana Sheth under the mountain of my loneliness. The poor fellow has been terrorized by his older brother all his life—so much so that he has not been able to talk freely with his own daughter! For the first time in his life, he enjoys talking to someone. And you know how silly a child sounds when it first starts talking! Well, then, this man never really had a chance to grow out of his childhood. Is it any wonder that he longs for a son? Or a son-in-law? His own daughter has been kept out of his reach, is he going to be deprived of a son-in-law that he can call his own? Can the world be that selfish and cruel, Ms. Tummy? Is it right for people to get happy by robbing others of their loved ones?'

Nana Sheth's heart chattered away as he leaned back and relaxed in his comfortable chair. The monologue came to an end as the phone rang : "Nanu Sheth? Khushaalchand here. I have some bad news for you. Sukhlal's mother just passed away. The mourners are gathering at my place."

"I-I-I-I... may I join you?"

"Certainly, if you wish."

Unable to say any more, Nana Sheth felt he had committed a grave blunder and he hung up. But the phone rang again and Khushaal's voice said : "Nanu Sheth, we are going to wait for you. Nothing will start until you arrive."

The phone disconnected before Nana Sheth could say a word. Now there was no way he could back out of going. He left the office without telling anyone where he was going. The man he asked to show him the way to Khushaal's place was instructed : "Nobody needs to know about this."

The unwritten rule of behaviour among the middle-class required that, even if one is not invited to weddings and other celebrations, one must show up on the occasions of illness or death in the families one knew well. Living under the dark clouds of his family's sudden affluence, the lightening bolt of this occasion served to reacquaint Sushila's father with this estranged social group that he had once belonged to. His starched white attire stood out among that gathering like a sore thumb. But if the group thought he was not one of them, they did not show it. It was he that felt ashamed of the gold chain around his neck and the gold watchband. He also realised that he didn't know how to behave on solemn occasions like this. He had the wrong expression on his face and laughed when he was supposed to express sadness.

Khushaal gave him further details : "She had been bedridden for a long time but this was kind of unexpected.

Her health was too delicate to survive the overdose of happiness and her heart gave out under that strain."

"Overdose of happiness?" Nana Sheth found that strange.

"It was only natural. Sushila's visit there was totally unexpected."

That hit Nana Sheth like a thunderbolt. Completely unaware that Nana Sheth may not have known about the visit, Khushaal carried on : "How long must she have pined for this—the wedding, the bride's arrival into their home! And then Sushila showing up like that and filling up that house with her charm and love! The joy was more than my aunt's fragile heart could take."

Khushaal had no way of knowing what had really caused the death. In his letter, Deepa Sheth had given no hint of what had transpired.

Nana Sheth's thoughts and imagination slowly turned towards the world of his childhood and he saw his own village of Tejpur and its neighbouring Rupaawati where Deepa Sheth still lived. He wondered how and why Sushila must have gone there. His elder brother claimed that Sushila hated the idea of marrying into that family and that was why he, Mota Sheth, was trying to make other arrangements!

"And listen to the words of praise for Gheliben in my uncle's letter." Khushaal started reading the whole letter aloud; his voice invariably paused at every mention of Gheliben (Bhabhu) in the missive. The gathered men started whispering to one another : "Who is this Gheli?" "Champak Sheth's wife." "Our Gheli from the village of Sudavad—don't you remember?" "One in a million." "The family riches never went to her head." "Can you believe she went all the way to Rupaawati to care for the daughter's mother-in-law?"

"And what can you say about the girl!" "All Gheli's training, I tell you." "How wonderful she must have felt in her last moments! In this day and age when nobody cares for anyone outside of the family!" "Departed with the feel of her unwed daughter-in-law's hand on her— one cannot ask for more from life!"

"My aunt died a happy woman. And Sukhlal here is standing on his own two feet. I certainly cannot ask for more!" Khushaal's words drew everyone's eyes towards the side of the room where Sukhlal was. He sat there quietly with the full gravity of his manhood. His eyes dripped like a cloud giving off its last drops after spending itself in a torrential rain. He did not sob, nor did his throat make any sound—he seemed to be drinking the nectar of his grief.

"I saw him sending registered mail at the post office just an hour ago." Unable to keep a solemn face, Nana Sheth was smiling as he talked : "How much did he want his mother to live through her illness! Such is life..."

"That's it, everybody! No more mourning. And my *Fua* has asked that nobody, not even the women, engage in any weeping and wailing. So please, bathe* yourself under the tap outside and let's be as quiet as we can."

As people took their turns at the community water-faucet, the others engaged Sukhlal in empathetic talk, trying to cordon off the past and to help him adjust to the new reality in his life. The entire group of well-wishers was there to partake in his feast of sorrow.

Nana Sheth tried to follow the men to the community water faucet outside but Khushaal stopped him : "You are not accustomed to bathing in the open. I have hot water for you inside."

A bucket of hot water awaited Nana Sheth in the bathroom. Khushaal provided the same arrangement for a few other frail and elderly people.

---

* The Hindu custom of cleansing off the 'touch' of death.

29

THE news of what had transpired at Khushaal's did not immediately get to the lone wife at the Sandhurst Road residence of the Sheth brothers. Nana Sheth spent a restless night with his nerve on the edge but he was temporarily spared the merciless badgering he had expected.

Intolerant of her spineless husband, Sushila's mother's unwavering attention and loyalty were centered on Mota Sheth, the macho brother-in-law who had placed Sushila atop their family inheritance. Ever since Mota Sheth had left town, the woman had lost interest in cooking. After posing difficult questions like 'Should I cook this ... or that?', she would decide on something plain and quick, like *rotli* and a vegetable, or *dhokla,* without waiting for any feedback from her husband. Able to say nothing more than 'Whatever you feel like or don't feel like making is okay with me.', Nana Sheth would quietly eat whatever he was served before leaving for work at ten in the morning. It was little wonder that, by early afternoon, he was ready for a restaurant meal.

That day, he had just finished his *dhokla* and oil and was chewing on *variyali* when his brother entered the house, back from out of town. The food in his stomach was replaced by a deep sense of fear.

As soon as Mota Sheth went to his room, Sushila's mother erupted into a frenzy of activity in the kitchen : three stoves were lit in preparation for a full meal of *rotli*, two vegetables, daal and rice.

"See what happens!" She was talking to the man-servant : "I got caught unprepared only because your Nana Sheth has no sense of food!"

In a few minutes, Nana Sheth was summoned into Mota Sheth's bedroom.

"Did you go to that beggar's mother's funeral meeting?" Mota Sheth's first question was intended to shock and impress his brother with how much he, Mota Sheth, knew. On his way from the railway station, Mota Sheth had stopped in at the office and had received a complete briefing from Praniya.

"Er ... yes. I thought ..." Nana Sheth tried to cut the matter short and kept chewing on *variyali.*

"Who asked you to go?"

"Er ... one has to do little things like ..."

"No, you will not. Do you want to live in this house or not?"

"What is the big deal?" Nana Sheth's face fell; the mere thought of being thrown out of the house shook him to his core.

"Are you trying to destroy me? Whose side are you on?" Champak Sheth's temperature and his voice continued to rise.

"But, what have I done that's so bad?"

"You have no idea what harm you have done! We have nullified and walked away from any relationship with that boy and his whole family. What you have done can help prove the existence of that dead relationship in a court of law."

"What court of law? I don't understand what you are talking about, *Motabhai* !"

"When did you ever understand anything besides filling your stomach and sleeping? That Sukhlal is going to drag us into the court."

"Impossible. He is not that kind of a person."

"You also know that we are trying to find another suitable match for Sushila. Have you given any thought to how all this would effect that?"

"I don't see why this would have any effect on it. Besides, why are we looking at anyone else? What is wrong with Sukhlal? He has started earning his own keep and more!"

"So! The goons have my own brother in the bag too ... " Mota Sheth gritted his teeth like grinding on sand.

"Even my *Bhabhi* and Sushila visited them in the village is what I heard. If Bhabhi approves, what else do we have to worry about?"

"I see. So the matters have gone that far!" And with that, Mota Sheth went to take his bath. When he returned, all he said was : "I want you to take the first train to our village—and I want to see you bring your Bhabhi and daughter back here the very next day! And I am warning you! Make the slightest change and ... do I need to spell it out for you?"

Nana Sheth habitually stayed away from his big brother and avoided talking to him as much as he possibly could. But even then, this was the worst humiliation he had experienced. He hadn't heard any thing close to 'do you want to stay in this house or not?' and '... the slightest change ...' ever and those words caused the throbbing pain one expects from a wound that is getting cold. Nana Sheth went to his room and started changing out of his working attire.

That was when Praniyo a.k.a. Pranajivan, the office gopher, made his appearance. With a "Here's your *ghee*, *kaki*, I had to go all the way to *Parla* to find it." He entered the kitchen and described the ordeal he had to go through that morning to Sushila's mother. That done, he asked her softly : "*Kaki*, I hope there hasn't been any thunder and lightening inside your house since Mota Sheth's return!"

"What thunder and lightening are you talking about?"

"Surely you jest! You know everything but pretend like you dont!"

"I swear I don't know what you are talking about!"

"Your beloved relative passed away, Nana Sheth went to the funeral meeting and you don't even know about it?"

"No. Which relative would that be?"

"He really didn't tell you?"

"Honest, I don't know."

"Attaboy, Nana Sheth! Finally he is paying you back! There is hope for him yet! You bullied him long enough; now it's his turn."

"Are you going to talk straight or not, you bum? What happened? Who died? Whose funeral was it?"

"Your daughter's mother-in-law passed away in Rupaawati."

"Must be someone else's mother-in-law; nothing to do with us."

"Is that why Nana Sheth went to mourn?"

"He did? He will pay for that."

"And what about the others who went all the way to Rupaawati and saved the occasion?"

"Who did?"

"Mota Shethani and Sushilaben."

"Don't joke with me, Praniya! I am warning you."

"I am not joking."

"You got a telegram about this, did you?"

"Not only me, and not a short telegram either."

"What are you saying?"

"A detailed four-page letter raving about how your daughter brightened the last moments of life for her mother-in-law and let her die happy were read to a hundred mourners. And do you know who got the credit for Sushilaben's wonderful upbringing? Not the one that carried her in her womb for nine months but the one who brought her up!"

"What are you blabbering about, you idiot? You are putting me on!"

"I am not! I am telling you exactly what happened. Your older sister-in-law got all the credit. She was the one that uttered the holy words at the moment of death; she took the three orphaned children to Thorewaad with her. If you find one thing wrong with what I just told you, punish me as you would."

For a moment these words from Praniya froze Sushila's mother like a figure in a painting. From earlier parts of this narration, the reader probably remembers Praniya as the odd-jobber who constantly strove to be the centre of attention with his hard work and running around.

It is well known that such Praniyas hold an irreplaceable position in every rich famiy's structure. These Pranjivans get along just fine with the women of these rich households because the things these women don't dare ask their husbands for, the Praniyas will get for them in a snap. The Praniyas remind the rich men about the household needs that are forgotten as soon as they reach their places of business. The men don't have the time to take the frequent phoned-in demands from home; the Praniyas attend to them. The Praniyas use their contacts to get the women tickets to plays and movies. Word on the latest fashions will not reach the women but for these Praniyas. The Praniyas are called upon to stay up nights at times of illness in the family. The Praniyas bring home all the gossip about what the men talk about away from home, their comings and goings, the highs and lows of business, etc. The Praniyas are knowledgeable about all the wordly matters ranging from what mangoes to buy in the summer to Kashmiri hand-woven woolen blankets. These Praniyas have free access to the kitchens, the freedom to joke and even to scold because they are able to do so while appearing to be polite and obedient. The Praniyas get their way because the otherwise subservient women of the rich can satisfy their desire to use affectionate addresses like 'bum', 'stiff', and such only with these Praniyas.

Having finished with his gossip for the day, Praniyo asked : "What bracelets did you want rewired? And the bangles that were to be redone?"

"Come back in the evening", Sushila's mother rushed him out and with a few minutes to go before her brother-in-law's lunch, went to her own room. Her husband had not finished dressing yet. With the pretext of helping him button his long coat, she stood there and spoke in her cold and authoritative tone :

"So you had to keep it hidden from me as if I was going to bite you! How long was it going to stay secret anyway? Was it my funeral you thought you were going to? And what right did *bhabhi* have to involve *my* daughter in a farce like that?"

"Now listen. You can tell me whatever you want but please don't say a word about *bhabhi*!" The husband's eyes glistened with tears as he spoke.

"You feel for your precious *bhabhi*—not for your wife! What kind of a husband are you? You are not even fit to shine your brother's shoes and are trying to order me around?"

"You want me to shine my brother's shoes? And what big damage has *bhabhi* done to invite your ire?"

"She has spoilt my daughter rotten. Is that not enough?"

"Has the girl done anything to disgrace you?"

"Why did Bhabhi take my daughter back into the relationship that Motabhai had gotten us out of?"

"She must have gone to their house because it was on the way to Thorewaad. And Sushila is as much Bhabhu's daughter as she is yours."

"Motabhai is the only one that has any right to do anything for Sushila, no one else. And what has Bhabhi ever done besides poisoning my daughter's mind against me, which I can understand, but also against her own husband? Besides pouring molten lead into Sushila's ears about that angel of a husband? Does plotting and acting behind the back of her husband she should kiss the feet of seem like the behaviour of a respectable woman?"

She went on and on. Brushing the dust of his cap, giving him a clean handkerchief, telling him to 'wear the other shoes, not these', she held him as long as she could and sang the praise of her older brother-in-law while missing no opportunity to slam her older sister-in-law. Her loudness made it clear that the brother-in-law was to hear her words as well.

"Lord! Oh Lord!" She whispered the final blow as her husband slowly left the room : "Does he think he is married to me ... or ... to her!"

Nana Sheth clearly heard the words spoken in the room behind him. He stopped dead in his tracks. He felt dizziness enveloping him and grabbed the door to support himself. The attack lasted a whole minute and then he regained control of himself. He walked to the elevator as if he was about to commit suicide, entered it and descended to the ground floor.

The car was waiting for him. The chauffeur opened the door for Nana Sheth.

"Thanks, but I am walking today." He told the chauffeur in Hindi, quickly walked to the corner and away from the street of his home.

30

LATER, after a lunch of hot *rotlis* served by his younger brother's wife—her head respectfully veiled—Mota Sheth belched and talked as he picked his teeth with a match-stick : "Isn't it a shame that even you had to scold the fool! What stupidity! How strong one should feel with a grown-up brother at one's side! But, can I trust this brother to do anything right?"

He stepped into the living room as he spoke, and was startled to hear someone address him with "Greetings!" He looked up to see Vijaychandra—respectable, handsome, clean cut, full of vigour and with not a hair out of place—standing there.

"Greetings." He reluctantly responded. "How long have you been here?"

"Quite a while. You must have worked up quite an appetite."

"Yes, I did have a leisurely lunch." The thought that Vijaychandra was probably present to hear the words spoken during and after lunch was unavoidable and extremely embarrassing.

"I am glad you are back. And not a moment too soon!"

"I wanted to be here yesterday but got into a car accident. Got tied up with that. How did your court appearance go?"

"I got a one day postponement. I am here right now to take you there with me."

"But ... I don't see how I can do anything to help." Mota Sheth's heart jumped into his mouth.

"Let me explain. I don't want any false testimony from you; I will not ask you to do anything unethical. All I want are a few words from you."

"What words?"

"Words to the effect that, through a proper Hindu ceremony, you have promised Sushilaben's hand in marriage to me, and that I was to go abroad for higher education with your help."

Champak Sheth struggled to laugh the matter off : "Surely you jest! Do you think any court is going to swallow that line? They are bound to ask why a person of my social standing would go through a hasty and secret engagement for his sole heir!"

"And we will have an answer ready for them." Vijaychandra spoke with the coolness of a confident attorney : "There was an earlier engagement that had to be broken. The reasons for that break, if made public, could cause irreparable harm to the reputation of the parties involved. To spare them from the gossip and any public embarrassment that might ensue, we chose to keep the new betrothal private. I have cleared all this with my attorney; there is no reason to worry!"

Mota Sheth continued to pick his teeth with the matchstick and stayed quiet.

"Please believe me that I empathise with you and have given much thought to all your concerns." The affected remorse in Vijaychandra's voice would have melted the hardest of hearts : "Today, I am not the proud and confident Vijaychandra that you saw six months ago. Today, I feel neither victorious nor like the bright full moon that my name implies; rather, I feel like the vanquished new moon. My life has stumbled in a big way, my steps have strayed from the straight and narrow. I don't want to take advantage of your daughter. And I have not come before you today with any claim to her hand. I wouldn't want to do anything that would hurt her innocent name. Today, I seek my own salvation with your help. In the lawsuit against me, the opposition has been able to obtain a closed hearing in the judge's chambers to protect their good name. Your own good name will be under no jeopardy behind those closed doors. And, if you so desire, I am willing to forego, in writing, any claim on your daughter. If you ask for it, I am ready this moment to write out the kind of medical statement that your doctor had provided for Sukhlal. And if·the seems to believe in my being betrothed to your daughter, I will be willing to go to the elders of the society and admit to my impotence and unfitness to marry any woman; that I do not wish to ruin anyone's life ..."

Vijaychandra's words were accompanied by big teardrops he willed from his eyes. The tears' flow, when seen through his eyeglasses, looked even more effective. That is the nature of some forms of beauty : it is emphasised even more when seen through a transparent medium like glass. The sight of those tears trickling down Vijaychandra's handsome face would create illusions in the mind of even an eyewitness to his bad deeds; one's heart would be tempted to believe that there must be some misunderstanding; this man couldn't possibly do those heinous crimes he was accused of committing.

"After today, I don't intend to stay here in Mumbai. I want to go and hide my blemished face in a faraway place like Ceylon, Burma, Sudan or Aden. I have brought a written confession of my misdeeds with me. Here, Sheth, I am putting my life in your hands."

He offered a sealed envelope to Mota Sheth. Written on it, in bold letters, was : 'The Statement of a Soul'.

Seeing the expression on Champak Sheth's face, he knew he had made headway and continued : "As a matter of fact, I have decided on recommending two educated young men from our caste as suitable matches for your daughter. The other day when I accompanied her on the train to Dadar, it was with the intention of talking to her about them. As God is my witness, I also want to admit to the terrible temptation I felt to force myself on her vulnerability that day. I came terribly close to using the letters she had written to me to blackmail her into submitting to my animal instincts but was saved in the nick of time by the Lord. That letter from your daughter is in that envelope, too. Some falsely believe that she loves Sukhlal. She had a different reason for visiting him in the hospital; she went there to get her correspondence back, the letters that she had written earlier. You can find all that in her own handwriting in that envelope.

"But, I have no intention of taking advantage of her feelings for me nor of your extremely kind treatment of me in the last six months. I did not deserve any of that. I have offended the Lord." The tears flowed again : "I am also glad that you left town when you did."

"Why?"

"There were plans afoot to cause you life threatening bodily harm."

"Whose plans?"

"Need I name names?"

"How did you find out?"

"Your daughter told me."

"When?"

"On the train to Dadar."

"How did Sushila know?"

"She must have overheard something when Khushaalbhai and Sukhlal came calling the night before. My own inquiries confirmed that."

Champak Sheth was shaken to the core.

"But, you can relax now. They were called into the police station and warned off. In fact, they can be in serious trouble if you tell the police some lies."

The arrangement was very much to Champak Sheth's liking : "When does the court hearing begin?"

"At noon. In less than an hour ..." His eyes went to the clock on the wall, the movement of its second hand reminding him of the steadily approaching hour of his doom. His quietly imploring eyes compelled Mota Sheth to get up and dress for the court. The sly old man had his own ideas : 'Let me go and see what the situation is. After all, I am going to have to decide on where my testimony goes. I am not going to say a word until I know which way the wind is blowing!'

"You may want to put this away in a safe place, Sheth!" Vijaychandra tried to hand him the envelope he had brought.

The calculated gamble achieved its intended effect on Mota Sheth, who countered with : "Why don't you take it back for now—what am I going to do with it?"

"I badly needed to get it off my conscience. Where would I keep it? If it falls into the wrong hands, I don't care what happens to me but it will destroy your daughter. Please keep it with you. I am ashamed to admit this but I have some more of her letters that I was going to keep, just in case! I had not expected you to be this generous with me and I thought I could use them as leverage against you. After the hearing, I would like you to stop by my residence so that I can turn it all over to you. It's only because we don't know how noble the other person is that we stoop so low in our own behaviour. You have shown me the milk of human kindness today and, because of that, my own low life mentality pains me even more."

And the tears flowed again.

31

"PORTER!" The chauffeur stopped the car outside the Bombay Central station and called out.

"I don't need a porter." Nana Sheth stopped the chauffeur as he opened his suitcase, leaving the poor chauffeur completely befuddled.

Nana Sheth closed the suitcase and got out of the car, carrying a couple of items of clothing rolled inside a bath towel. Before the chauffeur could ask him anything, Nana Sheth instructed him : "Take the suitcase and the bedroll back. If anyone asks, tell them I didn't think I needed anything more than a change of clothing for this short trip."

"But ... the bedding for the train ..." The chauffeur felt sorry for this man, more because Nana Sheth was fair-complexioned and fragile in appearance. Those two attributes, although more common among women, are sure-fire means to attract sympathy.

"Don't be silly! For years and years, I slept like a baby on those bare wooden train benches. Don't you worry about me; take it all back!"

And with that outward show of toughness, Nana Sheth started his train journey. After a hot summer day, the cool night air felt very comfortable but Nana Sheth could not sleep at all. He got off the train at every stop along the way and drank hot tea. His restless eyes kept roaming the wide expanse that sped by as the train moved. His face showed the expression of a famished person trying to break his hunger of days with one huge meal. The hoarse and toneless sound that came out from his lonely corner seat could not have been mistaken as singing let alone identified as a song of any kind. The other occupants of that train compartment would have laughed at the suggestion that he was actually singing a well-known sad song with the lyric that went something like 'The happy days don't last forever'. His voice seemed incapable of conveying sadness. His gestures that accompanied his 'singing' could have given the impression of a ballad portraying heroic deeds; the faces he made certainly suggested the attempts at a funny song. It sounded anything but sad. But, a sad song it was.

On reaching the Tejpur station next morning, he did not stop in at their branch office but immediately looked for transportation to Thorewaad. For a trip like this, he would normally have hired a taxicab, and, if one was not available, engaged a horse-cart. That day, for some unknown reason, he chose to go cheaper. He hired a one-ox cart and set out for Thorewaad.

On the way, he started reminiscing about the old times. He recalled his innumerable trips in such carts. In those days, they ran the small shop inherited from their father, selling dates by the handful and kerosene by spoonfuls from a single tin container. They bought stolen cotton in the dead of night; tempted the farmers' children with the promise of dates and other goodies if they stole cotton, grain and such from their homes. All along the way, the memories of those days of about ten years ago seemed to be arising one after another and greeting him with 'Hi there, been a long time ...'. The cart ride reminded of the return trips after buying clusters of dates and square containers of kerosene, on credit of course, when he would hire the single-ox cart only for the merchandise. In the scorching May-June sun, he would walk alongside and try to stay in the shade of the ox but wouldn't splurge the extra *anna* or two to ride in the cart.

The memory made him want to re-experience that walk in the moving shadow of the cart and he got off. Talking to the cart-driver, he found out that all the cart owners that he used to ride with, Wali Ghanchi, Kurji Thakkar, Gafoor Thakkar, Manako Koli, had all passed away.

"You know what I remember the most from those trips! We would make a stop by the pond and Kurji and Gafoor would start biting into their *rotla* and whole raw onions! My mouth watered so but most of the time I would turn down their offers to share the meal because I couldn't bear the thought of facing my Bhabhi after that. If I went home with the smell of onion on my breath,* she wouldn't say anything, but inside, I knew she would be deeply hurt."

The young cart driver had no interest in these talks about the good old days nor in his nerd customer's inhibitions about offending his *bhabhi* with the smell of onion on his breath.

"What do you know! Heerapaat is running full!" Nana Sheth saw the river swollen and overflowing with the waters from the recent rainfall. His ecstatic expression and behaviour would have caused suspicion of demoniacal possession.

He paid and sent the cart driver away right from there. He was going to renew his friendship with Heerapaat, his old lady friend. He used to jump right in in his younger days. Now, afraid that he may have forgotten the art of swimming, he stayed on the bank and bathed himself without going in. Then, his wet clothing in his hands, he started walking towards the village.

He started muttering to himself: "Looking at me, somebody would think I have been here for days! Even

---

* Jain dietary laws forbid consumption of anything that grows underground e.g. potatoes, onion, garlic, etc.

Bhabhi and Sushila shouldn't be surprised to see me now—I will just walk into the compound, hang my wet clothes to dry and call out : 'Bhabhi, when can we eat?'— and to Sushila, like when she was young : 'Yo! Santokdi, you chubby little girl!'"

And so he went, repeating those words to himself, trying to memorize them, trying to put courage in his heart : "You are going to keep a smiling face. You can talk business later, much later. Watch it now, don't lose that smile from your face. Only one thing can spoil it all. What if Sushila asks : 'How is my mother?' What will happen then? ..." The happy chain of thought fell apart at that last link. It was like watching a big crack run through one's smiling face in a mirror.

When he reached home, another realization brought him crashing back to earth. When he saw the newly built brick structure in place of the small clay house of his childhood, all his dreams, plans and those memorized words crumbled like a ball of sand on the riverbank in his hands. What he had imagined to be his last refuge turned out to be the product of his Motabhai's wealth. 'Not a brick in this place is the result of your effort,' was the cry that echoed in his ears repeatedly. If the old clay hut was still here, he could have claimed half ownership of it. The little brother who was the better peddler of kerosene by the spoon, dates and the stolen crops would have been the rightful co-owner of that old, dilapidated structure. But, he had contributed far less in the acquisition of their newer Mumbai fortune. His brother's words of just the day had assert just that : 'Do you want to stay in this house or not?' Even his wife had pointed out : 'You are not fit to shine your brother's shoes'.

The new and larger structure—which stood on additional land acquired by encroachment on a helpless widow's property—was his brother's; his brother could throw him out of it anytime he wished; in fact, he could be sued for unauthorized entry by his brother. He went in with these thoughts dominating his mind. He saw his Bhabhi but the pre-planned bravado had already gone up in flames; he looked at Sushila but the words "Santokdi, you chubby little girl!" were nowhere to be found in his mental sphere. Sushila was busy bathing two little children. She looked up, smiled a sweet, sad smile in his direction and continued washing up little 'Poti'. Bhabhu directed the woman servant to go get the brother-in-law's non-existent baggage.

"Not here yet. Should be here soon." He lied and went in. Bhabhu joined him in the sitting room with a glass of water for him.

"How are you, *bhai*? We didn't know you were coming. Is anything the matter?"

He saw this woman that addressed him as brother— not only addressed but treated him with the utmost care and respect like she would her own brother—and he thought of his wife. He remembered her belittling and insulting words, and saw for the first time the full extent of his worthlessness. Why hadn't he ripped the tongue out of her face the moment she said those insulting words about this saintly *bhabhi*?

He gulped the water down and answered : "I have been sent to bring you back."

"Who did?"

"My brother."

"Why so soon? What for?"

"For comforting the dying in Rupaawati."

Bhabhu stayed silent.

"We are to be on the next train back."

"I see."

"If not, he said he will not let anyone back into the house."

"Very well. We'll think about it."

The evening came. Bhabhi asked : "I thought you said the baggage was coming."

"Oh, I forgot that I had sent the baggage back."

"Back where?"

"Back with the car from Bombay Central."

"Why?"

"I felt I didn't own any of it. I was afraid my brother would snatch it away some day anyway."

It was finally dark. They talked at length. The brother said : "Bhabhi, my conscience is telling me to give it all up. To continue to live in a home that is not mine, to live the affluent Mumbai lifestyle that I did not help earn, and, as a result, to cause pain to my brother is something my inner being wants me to stop."

"Why are we *all* going insane?" Bhabhu smiled : "If you get so sensitive and start thinking like that, who will look after your brother, the poor soul?"

Convinced that, shunned by her, now her husband had lost even her younger brother, she felt sympathy for his helpless situation and 'poor soul', the habitual utterance of goodwill, slipped out of her mouth.

He pulled her aside and told her : "I saw Sukhlal and really felt very good about him. A son-in-law like him by my side can make up for the son that I don't have. I don't think, Bhabhi, that any modern or educated man will care for a good-for-nothing father-in-law like me."

"Those are brave words, Bhai! But, when you are sitting by the holy pyre to give your daughter in marriage and your brother screams for you to get up, will you or won't you?"

"If you are at my side, Bhabhi, I will not get up; I will be like a stake in the ground. I will not move an inch, I won't even breathe. Your presence by my side, Bhabhi, will make a man out of me again."

"That's all I have been waiting to hear from you, *bhai.*"

32

SUKHLAL had wiped the tears from his eyes, and within hours of the mourning assembly at Khushaal's, had gone back to work. The third night after that, he was sorting the merchandise for the next day's door-to-door sales. Selecting numbered pots and pans from the inventory on the shelves, he would freeze every so often on the steps of his ladder. But the next instance, he would shake himself out of his thoughts and rub his face hard as if trying to remove the still fresh scabs of his mother's memories.

"There you are, Sukha!" It was Khushaal's voice that got him out of his thoughts that time : "When did you slip out of the house? More people were over to offer their condolences to you."

"I have to make deliveries to the outer suburbs tomorrow and decided to get everything ready tonight."

"Aren't you leaving for the village tomorrow?"

"Not tomorrow. Maybe later."

"Why not?"

"I don't want to lose the *Diwali* business." His voice shook.

"Come down off the ladder. Let's talk."

Khushaal sat next to Sukhlal, patted him on the back and tried to comfort him : "Don't worry, I'll watch your business. Give me the list of your orders—I will personally make deliveries to every single customer of yours; isn't that what you want? Now, listen to me and take the morning train home."

"What difference does it make, especially now?" Sukhlal's voice almost broke at the end. The 'now' was a sarcastic shot at *Vidhaata*, the deity that preordains one's life. What difference would a few days make, *now*? His mother was gone forever and nothing was going to change that!

"Does make a difference. Your father needs you there; and your presence will help the children recover from the loss, my friend."

"But the kids are already with ..." He left the rest unsaid.

Khushaal did not need any further words anyway. He said : "That's precisely why I want you to go. Your father's letter did not completely explain the facts about the children going with them. We really have to piece together the *hows* and *whys* of the whole chain of events—the aunt and niece duo leaving Mumbai suddenly, their showing up at your house, the happenings there. One thing seems very clear—they left Mumbai in a big hurry. Running from the clutches of that devil Vijaychandra, I wonder? But why would they tread the path forbidden by Champak Sheth? Could it be that he is running scared and has changed his mind? And what a surprise that Nana Sheth came to mourn your mother's death! And here's something I just heard—Nana Sheth left for the village and sent all his baggage back!

"The bottom line is, we need you there to figure out the whole deal. It seems they may be in some big trouble and see things differently now. So we had better be ready too. All I care about is the girl; she is the real gem. Those thieves can stuff their money, we don't want any part of it. I don't think the two brothers have changed a bit from their Tejpur days when they were known for stealing food from the community feasts. Champak was the better thief of the two and he has acquired his Mumbai wealth the same way. We don't want to be even in the shadow of that ill-gotten money. But we cannot rest until we liberate that girl, that gem, from her dark surroundings. Until we have done that, living in Mumbai is going to feel like life in hell. Do you understand why I want you to go soon?"

Sukhlal didn't show it but found the whole monologue quite amusing. How nice of Khushaalbhai to renounce the thieves' ill-gotten wealth and to accept the girl! He made it sound like it was as easy as picking out the choicest sweets from a served platter, leaving the unwanted vegetables behind!

Khushaal continued his musings : "How many times did the two get caught stealing the food! I remember the day when I was one of the servers and the two tried to talk me into sneaking the *laadwa* out for them. But the girl seems to have inherited none of that."

Sukhlal's amusement continued—how do we know that the thieving instincts wouldn't resurface after marrying me? If I do get her, my first question to her on our conjugal night would be : "Do you have what it takes to steal *laadwa*?"

What will she say? Probably that "Only a thief's daughter like me would know how to sneak into your house like I did!"

What idiocy! The tears of grief are not even dry and I am already dreaming about the wedding night!

Even his mother's death did not make him homesick. Why? Because he wanted to wring every drop of the Champak-Sheth-introduced inferiority complex out of his being. His words to his father had been 'I am going to live and die in Mumbai'. He was going to make it big on his own and then flaunt his success in Champak Sheth's face : 'Look, I did not go out and steal from anyone; I have taken what fate gave me and built upon it with my own two hands.' Making that happen had become the obsession of Sukhlal's life.

Khushaal patted the determined Sukhlal's back : "What
are you worried about? If you think five lousy days away
from here are going to kill your dreams, you need to
have your head examined. And, remember your ambition
to put Champak Sheth in his place? Your chance to do
just that is waiting for you out there. Now then, will you
just go?"

Sukhlal was a product of the same environment that
had shaped Khushaal's thinking. It was only natural
that an appeal to his baser instinct produced a result
that no argument based on ethics and morality would
have : you want to strike a blow to Champak Sheth's
ego—you take Sushila—the apple of his eyes—away from
him, no matter what you have to do.

"Okay, but let me get all the orders ready."

"Good man! Do that. Meanwhile, I'm going to pay
Champak Sheth a visit. Let's see what he is up to!"

*   *   *

He rang the bell, and when the door opened he just
pushed his way in. For the situations that demanded it,
he had developed this *modus operandi* of not even asking
if his quarry was home, thereby depriving the door-opener
of an opportunity to deny admission. In his life, he dealt
with many households where, if you asked, you would
get the consistent 'he is not home' answer for months on
end.

Here too, he muscled through the half open door and
when the servant told him "Sheth is not home", he gently
tapped the man on his shoulder and said : "No problem
at all; I'll wait right here for him."

He entered the sitting room , took his cap off, and
made himself at home on the sofa. For the 'Sheth is not
home' situation, his bag of tricks included loud clearing
of his throat, coughing, the highly effective sneezing,
yawning, and when nothing else worked, his singing.

Khushaal's technique invariably worked and the 'not home' object of his pursuit miraculously appeared from within.

Here, two loud yawns was all it took. The whispered conversation in the inner room stopped, Champak Sheth entered the outer room and saw his nemesis Khushaal.

"Greetings, Champakbhai!"

"What are you doing here now, Mister? You shouldn't come uninvited like this! Didn't my servant tell you I was not available? Anyway, you will have to leave; I am busy right now."

Khushaal could tell that the man had not changed at all.

"You are getting excited again, Sheth!" Khushaal himself was absolutely calm, "You do remember that we have some unfinished business from the other night, don't you?"

"So, you are not going to leave peacefully," his eyes blazing, Champak Sheth started walking towards the telephone. Khushaal got up, grabbed Champak Sheth's wrist and smiled as he said "Come on, Sheth, sit down for a minute, won't you?" Khushaal's middle finger pressed down on a nerve in Champak Sheth's wrist, causing his eyes to roll up and the poor man gave up all resistance and sat down on the sofa like a man under a spell, completely drained of his anger.

Mother Nature has created some clever arrangements in the human body that are still largely secret. Strategically located in our bodies are some nerve points; the slightest pressure applied on one of those spots can reduce even the strongest among us to a rag doll. Khushaal had the expert knowledge of those points. That knowledge is all it takes to tame the raging bull of a man.

Champak Sheth's eyes rolled even higher as Khushaal smiled and maintained his grip.

"It's all right now, Sheth, just sit back and relax."
Khushaal said as he finally released the wrist.

The moment Khushaal let go of his wrist, Champak
Sheth cried out. A young man ran out of the inner room :
it was Vijaychandra. Khushaal took hold of Champak
Sheth's wrist again.

"Who the hell are you?" Vijaychandra tried to sound
forceful as he asked the smiling Khushaal.

"I'm Sheth's friend, a relative really. Do I look like a
robber or something? Why don't you ask him who I am?"

"Call ... police ..." Champak Sheth got the words out.
Vijaychandra walked towards the phone; Khushaal
begged him : "Wait a second, Mister, don't be hasty here
because you may regret it later. Trust me, I don't want
a red penny from you."

Vijaychandra stopped for a second, and then started
for the phone with contempt on his face. Khushaal
immobilized Champak Sheth with a hard squeeze on
the wrist and caught up with Vijaychandra in two
bounds. One touch on the back of Vijaychandra's left ear
was all it took to subdue the man and Khushaal brought
him back. The smile on Khushaal's face had not ceased
during all this. Having spent all his energy on making
his body attractive and his mind nimble, Vijaychandra
was physically no match for Khushaal even without
Khushaal's special training.

Champak Sheth had rescued Vijaychandra from his
legal predicament. For some reason, Sheth's attraction
for Vijaychandra had resurfaced. He had made a strong
resolve to wed Sushila to Vijaychandra at any cost. He
wanted to prove—as much to himself as to the world—
that he had made no error of judgment in choosing
Vijaychandra. His logic had succumbed to his ego; instead
of keeping his eye on Sushila's welfare, he had convinced
himself that what he had decided on was for Sushila's
good. Khushaal's untimely appearance had interrupted

the discussion of plans for Sushila's future with Vijaychandra.

Khushaal sat Vijaychandra down on a chair and addressed the two of them :

"Please understand this. Before any help arrives at this time of the night, one of you will have made his life dirt cheap. Now, I personally have no problem if your Santok were to marry this man here. I have no quarrel with that and, in fact, I will be happy to leave a wedding gift for her right now," Khushaal patted his wallet and continued. "Your son-in-law-to-be here will want to know what, then, do I want? What I want is really trivial and costs absolutely nothing. Just give me the two fake documents about Sukhlal that you are sitting on. I don't even want to keep them. I will rip them up right in front of you. How is that for what I want?"

"Give those to him! What do we need them for?" Vijaychandra obviously knew about the two documents.

"There you go! Good man, you," Khushaal's voice dripped sarcasm : "but bad papers, those! Sukhlal will die without a bride with those around. But, you know what? How is a poor doctor to ascertain Sukhlal's lack of manhood or this Vijaychandra's virility? Those matters are ... you know ... rather delicate and ... you know ... not something you would want to test. You know what I mean?"

Champak Sheth got up. Khushaal rose and brought Vijaychandra to his feet too : "Let's all go to the safe. I don't dare leave anyone alone, ha-ha-ha. Safe-ty matters, get it! Ha-ha-ha."

Champak Sheth's hands shook so much it took him five or six attempts to insert the key right. Khushaal's encouragements didn't help much either : "Don't worry, Sheth, there is absolutely no reason to be afraid!"

When the documents finally emerged, Khushaal said : "Tear them up with your own hands, Sheth! Or, better yet, get your precious son-in-law here to do it."

After making sure that the documents were gone for good, Khushaal folded his hands in apology : "Please forgive me, Sheth! I have also joined Mahatma Gandhi's non-violent group, sort of. It's only my hands that have remained outside—otherwise, would I go for even this much violence? Never. I have never liked any violence. I shy away from any kind of confrontation—ask the Police Department if you don't believe me. But you forced my hand. You went back on your word, Sheth! You insulted me, you ran for the phone. Calling the police in a domestic disagreement? Did I threaten to murder someone? Anyway, now excuse me, Sheth. And, by the way, I wouldn't take even the dirt off your floor from here."

He dusted his clothes and stamped his shoes and then turned to Vijaychandra : "Our meeting this time was shorter than a dream. I hope we can meet again and get to know each other a whole lot better than this."

33

THE two remained under the Khushaal-induced trance for some time after he left. On recovering from that, the smarting Champak Sheth spoke :

"Crooks—this Mumbai is infested with crooks and hooligans from Kathiawaad. They pay the police off with their earnings from gambling and then harass and blackmail honest citizens with impunity."

"I hope this does not change our understanding."

"Not one bit. In fact, I had told him to come and take the papers from me but he must have become greedy. This was nothing but a ploy to extort money."

"That's that, then." Vijaychandra tried to hide his impatience but he was anxious to continue their negotiations, now that the criminal charges against him had been dropped with the help of Champak Sheth's testimony.

"Let me ask you this. How can I be sure that you will make my Sushila happy?" Champak Sheth obliged him by getting back on track.

"I am not stupid enough to destroy my own or anyone else's life. Take a look at these." He pulled out a stack of letters from his coat pocket and offered them to Champak Sheth : "These are the offers from other interested parties. I am under siege from all these people. The last few were actually written after the police filed their charges."

Had Champak Sheth tried, he would not have discovered the phoniness of the letters. Each one was written in a different hand and with a different pen but the theme of each letter was the same—the father of a prospective bride was begging Vijaychandra to marry his daughter, enticing him with material offerings. Some fathers offered substantial cash dowries and one actually was willing to turn over his entire estate to Vijaychandra. It was not likely that anybody would even wonder whether these fathers actually existed in the real world outside Vijaychandra's pockets. The most helpless people in our society are the fathers of marrying young girls.

"I am not showing these to brag about myself or to impress you. That was why I did not produce these earlier. To press you in your state of distress will be to betray my upbringing and my education. I show these to you only to convince you of my innermost feelings. Today my name has become mud. You rescued me from complete ruin today and there is only one way I can repay that debt. All that I can call my own is my life's independence and I will gladly give that to you. I know what your family's single biggest burden right now is and I offer my shoulder to relieve you of that burden. A few days ago, I was trying to impose my conditions on you; today, I am willing to accept any and all conditions you propose."

"Are you prepared for an immediate wedding?"

"Please don't ask. Your wish will be my command."

"When do you plan to leave for England?"

"Whenever you grace me with your blessing."

"Alone?"

"I no longer have the courage to go there by myself. I will go only if you approve and send her with me, otherwise I would rather not go."

Champak Sheth's mind had already conjured up two images—one of a son-in-law leaving for England as a highly reputable firm's representative and the other of his flower-laden Sushila alongside the son-in-law, both boarding a P. & O. luxury liner at Ballard Pier. He created the imagery and fell in love with it himself. In it, he saw himself as the saviour of generations of his family. Pretty soon that image would be reality and his fame will know no bounds. Back in the village, his relatives and caste members will not stop talking about him. The affluent and the powerful of Mumbai—native and white-skinned alike—will all come to congratulate him with 'Champak Sheth, we had no idea that your family was this progressive'.

Were these merely the secret longings of a childless man? Or, were they the desires of a tree uprooted from its humble origins and trying to settle down in the garden of affluence among the elite of that golden orchard? Having forsaken the land of one's birth and still struggling to spread one's roots in an alien soil, does one seek to establish a measure of success like this? How would others understand the torturous desires of the heir-less, the childless! Or the restlessness that accompanies sudden and unexpected affluence! Such people seek ways to assert themselves, to justify their existence. They want to cry out and declare to the world : 'Look at me. I am not someone that doesn't belong, a nobody, someone to be ignored. I am here, I am somebody, I matter!'

"There is something you should be aware of," Champak Sheth tore himself away from the Ballard Pier dream sequence and reminded Vijaychandra : "Sushila was very upset about what your 'sister' told her ..."

"I reached there just after that incident and was unable to prevent it. Since I found out what had happened, I have given up the friendship of that friend and his wife— whom I had treated like my adopted sister—and have not gone near their place. I now know that I was taken in by their deceit for years. I was too loyal, too naïve and allowed them to play a terrible game with me. But that experience has done me much good to me as well.

I used to think of myself as very smart and shrewd; now I know better. Too late did I realize that they had taken every possible advantage of my trust. It was your daughter who opened my eyes to that deception and from that day I have known that the stupid, simpleton in me needs a woman to watch over my welfare; that what I don't need is a life partner who worships me and docilely agrees with everything I say. Since that realization, I have regretted my presumptuous demand to train and educate her to be worthy of me. Now, I wonder about my own worthiness."

Champak Sheth was under the spell cast by this striking mental transformation of the man he had first met six months ago. Had his rigidly old-fashioned wife— forever stubbornly arguing to keep the old betrothal— heard this, wouldn't the stupid and self-righteous woman be more inclined to change her opinion? And if Sushila had stood behind that door and heard this young man talk, the mental blocks inserted by her regressive Bhabhu would have vanished for sure. Both of them would have seen clear as daylight that his choice was impeccable. The happenings of the last few days were regrettable but nothing to be really concerned about. That crooked shopkeeper of Rupaawati must have taken the two women to his place under some false pretense. But now that he had shown his true colours, he, Champak Sheth, will show them who they were dealing with. The marriage ceremony will take place right in his face. And what was the community organization going to do about it? Impose a fine? He, Champak Sheth, will pay the lousy fine!

Turning to Vijaychandra, he asked : "Would you care about our community's reaction to a quick wedding in the next few days?"

"I don't care. I have no family and there is nothing they can hit me back with."

"Okay then. We leave for Thorewaad the day after tomorrow."

"I have one question."

"Ask away."

"I hope you don't mind my asking but I was wondering how your wife will take all this ..."

"If she doesn't like it, she can hit the road. One bellow from me and the tears will flow! You think I am the kind to take any nonsense from my wife? Forget it! Now remember : you board the morning train at Dadar the day after tomorrow and I will join you at the Borivali stop. A hundred things can happen and we can't be too careful about this. We can't rule out the possibility of the scoundrel Khushaal pulling a fast one if he finds out."

Vijaychandra steadily stared at him for a long time. As he had expected, his eyes glistened over and out came the scented handkerchief. Without a word and with a grateful expression in his moist eyes, he took his leave.

34

"BHABHI, *bhabhi!*" His voice breaking with fear, Sushila's father called out in the semi-darkness of the late evening.

A telegram from his big brother had been delivered earlier in the day with the instructions 'everyone stay there, letter follows' and he had gone to the Tejpur Post Office to get the mail. Scared out of his wits by the contents of the letter, he had just returned to Thorewaad and started searching for his sister-in-law to give her the news. Bhabhu sat on a small mat in the dark of a room. She heard his voice but did not respond.

"Sushila!" The father was almost hysteric : "Where is Bhabhu?"

"She is at her *Samayik.*"

"How much longer to go?"

Sushila brought Bhabhu's hourglass out into the waning daylight and said : "Looks like she just started another *ghadi.*"

That would mean another three quarters of an hour to go!

The seemingly endless forty five minutes passed but Bhabhu didn't rise. She turned the hourglass over and quietly told Sushila that she was starting on a third *ghadi.*

She ended the almost three hours of that peaceful introspection, folded and stowed the little floor-mat that she had sat on and gathered up her string of beads, mouth-cover and the hourglass. The brother-in-law just sat and watched from outside the room like a fascinated child.

"What's up, Bhai?" Bhabhu asked him.

"Why did you keep adding *ghadi*s to your *samayik*, bhabhi?"

"I lost my concentration when I heard you call for me and let my thoughts stray to what may have happened. I had to add two *samayik*s to get my mind back on track."

The brother-in-law was deeply embarrassed by his show of impatience. Although Bhabhu's explanation had carried no direct barb, his conscience felt the effects of the unspoken reproof.

"The mystery of the telegram is solved, bhabhi! My brother arrives here the day after tomorrow."

"Let him come."

"He is bringing Vijaychandra with him."

"That's OK."

"In the letter, he has instructed me to be ready for Sushila's wedding at a moment's notice."

"I see."

"And, Sukhlal has arrived."

"Where is he? In Rupaawati?" The ring in Bhabhu's voice was unmistakable.

"Yes. I have asked him to drop by tomorrow morning."

"He will come! His siblings are here after all."

The brother-in-law's words came out shaking and uneven like the wind blowing through the hollow of a bamboo shoot. Bhabhu's quiet and precise words were like a sharp knife cutting holes in that bamboo as if to get his beating heart to settle down and to produce the deep and even tones of a flute.

"What are we going to do, bhabhi? This is a catastrophe!"

"What is there to worry about? After all, don't we all— your brother, you and I—have to do what Sushila wants?"

"You must be joking! My brother is going to listen to Sushila?"

"He will if he really loves her."

"And what if he doesn't?"

"Then he will have to go home."

"He is going to make life hell for us."

"We'll need our courage to endure anything."

"What if he takes us back to Mumbai?"

"Nobody can drag you away against your will, Bhai!"

"Bhabhi, I am scared."

"I see that but what is there to be afraid of?"

"The thoughts that my brother will use force, get the help of the local law enforcement keep echoing in my mind."

"What can the law ask us to do? Sushila is the only one that has to answer to them."

"When she provides the answers, who or what is she going to stake her future on?"

"Certainly not you or I."

"Who then?"

"We'll get the answers tomorrow morning."

"From where?"

"From Sukhlal. Send someone to make sure he is here in the morning."

"What are we going to ask him?"

"Just this : 'Are you, Sukhlal, prepared to lay down your life to protect Sushila as your wife? They will punish you, beat you up, threaten you, put your father through living hell. Say yes only if you understand what you are getting into and are ready for it; if not, tell us now so that Sushila can look for protection elsewhere. We don't know what else you bring to the table, nor do we want to know; what we are looking for is the willingness to hold Sushila's hand and laugh in the face of your total ruin.' Sushila listens to his answers and then decides whether to take the plunge or not."

In the darkness that had fallen, that conversation must have sounded like a discourse between a teacher and a student. The mental spooks, fears and doubts haunting the brother-in-law's timid mind were slowly dissipated as his teacher continued.

"We can easily marry Sushila off but we can not be there to run her life after that. We know this : Sushila has really taken to the family from Rupaawati and she likes Sukhlal more than the other. What do we really know about how badly Sukhlal wants this? So, let's first ask Sushila where she stands. And then, let's talk to Sukhlal. We can throw our weight behind him, but he is the one that has to be out front and stand up to them. We are going into a battle here, *bhai*, this is no game! I have left my home in Mumbai fully realising the seriousness and finality of my actions."

Her mind's eye clearly saw the tragic lengths to which her husband would go to prevent the Sushila-Sukhlal wedding. She had followed all the threads of this complex web over and over, and now it was the decision time. Her worldly sense was steady, sure and quite simple. She knew what the bottom line in the qualification for a marriage was. She had personal knowledge of what made a marriage work. In her mind the final question to ask was :

'How ready is this candidate to sacrifice his all for this marriage? The tree of life does not yield fruits of a happy marriage with the mere sprinkling of love—it needs a solid feeding of blood, sweat and tears.'

Sukhlal arrived on horseback the following morning.

35

FROM where she stood on the elevated porch, Sushila watched Sukhlal arrive outside the gate and jump off his horse. He had a sash tied around his waist and his face was covered with another piece of cloth to keep the dust out of his breath. The white cap that he habitually wore in Mumbai was missing; in its place was a *paaghadi*.

When he entered the compound holding the reins of his mare, he had removed the covering from his face. His face, fuller from the one Sushila had last seen, looked good in the small coiled turban on his head.

He looked up and saw his three young siblings, sitting at the edge of the porch and brushing their teeth. Poti, the youngest one, was being helped by Sushila. He saw the hands, the fingers that were gently applying the *daatun* to Poti's teeth and Khushaal's words echoed in his head : 'That's the arm of a girl that works ... not the typical fragile Mumbai-ware.'

But it was not the absence of fragility that brought tears to Sukhlal's eyes. The little Poti made not a sound as this stranger brushed her teeth. You only have to remember your own childhood to understand how much children hate brushing their teeth, especially having their teeth brushed for them. The *daatun*'s softened end moved lightly on Poti's teeth, and the little girl, like a puppet on a string, turned her head and opened her mouth as Sushila directed.

"*Motabhai*, hey Motabhai, look, Chhuchhilabhabhi ..." The six year old boy jumped up and called out : "Look, look. Thichh ijh Chhuchhilabhabhi ... oul *Ba* went away—and Chhuchhilabhabhi came in ... look, Chhuchhi..."

As the boy chattered away, his one hand pointed at Sushila, the other held his *daatun* and his loose shorts had slipped down from his waist. As Sooraj, the older girl, tried to grab the little boy's hand and pull him down, Sukhlal just stood transfixed in the compound. A smiling Nana Sheth took the reins from Sukhlal and tied the horse in the shed in one corner of the compound. Sushila gave Sukhlal a sidelong glance and flashed a smile, but Sukhlal's eyes were downcast while his brother's words reverberated in his heart : 'Ba went away—and Sushilabhabhi came in.'

Back from tying up the horse, Nana Sheth said : "The children, I tell you, have mixed in like they were always here. Come on in and take a load off your feet."

"My brother talks a bit too much," Sukhlal responded as he threw loving glances at the boy. As if to prove the point, the little brother continued :

"I will be light back, OK, *Motabhai*! I will achhk Chhuchhilabhabhi if I can. I can't come without achhking hul."

Sooraj tried to cover the boy's gabbing mouth with her hand but the laughing Sushila stopped her. Sushila washed the faces of the two younger children and told Sooraj, "Why don't the three of you go say hello to your brother and then come in for your breakfast?"

What was Sushila's rush in sending the children to Sukhlal? Was it her do-gooder instinct prompting her to get the siblings to meet one another? But that question was answered by that do-gooder instinct itself : 'Who are you trying to fool! You can't go see him for yourself, so you are trying to get whatever satisfaction you can by watching the children meet him. We know what the big hurry is, you cunning little lady!'

Sushila took refuge in the kitchen to escape those wisecracking words from her inner self. But the loud cadence of someone's footfall seemed to come from right behind her; someone in a big hurry to get in, trying to break in through those walls around her.

But those sounds were really the loud beating of her own heart. Her mind was awhirl with the restlessness of an unbroken colt with a rider on its back.

"Sushila!" Bhabhu had just completed her morning devotional rites and her footsteps were soft and quiet : "Get some powdered *rotlo* and a bowl of yogurt ready. If he wants tea, you can make it later. I'll go see him and be right back. And listen, make sure the *rotlo* is crushed real fine, OK?"

She walked into the sitting room. Sukhlal got up, walked to her and bowed real low to her.

"Please sit!" Bhabhu was quiet for a while and then said : "Your mother was a lucky soul—a blessed soul. Her departure was a big loss for us. A bigger loss because we were instrumental in precipitating her sudden departure. The thought that she had lost her daughter-in-law proved to be too much of a shock to her heart."

The talk of this 'shock' was news to Sukhlal.

Bhabhu continued : "We inadvertently became the cause of her death. That must have been our destiny. But I brought the children here to atone for some of that."

Sukhlal was dismayed, his eyes flashed. So! The only thought behind bringing the children here was to provide a charitable refuge to the orphaned!

Bhabhu went on : "When we put out for someone or hurt somebody, our deeds are recorded in the celestial book of accounts and the mutual debts are created and developed. The relationships caused by those debts continue only as long as those debts exist. But it is easy to blame everything on those debts. What is not easy is to live by the courage of your convictions. That courage separates the winners from the losers in this world."

Sukhlal had absolutely no idea what this woman was talking about, nor about where he stood in her eyes. Was she merely asking him to face the loss of his mother with courage or was there something more that she was hinting at?

While this was going on, a bullock-cart pulled up in front of the compound gate. On hearing the driver call out 'Cart from Tejpur!', Nana Sheth panicked and blurted out : "Oh no, are they here already? How can that be?"

"Calm down, *bhai*, keep your cool," is all Bhabhu said to him. Meanwhile, the cart driver who was an employee of the Tejpur branch of their business, walked over and handed him a note. Nana Sheth read the note and told Bhabhu : "Says here, 'Per instructions from Mumbai, here are food provisions, cloth and miscellaneous items for use during the ceremonies.'"

"Wonderful!" Bhabhu smiled and Sukhlal's face fell. What ceremonies were they getting ready for? Couldn't be anything to do with him—it was not even five days since his mother's death! And if not for him, then who was it for?

"Our office manager says in his note here that the two of them will arrive from Mumbai around noon, spend the afternoon resting in Tejpur and come here in the evening." A disheartened Nana Sheth informed Bhabhu : "He has also attached the telegram sent when leaving Mumbai, so there is little doubt about their arriving tomorrow."

"Did we have any doubt, Bhai? Let's get the cart unloaded."

"The manager was asked to find out what the earliest auspicious date for the wedding was. It's the day after tomorrow!"

Sukhlal blankly stared at Nana Sheth as the older man continued to read the news from Tejpur. He was unable to break through the fog yet. Two were arriving, so who was the other person with Mota Sheth? Had they already found another candidate? Surely they were not going to even touch Vijaychandra after finding out what he had been up to! Who could the new lucky one be?

Nana Sheth answered his questions as he continued to read : "Vijaychandra insists on using *khaadi* for everything and they are bringing all needed clothing from Mumbai—including ready-made stuff for Sushila…"

"I get the picture." Bhabhu's tone left no doubt that she had heard enough. Turning to Sukhlal, she said :

"There are a couple of things I wanted to talk to you about.

"Think about this! Are a couple's engagement and marriage the ties that bind only the bride and the groom together? With her marriage, the bride adopts her in-laws' entire family, the household, the family traditions and beliefs—even the spike the family cow is tied to.

"Likewise, the groom weds not only the bride but her parents, her siblings, her kin, even the trees in her father's courtyard!"

Before Sukhlal could say a word in response, Bhabhu added : "The husband's father could be the village idiot and the bride would still treat him with respect and make sure he is properly fed and taken care of. And even if the wife's father is a ne'er-do-well, wouldn't the son-in-law do his best to carry him through the wilderness that is life? If he does not, where is the poor fellow going to go? To the shelter for the homeless?"

Sukhlal was more confused and lost now than before and just stared at the floor.

Bhabhu said : "Sukhlal, son, look at me!"

Sukhlal looked up.

"Sitting right there is my brother-in-law who has been like a son to me. To you he may be whatever you think he is. By tomorrow evening, the bricks of this house will be telling him : 'Get out of here, you bum! Go away; we don't care where; we don't care whether you live or die!'"

Her words sounded like a prophecy. Bhabhu went on :

"Don't worry, this is not an attempt to force anything on you. You need to understand what you are getting into before you make your final decision. I am only asking you to search your soul about all the blows you have taken, the stabs of insults that were aimed at your heart."

"Bhabhu!" Sooraj walked in and said, "*Rotlo* and yogurt are ready."

"Come, have some breakfast," Bhabhu escorted Sukhlal to the next room, had him sit down to eat and then left the room. Sushila entered the room with a plate and a bowl. Sukhlal had not even dreamt that Sushila herself would be serving him food. The first whiff of her presence made his blood rush and his manliness threatened to explode. On her side, Sushila felt committed to him and thought of him as her own. Modestly keeping her sari in place, she put the food in front of him and said : "I hope you like it." Her cheeks dimpled as she smiled.

Sukhlal pretended to eat. Instead of carrying the food to his mouth, his hand itched to slap this girl around for no reason.

Sushila said : "I wanted to ask you just one thing."

"Go ahead." Every cell in Sukhlal's body was alive.

"Are you really prepared?"

"Prepared for what?"

"To face what may be coming?"

"For you?"

"Not only me."

"Then?"

"For all of us."

"If I was not prepared, why would I keep after it?"

"Does *Bapa* agree?"

"I haven't specifically asked him."

"Will you go get him here? Before tomorrow morning?"

"What is happening tomorrow morning?"

"My *Mota Bapuji* is arriving with Vijaychandra—to marry me off to him. My father and Bhabhu are determined to stay with our betrothal. The two of them have left our house for good and come here—for us. Please hurry up and bring your father here." Her voice shook with terror.

"My father?"

"Yes, yes. Bapa, your father" Sushila emphasised.

"But ... why? I myself take the full responsibility— what do we need him here for?"

"No, no, I'm not going there just for you. I want to go there ... because Bapa is there, the children are there, the house is there and because the little calf is there."

"What if he wasn't around?"

"Then I might not have been this determined."

"But he will never say no!"

"He will not refuse to take us in, but as soon as he does, my Mota Bapuji is going to descend on all of us like a ton of bricks. Who knows what he ... oh God!" Sushila exhaled in desperation.

"I want to talk to Bhabhu and then decide."

"One way or the other, please decide by tomorrow."

Sukhlal ate hurriedly and then went to see Nana Sheth and Bhabhu. His proposal to them was : "Can't we perform a quick wedding ceremony today? In a couple of hours?"

"But of course!" An ecstatic Nana Sheth jumped at the thought : "I never thought of that, Bhabhi!"

"But I did, Bhai!"

"All right then, Bhabhi! Let's do it. That will cool my brother off, won't it, Bhabhi? Let's get the local priest to perform the ceremony. All we need to do is to find an auspicious hour today, right Bhabhi?"

"No, Bhai! Absolutely not!" Nobody had ever heard Bhabhu speak that forcefully in her life.

"Why not, Bhabhi? Sukhlal himself is ready."

"No, not even if his father wants it."

"But I don't understand why not, Bhabhi!"

"Because, it was not a stray animal that passed away the other day, brother mine! It was his mother, for heaven's sake. Another thing to keep in mind, I don't want my little girl to be married off in secret. Sushila has done nothing to be ashamed of. No, I want our entire community to be there to witness her nuptials. I want my darling girl to get the blessings of every elder. I want everyone to celebrate the greatest day of her life with all due fanfare. No way, no how, is she going to be married in the dark of the night and run as you propose."

"But, Bhabhi, there will be a hundred obstacles to overcome later if we don't do it now."

"This life would not be life without obstacles. Overcoming obstacles makes the fruits of that labor taste even sweeter."

"We'll be taking a big risk ..."

"Think positively, Bhai, and everything will work out. We are not thieves or criminals; we are not doing anything unethical. Why should we be afraid, then?"

"What if the local regime gets involved?"

"Not to worry. What are those poor souls going to do to us? Sushila is legally of age and has the right to choose a husband and the family she wants to marry into. You are her father and give your consent to her choice. And nobody is going to accuse Sukhlal of being *too old to marry* Sushila!"

"I am worried about what other tricks there may be up their sleeves, Bhabhi!" There was a hidden meaning behind those words. Sukhlal had no trouble recognizing the reference to the faked documents attesting to his impotence.

"Whatever stunt they may try to pull will matter little because you are the girl's father and she is of legal age to marry." Bhabhu understood the reference too.

Nobody spoke for a while. Sushila's father was still anxious and scared inside. He wanted the whole thing to be a done deal before his brother arrived. What treacherous terrain was Bhabhi leading him into? Will he survive the obstacle-ridden trek? Will he measure up to the opposition? But he was not going to be alone in this! Bhabhi was going to be there, too. And she had a lot more to lose in this. With Bhabhi on one side, Sushila on the other side and Sukhlal in front of him, what was he afraid of? The timid father of Sushila finally followed Bhabhu's lead over the burning chasm in the wilderness of his mind, leaving those growling demons of fear behind him.

"The immediate thing to do, Sukhlal, is to go and talk to Deepchand-*mama*. Discuss the matter with him, get his opinion and come to a final decision yourself. If you decide to follow through on Sushila, come back good and early tomorrow morning and bring a cart with you. If you choose not to come back, we will understand."

When Sukhlal mounted his horse, on his forehead was a *chaandalo* with grains of rice stuck to it, and melting slowly in his mouth was a piece of *gol,* good omens both to wish him success in his endeavour.

36

IN the late evening of that same day, the narrow market street of Thorewaad was lit up as if the mythical diamond-bearing King Cobra was on the prowl there. Tejpur's feudal prince's car arrived with Champak Sheth and Vijaychandra on board, leaving a trail of startled homeward bound oxen and a muster of loudly protesting peacocks. Accustomed to the sight of the prince's car, the villagers got up from their shops and porches and saluted. This pleased the vain Champak Sheth no end, thinking the honour was directed at him.

Determined to intimidate his brother and his wife into submission, Champak Sheth exchanged not a word of pleasantry and escorted his guest to the upper floor of the house. In the quiet of the evening, he heard the rhythmic sound of a swinging cradle. This sound that millions of people consider the sweetest in the world stabbed Champak Sheth in the ears. He asked Nana Sheth, who was standing meekly on one side, none too gently : "Who is in the cradle?"

When there was no reply forthcoming, he loudly cleared his throat : "Well!" Bhabhu replied from the adjoining room : "It's the younger daughter of my Roopchandmama—from Rupaawati."

"His wife passed away, you know, and the children are here with us," the temporarily nonplussed Nana Sheth finally found his tongue. He had not been aware that Bhabhu was in the next room.

"Send them back first thing in the morning," Champak Sheth ordered his brother. He totally ignored his wife, standing in the doorway and brightening up the entire room with her presence.

"I want you to get up early tomorrow and have the sitting room cleaned up. There will be fifteen people for lunch. Inform whoever is managing the kitchen not to prepare any sweet; just have them prepare the normal meal of rice, vegetables, lentils and fritters of some kind. The sweets have been ordered and will be delivered in the morning."

With those instructions to the younger brother, Champak Sheth stretched out on the bed and turned away from him. Vijaychandra hung up his coat and hat and then asked Nana Sheth politely : "Where are the toilet and other facilities? Would you mind showing me around?"

When the unhappy Nana Sheth descended the stairs with Vijaychandra in tow, Bhabhu was right there and told the servant : "Please show the guest where the facilities are. The drinking water is right in the room upstairs."

Though thwarted in his effort to talk to his father-in-law-to-be, Vijaychandra's unshakable faith in the principle of 'no pain, no gain' didn't let him quit. He spoke to Nana Sheth but his words were really meant for Bhabhu's ears : "You have a very nice place here. Everything one could ask for! By the way, may I have water and some salt? I better rinse my mouth before I forget."

Bhabhu got the salt and water from the kitchen and handed it to him without a word. Vijaychandra's mouth and throat received extra good care with a prolonged gargle that night. But he did not get even a glimpse of Sushila. Only the rhythmic swinging of the cradle sounded. Neither the cradle nor the hands swinging it were in sight.

'One day, the same sound ...' The thought flitted through Vijaychandra's imagination and quickly disappeared. He went to the upstairs room and fell asleep. All kinds of dreams tortured the peace of his mind all night long.

Bhabhu woke Sushila up at the crack of dawn and fired the kitchen up. She had not told Sushila what had transpired upstairs the night before. She immersed herself in the kitchen chores with her habitual attention to detail, chirpy but not especially forthcoming about the developments. "Did you know, girl, that all the sweets were specially ordered from Tejpur?" "Wait till you see the *bhajiya* and *dhokla* that I prepare for the big day today!" More such hints and the interest Bhabhu showed in the cooking arrangements left Sushila perplexed and deeply worried. Sushila did not appreciate Bhabhu's attempts at humour like 'Let's see how Vijaychandra compares my bhajiya today with what you served to him in Mumbai!' This was a repeat of the torture Sushila had undergone during the train journey from Mumbai.

To add to all that, Bhabhu, who otherwise never sang, today kept humming lines from a wedding song that went :

The word has come of my dearest's arrival;
O what a beautiful moment this is!'

Listening to all this, Sushila became so paranoid that she came close to crossing the bounds of decency and tried to—directly and indirectly—find out whether Bhabhu had paid a nocturnal visit to Mota Bapuji's room. Bhabhu was, of course, too smart to respond to any of that.

New seating mats, new knee-rests, shiny new dinner sets and other paraphernalia kept coming out of their storage and Sushila felt more and more suffocated.

Even in her worried state, Sushila looked in on the children every so often. Sooraj, the older girl, even asked her : "Why are you looking sad, Bhabhi? Has anything happened?"

The little boy would ask her : "Why aal you not talking to me, Bhabhi?"

"Who said I'm not talking, Bhai?" Sushila would force a smile.

"Hey, bhabhi, I can chhee wotal in youl eyejh! Look Poti!"

Sushila ran from the room, afraid that she may not be able to hold the tears back. Champak Sheth happened to come down the stairs at that very moment. His eyebrows went up and he snapped at Sooraj : "Go sit in the back!"

Sooraj took her brother and sister to the back porch, tried to make themselves melt into a corner and waited for Sushila's next visit. When Sushila showed up, Sooraj whispered to her : "Will it be better if we went and waited at the neighbour's house, Bhabhi?"

"No, why?"

"So that we are not in the way here."

"You are not in the way. Did someone say something to you?"

"No."

"Don't you like it here?"

"Why wouldn't we like it here? If we don't like it with you ..."

"Go on, say it. You can be with your brother."

"Bhai will always be there—but you come ahead of him."

"Really? Then remember, don't be scared no matter what happens, no matter what anyone says to you. Can you manage that?"

"Let anyone say anything to us and we won't mind; but we will be scared if we see you get into trouble."

"You have to be brave and stick it out for the day, even if you see me in trouble. Tomorrow we will go home."

"Is my brother coming here?"

"He said he was, but we will go tomorrow even if he doesn't come." There was a touch of anger and doubt in those words. He left here yesterday afternoon; what was keeping him now? Did he get scared off and decided to throw in the towel? Made a big show of riding in like an outlaw, face-wrap and all! What if his father nixed the deal? If so, it wouldn't be his fault. But of course it would be his fault, nobody else's but his. Was he frightened away by Bhabhu's test?

She asked Sooraj : "Is your brother afraid of anyone?"

"Only of the house-lizards, runs at their sight. Of nothing else."

The tragedy was instantly transformed into a comedy. Sushila walked away from the children with the naughty notion of someday using a house-lizard for some real fun.

At that instant, the borrowed princely automobile made its appearance again, inciting a ruckus among the peacocks, frightening the cattle, getting the people to get up and salute and stinking up the little town with its smoky exhaust.

Six or seven affluent looking men entered the compound. The loud voice of one of them filled the space of Champak Sheth's residence with its booming quality.

The manager from the Tejpur office arrived about that time with some men carrying baskets full of sweets. He went into the kitchen and expressed his pleasure : "What a wise thing to do, Gheliben! The old arrangement would never have worked. Did you know that Mota Sheth stopped to see Deepa Sheth on his way in yesterday? Deepa Sheth said the same thing : 'The elders should do what the girl wants. I will be happy to go along with her wish.' What could be more wonderful! I say, make hay while the sun shines; get the engagement and the wedding over with in one shot."

"Oh absolutely, bhai! Everything is coming together. Everything will be resolved today. Today is the day to get it all settled, once and for all." Bhabhu's enigmatic words bothered Sushila more and more. Bhabhu opened up the baskets of sweets and started sampling the contents of each. The deliberate smacking sounds she made stung Sushila's ears just as Bhabhu intended. Sushila pretended to be busy with cooking but Bhabhu had long since sensed her snappy mood. Stirring the pot of *daal*, she would bang the ladle. Reaching for the container of the *bhajiya* flour, she managed to spill some.

"Come here, girl! Try some of this." Bhabhu called Sushila as she herself put a piece of sweet in her own mouth.

"I am busy with the stove here. What do you want?"

"I want you to try this. My, this is delicious!" The sluggish words coming out of Bhabhu's food-filled mouth crawled into Sushila's ears like a centipede.

"Not now."

Sushila's attention was on the stove when Bhabhu sneaked in from behind her and stuffed a big piece of sweet in her mouth. Ignoring the choking Sushila's 'No—please don't', Bhabhu prodded her with, "Come on, girl, think of the sweet as coming from Vijaychandra!"

"In that case ...," Sushila spit the stuff right out of her mouth. Seeing the anger in her big eyes, Bhabhu backed away from her in mock terror and started singing with her claps keeping time : "Spare me ... forgive me, o Goddess, Bhawaani the fearsome ...!" Slowly and deliberately, she got another helping of sweet and sat down in front of Sushila. From her stuffed mouth came the garbled words of a country lyric :

> *Send that leaf fluttering on its way,*
> *For the leaf does not belong here.*
> *Her husband has arrived to claim her,*
> *For the leaf does not belong here.*

He gave the vamp seven lashes,
For the leaf does not belong here.
And she quickly climbed into his cart,
For the leaf does not belong here.

"How is one to know what's going on inside that young head!" Bhabhu tried to break through Sushila's wrathful silence : "Changed your mind overnight, did you?"

"Who changed her mind? You or I?" Sushila stormed into the kitchen : "Get me an ounce of iodine, so that I can put us all out of our misery!"

"You can't find any iodine around here, girl mine!" Bhabhu was cool as a cucumber : "Down the country way here, the only way out is opium; a fifth of an ounce or the weight of a small coin would do the trick."

"So get me that."

"It's coming," she paused and then added in a low voice : "all the way from Rupaawati." Another pause and then : " That worthless bum! Why would he come back? Walked out of here and just disappeared. But then, where would he find the backbone for something this big?"

That was when Nana Sheth came in asking : "Bhabhi, they want to know how much longer before we eat."

"As soon as I start frying the fritters, Bhai! Here, try some of this sweet!"

"Sweet, Bhabhi! I find the very thought of it appalling. Upstairs, my brother is telling the elders all kinds of lies. As for me, he has totally ignored me and kept me out of the picture. I can not take this any more, Bhabhi! I took a walk to the centre of the village. The father and son have arrived with the ox-cart as we requested."

"The poor souls!" Another piece of sweet went into Bhabhu's mouth, "Just this moment I was calling them names! So they are here, but now your darling daughter is acting up."

"What's the matter?"

"For some reason, she seems to have changed her mind overnight."

"When did I say that? Why are you torturing me like that? Cut me to pieces and I still won't change my mind. I am ready to leave now." An exasperated Sushila blurted out.

"If you haven't changed your mind, here, eat this."

"Throw your sweet into that *chulo*! Have you gone mad, Bhabhu?"

"Call me whatever you want. But eat this sweet and prove to me that you haven't changed your mind. If you take it out of your mouth, I will know that you are still wishy-washy about this."

Bhabhu put a big piece of sweet in Sushila's mouth and then kissed her on the swollen cheek, gently caressed her and said : "You have yet to know your Bhabhu, my sweet! And you are right about one thing—I have gone crazy today."

> '*O what a beautiful moment this is!*
> *The word has come of my dearest's arrival;*
> *O what a beautiful moment this is!*'

37

THE big lunch was in its final stages. Amidst the loud slurping sounds of *kadhi* and curried vegetables being consumed, the group had spent the first fifteen minutes discussing the progress being made in girls' education and the deplorable shortage of appropriately educated young men. For the last ten minutes, the group had concentrated on pressing Champak Sheth on the size of his donation for the local shelter for old cows.

"If that is what you need, two thousand is no problem."

Champak Sheth's words were greeted with a chorus of belching noises from the overindulgent group.

"Finish up here and then come up as soon as you can," Champak Sheth instructed his brother, who had been busy with serving the lunchers and had yet to eat. The brahmin priest arrived a little later and asked for the paraphernalia that went with a religious ceremony— rice grains, red turmeric paste, multicolour cotton thread, brown sugar, etc.

Just then, the distinctive sound of gravel being crunched by hard shoes came from the compound gate. Sushila looked for the origin of the sound from the kitchen window when the little boy called out : "Bappa, my Bappa! Chhuchhilabhabhi, my fathal ijh hiyal to take uchh home! Come on, let uchh go!"

With those words, Sukhlal's brother ran to Sushila and grabbed her and started pulling : "Get leady, *bhabhi*! Let ucch go!"

"We will, very soon now, OK, *bhai*?" Sushila pressed the little brother-in-law to her bosom.

Sushila's father had not met Deepa Sheth in a long time and came forward to greet him as the latter mounted the steps of the porch. They had barely seen each other when Deepa Sheth was in Mumbai and Nana Sheth held back because of that limited acquaintance. But Deepa Sheth followed the village custom—also feeling genuine warmth for the man—and embraced Nana Sheth with the words : "How are you, Sheth? And daughter Sushila is well, I hope? God bless her for brightening my life and the lives of my next seven generations! Where is everybody, upstairs?"

"*Mama!*" Bhabhu emerged from the kitchen and addressed Deepa Sheth : "Please sit down and have some lunch."

Deepa Sheth noticed the stack of dirty dishes from the just finished lunch and begged her to excuse him : "I ate just before we left home, Gheliben!."

Sushila heard that and wondered how early the aging gentleman must have risen and fired up the stove to cook!

"Please come in, Sheth." Nana Sheth escorted Deepa Sheth inside, took a square of *mesub* and told him : "Please open your mouth."

"I can't, please. Not just yet, not today." He was referring to the recent death of his wife and the conventional mourning period.

"Today is the day, Sheth. If Sushila's mother-in-law objects to this from her abode in heaven, let the burden of that sin be on me—but please accept this from me, Sheth. My Sushila, my only girl, the apple of my eye ..." —Nana Sheth's voice cracked—"Please take good care of her, Sheth! Please open your mouth—promise me!"

"Sushila will forever be more than a daughter to me; and you, Sheth, will be no less than my blood brother," Deepa Sheth took the *mesub* piece and ate it.

Like an underground stream searching for millennia for a way out of the strata of rock and hard ground, a surge of humanity burst through the layers of Nana Sheth's dense and dull intellect. He bowed deep to Deepa Sheth with folded hands and said :

"I am giving you my all. This is not a mere pledge to give my daughter's hand in marriage, Sheth, consider this to be my formally giving my daughter away to your son, right now! No matter what happens, I will not lose heart now. Not when my Bhabhi is with me!"

"I am with you and so is Deepa Mama, Bhai! We are all together in this, there is no cause for worry."

"Gheliben! Can I see Sushila for a moment?" Deepa Sheth asked.

"Come on out, my girl!" Bhabhu called out.

Sushila came out but stood respectfully without facing her father-in-law.

"Please, my daughter, look at me."

Sushila hesitated : what did her villager father-in-law want?

"Please look at me, daughter! I am but a village simpleton. But, even I know that until you are married to my son, you are the embodiment of *Goddess Shakti*, someone to look at, someone to worship. Let me look at you, o Mother!"

Sushila faced him. Deepa Sheth raised his arms to offer his blessings and then said : "Now bless me, daughter. Grant me the strength to be myself. Pray for me, daughter, that I don't lose my humanity even if thrown into a cauldron of boiling oil. And, please trust me."

With that, he beat his flat palm on his chest three times. His chest seemed to get broader and his palm struck it like the stick of a war drum. He smiled with some mirth : "Now I will see those elders from Tejpur. I want to get the measure of those charity thieves!"

He climbed the stairs to the room above. Nana Sheth followed him to lend his support but, in reality, needed to hold Deepa Sheth's hand to borrow some courage from him.

The moment the gathering saw Deepa Sheth, the faces of these elders of the local Jain community adopted the gravity befitting a court of law.

"Please take your seat." The elders, themselves occupying mattresses covered with white sheets, pointed Deepa Sheth to the floor mat. Deepa Sheth went beyond that and sat at the edge of the mat.

When Nana Sheth sat down right next to him, Champak Sheth glared at him to get him away from there but the younger brother refused to even look at him. His eyes were on the door to the inside stairs. From where he sat, he could see the face of Bhabhu above the stairs. The rest of her body was out of sight.

The Brahmin priest started anointing people's foreheads with turmeric paste dripping with oil. When Vijaychandra's turn came, he quietly told the priest to let the oil drain out before applying the paste to him.

"This is something to rejoice about," the lead elder started the conversation : "This is indeed a progressive step. By signing the annulment, Deepa Sheth has prevented two lives from being condemned to a living hell."

"What living hell are we talking about?" Deepa Sheth laughed.

"What was it then, a life in paradise that she was going into?" Champak Sheth was boiling mad.

"But..., wait ..., annulment, er, I never ..., don't I have any say?" Nana Sheth made a feeble attempt to assert himself.

"You stay out of this, I will handle this." Champak Sheth spoke without catching the significance of his brother's words.

"No. I want a clarification ..."

"Do you want a smack on your face?" Champak Sheth had reached the point of no return.

"Calm down, there is no need to get violent." Deepa Sheth tried to intervene.

"Ah, yes, a smack from you! I got plenty of those when I was young, Motabhai! One today will be nothing new to me. But Sushila's welfare means a lot, an awful lot to me. I love my girl, my only girl ..."

"Is that right?" Champak Sheth jumped up and quickly moved towards Nana Sheth. Without listening to the protests of 'Oh no, wait!', he lashed out at his brother's cheek. When the blow landed, everyone realized that it was Deepa Sheth who had been hit when he tried to intervene. The sound of the slap was followed by just one word from Deepa Sheth's mouth : "Lord!"

Everybody got up and tried to hold Champak Sheth back and to pacify him, when penetrating all the commotion came the words :

"My respects, Somchandkaka, Pitambarfua, Anupchandbhai! Greetings, everybody!"

Standing in the doorway, Bhabhu addressed the elders of the Tejpur Jain society according to her relationship to them. Her face was covered, as best as she could under the circumstances, in deference to the elders who were relatives from her husband's side of the family.

This couldn't be happening! A woman had come into the meeting of the elders; something that would be a no-no even in the progressive Mumbai city had happened in this remote backward village! Bhabhu, the middle-aged wife from a respectable family—who had never stepped anywhere close to such exclusively male assemblies, one who had chosen never to even bare her toes in the presence of men, that 'Gheli'—was standing there. The sight of her face created much unease among the elders.

Her hands still folded in humility, she asked : "May I say something to the assembly here?"

"Go downstairs right now!" Champak Sheth bellowed.

"This is the first time in my life that I am going against my husband's wishes—for the very first time." Bhabhu continued to address the elders. "For the first and the last time, all I want to say is : even if Deepamama granted an annulment, Sushila or her father never did. On one hand, there is absolutely nothing wrong with Sukhlal. On the other, our Sushila lays no claim to being a Mumbai sophisticate deserving of something better than the Rupaawati family or the boy she was betrothed to a long time ago. You will actually be condemning two lives if you match her with another, supposedly more deserving man. Sushila has given her solemn word to her mother-in-law on her deathbed, has already taken over the responsibility for the deceased's children and accepted refuge in my Deepamama's household. If we had wanted, this wedding—Sukhlal and Sushila's—it would have happened before you knew it. We saw no reason to do it in secrecy. Besides, Sukhlal's deceased mother deserves more respect than a surreptitious wedding before her ashes are even cold. Being that you are here, I urge you, our respected elders, to offer your blessings to Sushila and Sukhlal. I want everyone present to know that nothing or nobody is going to change this an iota. Those who want to test us are most welcome to try."

With that she withdrew from the room.

"Get Sushila over here," Champak Sheth snapped.

Sushila came into the room and respectfully stood facing away from her father-in-law.

"Who has put you up to all this?" Champak Sheth roared. Sushila said nothing.

"What is your decision? One word and you'll be begging in the streets, all of you!"

"Heh-heh..." That sarcastic giggle from Deepa Sheth carried the force of a thunderbolt from heaven. In that mocking laughter, Sushila heard the confirmation of his battle-readiness. Without looking at her Mota Bapuji, she told the elders :

"Whether my father-in-law approves or not, I am going to his house; even if he refuses to take me in, I am going no place else."

"That does it! I thank you all for coming—now you will please excuse us." Champak Sheth told the elders and then turned to his brother : "You, your daughter, and this—whatever she is to you—low-life, get out of my house! If you stop for even a drop of water, I will make you regret it."

"I want to ask your permission for one last thing," Bhabhu's voice was calm.

"You have my permission to drown yourself in a well."

"You'll still be my husband and master; permit me to take the oath of renunciation ..."

"You are free to become a whore, is that enough?"

Everyone present gasped with horror at his words.

Bhabhu calmly said : "More than enough! Bhai, Sushila, Mama, let's go."

Nana Sheth folded his hands and told his brother : "Everything was yours, Motabhai! I was only a guest, a freeloader here. You supported me all along. I will forever be in your debt, Motabhai."

With that, Nana Sheth bowed low and tried to touch his brother's feet when Mota Sheth pushed him away and said : "Get lost, try your act someplace else."

"This is totally unacceptable." A stunned Vijaychandra finally saw a chance, his last chance, to speak up : "I am not going to give up just like that. I have sacrificed my entire career for this, you know? I will go to court on this."

"Go for it, young man! By all means, go for it." Bhabhu laughed with utter disdain for the man : "You know, we have never seen the inside of a court before! This will give us a chance to see it!"

The Jain elders were totally dumbfounded by all this. They looked at one another and one spoke everyone's mind : "Had we known, we would have avoided this place like the plague!"

A short while later, an ox-cart driven by Deepa Sheth left for Rupaawati. Sushila and the three children rode in it. Sukhlal, Bhabhu and Nana Sheth walked behind it. Sukhlal supported the suddenly aged Nana Sheth with his shoulder, contemplating the debt of gratitude he owed his father-in-law for the bravery shown by this once-considered 'spineless' man. The cart carried not a stitch of extra clothing.

Three days later the mailman delivered a bulky piece of mail addressed to Sukhlal. The letter was from Khushaalbhai and also contained a photograph. A toothless and elderly looking woman's face smiled from the picture with the inscription reading 'To my darling son Smarty, with love from Leena.'

Khushaal's letter explained :

"I went to her place to give her your news. When I saw her, I was absolutely flabbergasted by her toothless appearance. She said an epidemic of plague had broken out in the Ratnagiri District and that she had volunteered for an assignment there. She said she herself might not come back alive and wanted you to have this picture. She also gave me a diamond ring for your bride as her wedding gift."

Sukhlal's tears almost washed the letter unreadable where they fell.

Glossary

Anna : Sixteen annas equalled a rupee until the mid 1950's

Ba : mother

Bapa : father

Bathing : here in context of the Hindu custom of cleansing the unholy touch of death off.

Ben : literally meaning sister, also used as a suffix to show respect to women.

Bhabhu : father's older brother's wife.

Bhabhiji Bhabji : the respectful version of Bhabhi (brother's wife), in this case husband's older brother's wife.

Bhai : literally, brother; used to show respect to a male of greater age or higher standing.

Bhajiya, dhokla : side delicacies in the general category of *'farsacn'* that embellish a special meal.

Ceylon, Burma : Now Sri Lanka and Myanmar.

Chaandalo : a ceremonial red dot on the forehead topped off with rice grains.

Chattari Mangalam : A Jain invocation for auspicious occasions.

Chhaana : Dried cow-dung cakes burned as fuel for cooking and heating.

Chorso : a shorter than sari piece of coarse cloth.

Choti : A solitary long lock of hair in the back of the head.

Chulo : cooking stove that burns cowdung cakes.

Confined to a corner : the extended mourning period during which a widow's activities were severely restricted

Cover the head : women traditionally covered their hair with the sari when in presence of elders, especially men.

Daal : Lentil soup

Daatun : a piece of a slim branch, usually from a Baawal tree, made into a toothbrush by chewing on one end until soft.

Dadar : a railway station, also a Mumbai suburb.

Dhoti or *dhotiyu* : a long plain white sheet wrapped around the waist and tucked in.

Diksha : the renouncement rite; here the formal ordainment into Jainism's priestess ranks.

Dilruba : a violin-like stringed instrument

Diwaali : Festive days at the end of the Lunar year, generally falling in mid/late October observed in much of India.

Fua : Father's sister's husband; Deepa Sheth was a distant relation of Khushaal's.

Gaadi : the seating commonly used by traders, consisting of a sheet-covered-mattress spread on the floor with a round bolster used as a backrest.

Ghadi : Used here to indicate 48 minutes, the typical *Samayik* 'hourglass' duration. The strict meaning of *ghadi* is one-sixtieth of a 24-hour day or 24 minutes.

Ghee : clarified butter

Gol : hardened molasses, brown sugar.

Harmonium : a musical instrument similar to a small organ.

Hindolo : a swinging cot.

Hiranyakashyap : A demon in Hindu mythology, immune to all weapons, eventually killed by Narsimha, the man-lion incarnation of Lord Vishnu.

Indhoni : a ring made from cloth or woven from soft rope to balance and carry round containers on one's head

Irani : Restauranteurs of Persian descent who cater to the snack and beverage needs of Mumbai.

Kaka : uncle; used as respectful address for elderly men.

Kaki : aunt; used as respectful address for elderly women.

Kansaar : coarse ground wheat cooked with molasses.

Karela : A green vegetable with a unique bitter taste.

Kathiawaad : Saurashtra, the half-moon shaped peninsula in the Central Western state of Gujarat.

Khaadi : hand-spun and hand-woven cotton cloth popularized by Mahatma Gandhi as a patriotic alternative to the imported mass-produced cloth.

Khansa'ab : colloquial for Khansahib; generally used for Muslims of influential families.

Khar, Santacruz : Suburbs of Mumbai

Khes : loose cloth worn over one shoulder.

Laadwa : laddoos, sweetballs—a favorite sweet for the community feasts.

Lifting shoes in one's mouth : the phrase to indicate the height of humiliation.

Mama : maternal uncle. Sukhlal's father was a distant uncle of Bhabhu's.

Marathi : the regional language of the State of Maharashtra.

Meend : a range of notes produced from one pluck of a string instrument by varying the tension of the string.

Memsa'ab : Madam; used to address Western women.

Mesub : sweet made from roasted gram flour, clarified butter and sugar.

Miyan Then-tha-nen-then : Mr. All-talk-no-action

Mota Sheth : literally, the older owner; used throughout the book as an address.

Motabhai : older brother, Mota Sheth.

Nana Sheth : literally, the younger owner.

Navkar Mantra : The holiest chant in Jainism.

Odhani : a shorter length and colorful sari generally worn by young girls and women.

Paaghadi : a turban; several yards of white cloth twisted and wrapped around the head.

Patlo: A low wooden stool

Pranaam : the folded hands gesture of respect for one's elders.

Queen of the Night : Raatraani, highly fragrant flowers that bloom at night.

Raosaheb : Used to address a prominent Marathi man; used here to inject light sarcasm.

Rotla : plural of *rotlo* — home-made millet-flour bread.

Rotli : thin rolled and pan-roasted wheat flour bread.

Rotlo and yogurt : a favorite Kathiawaadi breakfast.

Saadhvi: priestess, especially in Jainism.

Samayik: A daily Jain religous rite of meditation, not interrupted before the preallocated time, in multiples of 48 minutes.

Santokdi : a diminutive form of Santok — Sushila's original old-fashioned name.

Sari : The five or six yard long wrap-around garment worn by Indian women.

Shakti : energy

Shreefal : dry coconut; used in various ways on auspicious occasions.

Soodi : The steel nut-cutter used to crack or finecut beetle-nut.

Sukha: A loving short address for the younger Sukhlal.

Sukhlo : diminutive for Sukhlal

Tasbi : a string of beads, like a rosary, used by devout Muslims.

To touch feet : a gesture of respect for an elder.

Vaitarani : the river in Hindu mythology that all souls must cross after leaving the body.

Vanik (also Vaania) : a member of the merchant caste.

Variyali : Fennel seeds used for mouth freshening after a meal.

Vijaychandra: Victory-moon

Vile Parle : a suburb of Mumbai

Virpasali : A Hindu traditional observance when a brother gives a gift to a sister for the Rakhi thread she ties on the brother's wrist.

Vithoba : Lord Krishna.